Hello, friends!

As I write this n

of central Pennsylv

African violets an

my spirits. O

the smal

peepi

but

...te, we have snow in the mountains
...ania. But in my office, the blooms of
...d Christmas cacti in myriad hues perk up
...n the windowsill behind me, I have several of
...l angel figurines from the Willow Tree collection
...ng over my shoulder. (Mine all are holding animals,
... that's beside the point.)

Shining Forth, my latest installment in the Miracles of Marble Cove series, is chock-full of angelic themes. Beverly is rescued by yet another unexplainable beam from the lighthouse, prompting Margaret to suggest that Beverly has an angel sitting on her shoulder. Shortly afterward, Beverly herself acts as an angel of generosity to help Margaret, and all the friends gather together to support Shelley after a bad fall. And then Margaret's daughter Adelaide finds angels... well, I don't want to give away the story! But suffice it to say the theme of looking out for one another, of stepping in to help, runs throughout each character's story in *Shining Forth*.

Do you have you an angel in your life you'd like to thank? Or perhaps you are moved to step into a supportive or helpful role as an angel for someone else in need. Whatever the source of the angels in your life, I hope you'll enjoy this eighth visit with our little fictional community of Marble Cove, Maine.

Wishing you miracles,
Anne Marie Rodgers

Dedicated to my husband Andy.
How could I not love a man who says yes
to adding a nine-year-old mastiff to our pack?

MIRACLES *of*
MARBLE COVE

Shining Forth

ANNE MARIE RODGERS

New York

Published by Guideposts Books & Inspirational Media
110 William Street
New York, NY 10038
Guideposts.org

Acknowledgments

Every attempt has been made to credit the sources of copyrighted material used in this book. If any such acknowledgment has been inadvertently omitted or miscredited, receipt of such information would be appreciated.

"From the Guideposts Archive" originally appeared as "To Save a Lighthouse" by Giorgina Reid in *Guideposts* magazine. Copyright © 1989 by Guideposts. All rights reserved.

Cover and interior design by Müllerhaus
Cover art by Jeremy Charles Photography
Typeset by Aptara

Printed and bound in the United States of America
10 9 8 7 6 5 4 3

Chapter One

Beverly Wheeland-Parker smiled as she saw the familiar sign. Marble Cove: 10. As she turned off Maine Route 1 onto the smaller road that wound along the coast, anticipation rose. As soon as she came around the next bend, she'd be able to see the lighthouse.

The sign and the sight of the lighthouse had become a part of her weekly landscape as she made the drive from her office in Augusta, Maine, to her new home in the tiny coastal town.

Although she hadn't grown up in Marble Cove, her parents had moved there some years ago after retirement, and her aging father still lived in the same house they'd shared. Beverly had recently moved in with him. With her boss's blessing, she had found a way to do much of her work from home, only traveling to the office one, sometimes two days a week. Today was the first Wednesday in January, the kind of bleak winter day that made her really glad she wasn't making the daily drive anymore.

She steered into the curve, her eyes on the spit of land where the lighthouse stood, stark against the steely sky. She suspected there would be snow by morning, and she was grateful she'd be settled back in Marble Cove this evening.

The world appeared in shades of black and white during these short days of midwinter, and the ocean was a dark, gun-metal gray, boiling with whitecaps that foamed up around the rocks along the shore. When she'd decided to telecommute, she hadn't considered how grueling the drive to and from Augusta could be when the winter weather turned bad.

And heaven knew the weather in Maine could be unpredictable. What appeared to be a dazzling sunny day when she left in the morning could turn into a howling blizzard by the time she headed home. So far, she'd been fortunate that she hadn't been caught in anything too terrible. And she'd been working hard to limit her travel.

Wait! What was that? A light had flashed from the window at the top of the lighthouse that housed the Fresnel light— the light that had been deactivated for nearly sixty years now. It flashed again, and she caught her breath as an insistent presentiment of danger rolled through her. Adrenaline surged, and she sucked in a breath as her fingers tightened on the wheel.

A blur of red whizzed around the sharp turn *in her lane*!

Instantly, Beverly wrenched the wheel to the right, reflex kicking in milliseconds after she perceived the threat. The red car's brakes screamed, and the car fishtailed, the rear of the driver's side sliding inexorably toward her.

Lord, help! It was all the thought she had time for. As her car shot off the road and bounced into a rocky ditch, the undercarriage scraped and clanged over small boulders.

Just when she was sure she was going to be hit, the red car fishtailed again and missed her by inches. As Beverly jounced to an abrupt halt, the red car roared past. And her airbag exploded into her face with a sound like a shot.

Stunned, Beverly didn't move for a moment. The car's engine was still running, and she automatically reached for the key to shut it off, but her arm was pinned. Then she realized her eyes were closed. She opened her eyes and blinked at the cloud of dust swirling around her. Smoke? Her pulse surged. Moments later, though, she realized that it wasn't smoke but the powder from the airbag that had deployed.

Coughing, she fought her way free of the rapidly deflating airbag enough to turn off the engine. She stopped then and took a careful inventory of herself. Nothing seemed broken. *Thank You, God.*

Relieved to note that she didn't feel pain other than some deep aching where the seat belt had restrained her, she reached down and unbuckled herself. The door handle was blocked by the remains of the airbag, so she had to grasp handfuls of the thing and shove it out of the way until she could open the door and step out.

Whoa! To her shock, she stepped into thin air. She landed on her hands and knees on the ground with a jolt, still coughing as she blinked to try to clear the airbag powder from her eyes. When she looked around, she saw that her car had come to rest at an angle, the left front corner off the ground with the tire in the air. It explained why she'd fallen so hard when she stepped out of the car.

Slowly, she stood and straightened. She hoped the other driver hadn't been injured.

And then she realized she was alone on the side of the road. He didn't stop! Beverly couldn't believe it. She could be injured, or worse, and that careless road hog hadn't even stopped!

Quickly, she took stock of her aches and pains again. Knees and palms stung from the fall in addition to the bruises she'd noted earlier, but thankfully, she hadn't been badly hurt. She shuddered, recalling a red fender sliding inexorably across the road straight at her. It could have been much worse.

She shivered as she buttoned up her coat. The temperature was January-frigid: she'd heard the high today had only reached eighteen, which probably explained why there were so few people on the road.

Squinting against the snow-brightened landscape, she checked the highway in both directions. Nothing coming.

She sighed. She really didn't want to call 9-1-1. She wasn't injured. But she sure wasn't going anywhere until she got her car off those rocks.

She patted her coat pocket and drew out her cell phone. Grimly, she smiled as she hit her list of contacts. It paid to be prepared. She had both the nonemergency number for the state police and the number of a body shop just outside Marble Cove. After two short conversations, she slipped the phone back into her pocket and pulled out her elegant leather gloves.

Slipping on the gloves as she walked, she returned to the car. Fortunately, she could reach the back door on the driver's side, where she knew a warm hat and scarf lay on the seat. Moments later, she was swaddled in both.

To keep warm, she paced back and forth along the berm of the roadway. She supposed she might be able to get back in the car and turn on some heat, but given the odd angle at which the car was perched on the rocks, that might not be smart. The ground dropped away on the far side of the stranded vehicle.

She hoped there was no significant damage to the undercarriage. The car was still in excellent shape, a dark metallic gray Ford Fusion she had purchased in 2010, and although her insurance would cover most of a repair bill, she worried that a damaged-and-repaired car might never be the same.

A car with flashing lights atop had come around the bend while she was engrossed in her dismal thoughts. Moments later, the state police cruiser drew to a halt near her, and an officer emerged. As she was giving him the story and the limited description she had of the red car, a minivan rounded the curve. It slowed to pass and then suddenly pulled over to the side of the road just beyond the cop's car.

A short, round woman bounced out of the driver's seat. "Beverly! Are you all right?"

A flood of relief spread through Beverly as she recognized her friend Margaret Hoskins, who lived just down the street from her. She excused herself from the policeman and went to meet her friend, accepting Margaret's warm embrace with far less reserve than she normally would. "I'm okay." She explained how the accident had transpired.

"Let me drive you home," Margaret urged. "It's freezing out here."

"Thank you, but I need to wait for the tow truck."

The officer overheard the comment. "If you'd like to go on home with your friend, I'll supervise the towing." He pointed down the road. "I think that's the truck coming now."

Beverly hesitated. It went against the grain not to handle her problems herself. But it was *cold* out here! Finally she handed the officer her keys. "Thank you."

Quickly Margaret hustled her to her van.

"Wait," Beverly protested. "I've got to shake off this powder."

"Forget the dirt," Margaret told her. "This van has seen worse."

All the same, Beverly brushed down her stylish, lined trench coat to remove the residue before Margaret bundled her into the passenger seat. Margaret hurried around to the driver side and hopped in. She turned up the heat until the welcome warmth was blasting out at Beverly's chilled cheeks.

"Wow," she said. "I didn't realize how frozen I was getting."

Margaret nodded. "It's deceptive. By the time you figure it out, you're one icicle away from frostbite." She put the vehicle into gear and, after a cheery wave to the helpful police officer, accelerated onto the road toward Marble Cove.

"Thank you for stopping. It's lucky you were traveling this way today."

Margaret nodded. "We have Louellen Lumadue to thank for that."

"Lou...who?"

Margaret chuckled. "Louellen Lumadue is an artist. Her work inspired me when I began to paint again. The first time I went to a showing of her work, I was absolutely captivated."

"What appealed to you?"

Margaret shrugged. "She's an impressionist, and there's just something about the way she uses color that's unique. I could look at a lineup of paintings and instantly pick out a Lumadue." She smiled. "It sounds rather mystical to say that her work called to me, but there was something in the paintings she created that I couldn't stop thinking about. And from there, it was a short step toward trying it myself."

"But I don't understand what that has to do with your being on this road."

"Oh, sorry." Margaret shook her head. "I forgot where I was going with that story. I read in the paper last week that Louellen is exhibiting during January and February at Colby College's Museum of Art. They have a nice collection that focuses on American artists. So I thought I'd go up to Waterville to see it."

"How was it?" Beverly was eager to distract herself from the unsettling memory of metal scraping over rock as she veered off the road.

Margaret sucked in an enthusiastic breath. "Oh, it was wonderful! She still has such a unique command of color, although she's moved from impressionism into expressionism." She made a face. "I have to say I prefer her earlier pieces. Why, I still can recall one series she did in which she incorporated hidden images that reflected the theme of the painting. Very, very subtle, and absolutely riveting. Her newer work doesn't speak to me like that, but the exhibit was fascinating all the same. And here's something even more wonderful: she's going to be giving a lecture at the art museum next week."

"Are you going to attend?" Beverly rubbed her hands together. She could feel her fingers and toes thawing, tiny pinpricks of sensation stinging her extremities.

"I'm hoping to. Though I wouldn't dare commit to something without checking my calendar first." Margaret made an exasperated noise. "Enjoy your memory while you've got it. This aging stuff is for the birds."

"Oh, Margaret, I'd say you're aging as gracefully as anyone."

They shared a laugh as the lighthouse loomed large on its rocky promontory near the town limits.

The sight triggered a memory. "Margaret." Beverly caught her breath. "I saw a light."

Margaret glanced across the console between their seats. It was obvious she'd made the connection between Beverly's words and the solitary structure. "Do you think it was a warning?"

"I do," Beverly said in a wondering tone. "Right before the accident, it flashed twice."

Margaret appeared unsurprised. She smiled. "Another miracle to add to our collection. Wait until Shelley and Diane hear about it." Her smile faded. "Thank heavens for that light. Your accident might have been much worse."

"You're right. Because it caught my attention, I was looking that way when the car came around the curve. If I hadn't seen it as soon as I did, the car probably would have hit me head-on."

"It does seem there must have been an angel on your shoulder." Margaret glanced over at her friend and raised her eyebrows. "If you'd spun a little farther, you'd probably have flipped over going down that embankment."

CHAPTER TWO

Shelley Bauer was doing laundry. Again. She grimaced as she carried yet another basket of dirty clothing into the upstairs hall late on Wednesday afternoon. How could four people, two of whom were quite small, generate so many dirty clothes?

She suspected women all across the country wondered the exact same thing on a regular basis.

Glancing into her daughter Emma's room, she saw that the toddler was still sleeping. Her afternoon nap rarely lasted this late, but Shelley had taken the kids to the library right after lunch, and they'd lingered longer than usual when they ran into Aiden's friend Jeremy and his mother.

She headed down the stairs, thinking she'd better get dinner started. On the third step from the bottom, she used her foot to nudge aside one of her son Aiden's miniature cars. Her son's fourth birthday was in two days, and he'd probably get quite a haul of brand-new toys from his extended family. They were planning a celebration during the usual after-church Sunday lunch at her in-laws' house.

"Aiden?" she called. "I need you to move your toys off the stairs." *Someday,* she thought, *one of us is going to break a leg tripping over one of these things.*

Hearing no answer, she started for the kitchen. Aiden had been manipulating Play-Doh into various shapes a few minutes ago, with their puppy Prize snoozing beside his chair. "Aiden?"

"Mama!" She heard little feet hit the floor and come rushing her way. Before she could caution him to slow down, Aiden barreled through the kitchen doorway. Seeing his mother in his path, he put his arms out to stop. Just then, Prize rushed between his feet, barking at this new game, and Aiden tripped. His outstretched hands flailed, hitting her thighs, and his head connected with her knee. As he did so, she heard a distinct popping sound in her left knee.

"Aiden!" Shelley felt herself falling, off-balance as she tried desperately not to drop the heavy clothes basket on either her son or the puppy. "Watch out!"

The clothes basket went flying as she toppled awkwardly to the side. She tried to break her fall by grabbing the edge of the couch, but she still landed on the floor.

"Ohhh," she yelped, then groaned, rolling to her side and grabbing at her leg.

Aiden began crying. "What's the matter, Mama? Is your leg hurt?"

Shelley bent her head, forcing back a wave of nausea as searing pain engulfed her leg. "Yeah," she managed.

Prize was barking wildly, and she waved a weak hand in the direction of the kitchen. "Put her out in the yard, honey."

Her son hurried to obey, tugging at the puppy's collar until she went with him. When he returned, he sounded distressed as he asked, "Do you need a Band-Aid?"

She registered his concern, but she was unable to answer him, rocking slightly back and forth as she tried to breathe through the pain.

"Mama?" Aiden's sobs grew louder as his distress grew.

"Come here, honey." Shelley reached out a hand, ignoring the pain in her knee. She inspected the lump growing on Aiden's forehead. He was definitely going to have a goose egg. She hugged him to her and kissed the spot, gritting her teeth as the pain clutched at her knee. "You're going to be all right. We just need to put an ice pack on there. Hold on a minute." She fished her cell phone from her pocket and hit the speed dial for Dan.

"Hey, honey." Dan sounded happy and jovial when he answered. "What's up?"

"Dan." She tried to keep her voice calm. "I...fell. Hurt my knee. And Aiden bumped his head."

There was a moment of silence. "Fell where?"

"In the living room. I don't think I can get up."

She heard an intake of breath, and she realized he must be able to hear Aiden sobbing. "I'll be there in a couple of minutes. Just stay where you are." All traces of levity were gone. "Where's the baby?"

"Still napping."

"I'll get there as fast as I can." And Dan hung up.

Shelley rubbed her fingers over the smooth surface of her phone. She should get someone to help. Before she could talk herself out of it, she dialed Diane's number.

When her friend answered, Shelley again explained what had happened. The throbbing in her knee was still fierce, but slow, deep breathing helped.

Diane must have run across the street, because Shelley had barely ended the call when her friend burst through the front door and skidded to a halt next to her.

After a cursory greeting and one quick look, Diane dug into her pocket for her own cell phone. "Did you call 911?"

"No! Wait." Shelley shook her head frantically. "No emergency services. We can't afford that bill." She swallowed, suppressing a whimper as even the slight motion sent another burst of pain through her knee. "It's not that bad. Dan's coming. Just let me sit for a bit."

Diane's eyebrows rose, and she looked like she might argue. But then she simply nodded. "All right. What can I do?"

"Check on Emma. Get Aiden an ice pack for his head and a snack. I think supper's going to be delayed." Diane didn't even smile at her weak attempt at humor.

"How about if I feed the kids and the dog while Dan takes you—wherever." Diane stopped abruptly, and Shelley realized her wise friend hadn't wanted to worry Aiden with talk of hospitals.

"That would be wonderful. But please ignore the mess in the kitchen."

Diane chuckled, although worry lurked in her gaze. "I'll keep my eyes closed." She looked down at Shelley's knee, which appeared to be swelling a bit. "Maybe I should get you an ice pack too."

As Shelley was gingerly settling the ice pack on her knee a minute later, Diane asked, "Who's your doctor? I think you'd better call right now, so that when Dan gets here, you can leave."

Alarm raced through Shelley. "Oh, but I don't need—"

"Shelley." Diane was using her "mother voice." "This is not something that's going to get better in a day or two. You can't even walk." Shelley felt tears well again. She tried not to cry with frustration and worry, but she couldn't shake the feeling of apprehension. They couldn't afford a huge medical bill!

Diane's tone softened. "Let me call the doctor and tell him what's going on. Then he can decide how to handle it." She eyed the knee again. "You don't want to risk doing more damage and possibly injuring something permanently, do you?"

"No." Shelley exhaled, and her breath hitched. "Go ahead. I'm just so worried about what this might cost."

"I know." Diane stroked her hair, a sweet gesture that made Shelley want to simply lay her head against her friend and let her take care of everything.

After a few minutes, the ice began to numb the worst of the pain. Diane checked on Emma, who was still sleeping. She took Aiden into the kitchen, and Shelley could hear him explaining his Play-Doh creations to her.

Then Dan burst through the kitchen door, calling, "Honey?"

Shelley heard Diane say, "She's in the living room."

"Daddy, I hurted Mama. And I banged my head." Aiden's high treble voice wobbled as if tears were imminent again.

"I see." She heard the sound of Dan giving Aiden's boo-boo a healing kiss.

"Mommy's going to be fine, Aiden," Diane said firmly. "Accidents happen. You didn't do anything on purpose."

Dan appeared in the doorway then, and Shelley forgot all about the conversation in the kitchen. "Oh, baby," he said, "what happened?"

"Aiden barreled into me. It was an accident," she hastened to say. "I just fell wrong, and I felt something pop in my knee." Carefully, she lifted the ice pack so her husband could assess the injury.

Dan surveyed the leg. "Can you walk?"

"I haven't tried." With his help, she managed to get to her feet. But she couldn't put weight on the knee, and just the effort of rising had her gritting her teeth.

Dan looked at her, his eyes concerned. "I think we'd better go to the ER."

"Diane called the doctor, and he said we could come to his office first."

But Dan shook his head. "He's going to take one look at this and send you straight to the ER anyway."

"Really?" She felt tears rising again. "I'm so sorry, Dan—"

"Nothing to be sorry for." He leaned down and kissed her. "You didn't wake up and decide to injure your knee today, did you?"

"Of course not." She smiled reluctantly. "Okay. To the ER we go, then. Help me to the car."

Dan lifted a skeptical eyebrow. "Um, Shel, I don't think you want to walk on that. I'll carry you."

"Oh, that's silly. I can walk." She extended a hand to her husband.

Dan heaved a sigh. "Okay." He looped an arm around her and took her weight.

And still, an involuntary cry ripped through her when she tried to put weight on the knee. "Owowowowow!"

"Let me carry you." Dan offered sweetly.

She couldn't prevent the pained sounds that escaped when Dan carefully lifted her and her foot dangled over his arm.

Diane heard her and supported the foot until Dan placed her on the backseat of the white station wagon so she could keep her leg up on the seat.

Dan drove carefully during the fifteen-minute trip to the emergency room at Sailors Memorial, the hospital that served the local area. It was only a few miles outside town, but to Shelley, every tiny bump along the highway felt like they were bulldozing over boulders. Her knee seemed to swell more with each passing moment.

He parked in an emergency space right outside the door and ran inside before she could stop him. Minutes later, attendants with a stretcher returned with him, and Shelley suffered through another bout of jolting. Dan gave her his hand as he hurried along beside her. "Squeeze," he encouraged. "Go ahead."

Despite the pain, the words tickled her funny bone and she snorted out a laugh. "Reminds me of being in labor."

Dan grinned. "Didn't I say the same thing then?"

Two hours and one MRI later, she had both a diagnosis and a treatment plan. The doctor had manipulated her knee until she thought she couldn't stand it, paying particular attention to how the inside of the joint felt when pressure was applied to the outside—at the point where Aiden's head had connected with her leg. The spot was already bruising and the knee had continued to swell.

"You've got what we call a grade two tear of the medial collateral ligament in your right knee. A grade two MCL tear is an incomplete tear, with a little looseness in the knee." He demonstrated by showing her how easily her kneecap moved back and forth—a less than pleasant sensation. "The good news is you won't need surgery."

Her eyes widened. "I hadn't even considered that. Will I need a cast?"

"No." He shook his head. "Not a cast, but for at least three days, I want you off your feet around the clock. Follow the RICE treatment—rest, ice, compression, and elevation. You'll need to ice it every four hours for twenty minutes, keep this brace on it, and elevate it—higher than your heart, if possible. That means lying down. After the third day, you can start some limited use wearing a brace."

"I have two small children. I can't lie down for three days," she protested. "And a job I need, and—"

"You have to." He smiled at her expression. "What kind of job do you have?"

"I'm the baker at the Cove."

His eyes lit up. "Really? You make their desserts?"

She nodded.

"Your blueberry crumb cake might just be my favorite sweet in the world."

"Thank you." She was genuinely delighted. She was still getting used to exuberant praise.

"Much as I hate to say it, the Cove will have to get along without you for at least a week, Mrs. Bauer."

"A week! I can't be off work for a week." Anxiety began knotting her stomach. They couldn't afford the loss of income...and what would Rusty, the Cove's owner, do without her?

"We'll figure it out, Shel." Dan laid a comforting hand on her shoulder as the doctor nodded.

"Sorry, but if you want this injury to heal, you're going to have to give it some time. Three days of wearing the brace full-time, and then you could begin to use it just when you are going to be on your feet. After that, you could use crutches for a week or so. You'll need to continue to wear that brace for a while."

"What, exactly, is a while?"

The doctor smiled. "It'll depend on your progress but probably about a month. After the swelling subsides, we'll give you some exercises you can do at home to regain mobility and strength."

That's going to cost a fortune, Shelley thought, even with their co-pay, which was quite a chunk of change in itself.

Dan must have seen the look on her face, because as soon as the doctor left the room, he said, "Don't worry so much. We'll deal with this."

"Not if our income is reduced because I can't work," she said gloomily.

"The doctor said you wouldn't need to be off long." Dan's tone was encouraging. "And I can find another side job or two if I have to."

"But what about the Cove? Oh dear, I have to call Rusty right away." The owner of the little eatery depended on her.

Shelley sighed as Rusty answered. She explained the situation, finishing with, "And I'm so sorry to leave you in the lurch, but I don't think I can—"

"Stop worrying." Rusty's tone was calm, and it reassured her. "Before you, I bought pastries from out of town, remember? Folks like yours better, and I like your prices, but I can scare up something for a week or so until you can be on your feet again."

"Oh, thank you." She was so relieved she felt the weight lift from her shoulders. "I promise I'll be back as soon as I can."

But as she concluded the conversation, another thought struck Shelley. "Oh no! What about Aiden's birthday?"

"What about it?"

"Dan." Shelley shook her head at his total lack of concern. "I was going to make the cake with Prize's picture on it, remember?"

"Oh, right." Dan shrugged, clearly unworried. "He'll understand why we can't have it. And he's having his big party at Mom's on Sunday anyway."

"We can't do that to Aiden." She cringed at the mere thought. "Don't you remember what a big deal birthdays were when you were a child? He's been excited about this for weeks."

Dan frowned as he began to see the problem. "What if I buy a cake mix and icing and do it myself?"

Shelley grimaced, but even as she registered her distaste for a store-bought cake mix, she was touched that Dan would offer. "I guess that would work."

Dan snapped his fingers. "Hey, remember that little Spider-Man action figure he saw at the store last week?"

Shelley nodded, not sure how it was connected to cake decorating— "Oh! We could put it on top." She smiled. "That's a great idea. He'll be thrilled, even if it isn't up to my usual standards."

"Well, it's definitely up to mine." Dan snickered at himself. "And you can save the Prize idea for next year's cake."

CHAPTER THREE

Diane didn't know a whole lot about knee injuries, but she was pretty certain Shelley wasn't going to be cooking any supper that evening. A hunt through the cupboards netted her a box of macaroni and cheese mix, and there was leftover meat loaf in the refrigerator. Heating the contents of a jar of canned green beans in the microwave while the meat loaf warmed in the oven and the noodles for the macaroni came to a boil on the stovetop, she decided that there could be worse dinners.

Emma, who had awakened not long after Dan and Shelley left for the hospital, looked up from her high chair and gave Diane a wide, toothy grin. A shiny river of drool tracked down her chin and made a large wet spot on the front of the bib Diane had prudently placed around her neck before she'd settled her into her high chair with a handful of Cheerios.

"Miss Diane?" Aiden wandered into the room, Prize trotting close behind him. Diane found it absolutely endearing how devoted the little boy and the puppy were to each other.

"What's up, buddy?" She smiled as she lifted him into her arms and rubbed her chin over the top of his head.

"I wanna draw a picture of the lighthouse."

Diane's eyebrows rose. "Okay. Do you know where there's some paper and crayons?"

Aiden nodded, pointing at a cupboard high out of his reach. "Mama keeps some of my things up high so I don't get into them and get in trouble."

His tone was so serious Diane had to suppress a giggle. She nodded, trying to match his sober tone. "That's a good idea. I wouldn't want to see you get in trouble."

Going to the cupboard Aiden had indicated, Diane found the requested supplies, and soon the little boy was sitting at the table happily coloring.

Diane worked on the meal while Aiden colored, setting the table around him.

As she filled glasses with milk for the children and water for herself, the back door opened. Shelley stood in the doorway, propping herself awkwardly on crutches, while Dan hovered behind her.

"Mama, Mama!" Aiden shouted.

Emma shouted too, although the garbled sounds didn't resemble anything intelligible.

"Hi, guys." Shelley made an effort to smile for her children, but her face was wan and the expression looked forced. "Are you having dinner?"

"You're just in time," Diane said. "It's not going to win any culinary prizes, but I made plenty because I hoped you'd soon be home."

"Sounds great," Dan said. "I'm starving."

Shelley clomped forward with the crutches. As soon as Dan was inside, he slipped around her and snagged her chair at the table, pulling it out so she could lower herself gingerly into it. Then he pulled another one close and gently lifted her braced leg onto it.

While Dan settled Shelley, Aiden stood nearby, his initial jubilation at his mother's appearance fading. His little face looked dismayed, then distressed, and before Diane could figure out what was wrong, the preschooler burst into tears.

"Aiden? Honey, what's the matter?" Shelley held out her arms.

But Aiden didn't rush into her embrace as he usually did. "I'm s-sorry, Mama." His little chest heaved; Diane wondered what possibly could have upset him so much.

"For what, Aiden? You didn't do anything." Shelley sounded as bewildered as Diane felt.

"I hurted you." It was a wail of misery.

Shelley winced when he finally threw himself against her. Dan tried to remove him, but she shook her head. "Aiden." She lifted his chin with a finger. "It was an accident."

"But I hurted you!"

"Did you mean to?"

He cast her an incredulous look. "No."

"So it was just something unexpected that happened."

He nodded vigorously.

"So you don't have to feel bad," Shelley assured him. "Sometimes, we just have accidents."

"Like sometimes I do when I can't wait for the bafroom." Aiden looked a little startled when all three adults burst into laughter.

"So what's the story?" Diane asked as she set a bowl full of green beans on a trivet and returned to get the platter of meat loaf. "What did you injure?"

"I tore a ligament in my knee," Shelley told her. "I don't need surgery, but I have to be off my feet with this leg up for two days—"

"Three." Dan scooped mac and cheese into a bowl for Aiden.

Shelley rolled her eyes. "And I have to wear this brace, use crutches, and go to physical therapy." She sighed. "I don't have time for this."

Diane wisely resisted smiling. "It's not like you have a choice. Look at it as a heaven-sent opportunity to relax. When was the last time you were off your feet for three days?"

Shelley thought for a minute. "When Emma was born. And actually, not even then, because I was released from the hospital the day after she arrived." She sighed. "I guess I'll have to resign myself to ignoring the mess in the house."

"I can help out," Diane said. "And Adelaide can do a few more things, I bet, if you ask her."

Dan cleared his throat. He was keeping an eye on Emma, whose enthusiastic eating habits included flinging food across the room if she wasn't watched carefully. Diane noticed he didn't look at Shelley. "While you were getting the MRI, I called my mom to let her know what happened.

She is rearranging her commitments for the next couple of weeks so that she can give you any help you need."

"Dan!" Shelley sounded aghast. "I can't believe you waited until now to tell me that."

Diane could. It was obvious that Dan hoped the presence of other people might keep the explosion to a minimum.

"She has plenty of time." Dan shrugged. "She can't start until Monday, because she's helping Samantha wallpaper her kitchen. Come on, Shel, you know she loves taking care of the kids."

"Who loves taking care of me?" Aiden demanded.

"Your grandmother." Dan grinned at his son. "Would you like to have Meemaw come and help for a little bit while Mama's leg gets better?"

"Yeah!" Aiden shouted. "Meemaw-Meemaw-Meemaw!"

Emma said, "Me-me-me-me!"

Diane laughed. "You little mockingbird." But she noticed how strained Shelley's smile was. Somehow, she doubted it was only the injury. Shelley found her mother-in-law overwhelming in the best of times. Having her around when Shelley was going to have to depend on her help...yikes!

To Shelley, she said, "Why don't you get settled on the couch or in bed, wherever you plan to rest, and let me bring you a tray?"

"Oh, I couldn't—"

"Great idea," Dan said. He rose and lifted Shelley into his arms before she could protest. "Bed. He said he wants the leg elevated higher than your heart, remember?"

"But I can't eat lying down!"

"Well, I guess you can sit up long enough to eat." Dan's voice was teasing. Either he had no idea that his invitation to his mother was a really bad idea, or he was trying to smooth the waters.

Diane couldn't hear Shelley's words as they moved through the house, but she could imagine what her young friend was thinking. How on earth was Shelley going to deal with *this* wrinkle?

★ ★ ★

As Diane left Shelley's and walked out the short front path to the gate, a van turned the corner from Main Street and began to cruise slowly down Newport Street. Although it already was growing dark, she saw that it was Margaret. And as she slowed and waved, Diane saw that Beverly sat in the passenger seat.

Beverly? Diane was almost positive she had worked that day.

"Hey there." Margaret braked to a stop.

"Hey." Diane let herself out of the gate, closing it behind her. "We had a little excitement here this afternoon."

"Oh?"

"Shelley fell and hurt her knee. She isn't going to be getting around much for about a month."

Margaret's eyes widened. Beverly leaned forward so she could see Diane better and asked, "What happened?"

Diane gave them a short version of the fall and hospital visit.

Margaret shook her head. "I'll have to tell Adelaide. She could do a few chores she doesn't normally do when she's over there."

"We all may want to pitch in," Beverly said.

Diane nodded. "If there's a need, I certainly am willing. But Dan, bless his oblivious heart, asked his mother to come in and help."

"For the whole month?" Beverly sounded horrified. Shelley tried to be circumspect about her mother-in-law's critical comments and tendency to take over any plans, but from the few times each had observed Mrs. Bauer, the three friends had a fair idea of how Shelley would feel about that.

Diane shrugged. "I don't know. I guess it depends on how long Shelley needs help with the children."

Margaret shook her head. "Oh, that is just awful. Poor Shelley. Before I go in to the gallery tomorrow, I'll pop in and see how I can help." Then she gave a start and turned to Beverly. "Heavens. I am so sorry! I know you're anxious to get into a warm house." She peered back out the window at Diane. "Beverly was run off the coast road on her way home from work. I stopped and brought her home."

Diane was shocked. "What?"

"And she saw a light!"

Beverly cleared her throat. "Why don't you both come to my father's for a bit, and we can continue this conversation there?"

"Excellent suggestion." Margaret nodded.

Diane hesitated. "Maybe we should wait until Shelley can join us to hear about that."

Margaret chuckled. "She does love that lighthouse. But I doubt she needs us barging in on her this evening. One of us can fill her in later."

Margaret was right. And Diane was dying to hear about Beverly's light sighting. Beverly wasn't dressed for walking in the frigid air, so Margaret dropped her off at her house before returning to park the van at her own home. Then she joined Diane, and they both hotfooted it down the street to the Wheelands'.

Diane sighed with pleasure as Beverly held open the door and they stepped into the entry. It was nice to be out of the biting weather. The temperature had dropped steadily as the day went on, and a big snow was in the forecast.

She looked back at the drifts, tall enough to bury her, that surrounded the houses and repeatedly tried to encroach on the hard-packed snow of the roads. More snow. It was a good thing she had made dear friends and loved her little cottage so much. Maine winters definitely were not for the faint of heart.

Beverly's father was sitting in his recliner, as he often was when Diane visited. She went in to talk to him while Margaret volunteered to make some hot tea and Beverly raced upstairs to put on some warm clothes.

Mr. Wheeland smiled when he saw her. "Hello, Diane. How are you?"

She pretended to shiver. "Chilly!"

He chuckled. "Nah. This is jacket weather."

"For you, maybe. For me, it's wool sweaters and long johns weather." She grinned.

"Did I see Beverly come in?" He peered toward the hallway. "She's late coming home."

Diane nodded. "She had a little hitch in her commute today. She'll be down in a minute. How are you?"

He waved a hand dismissively. "About like anyone who's pushing eighty. I used to love winter, but now it keeps me housebound, so I don't enjoy it much."

Diane didn't quite know what to say. Aging changed so many things that one took for granted. She'd have to try to visit him more often.

"How's your new book coming along?" Mr. Wheeland always enjoyed discussing her literary endeavors, and she accepted the change of topic gratefully.

Moments later, Margaret came into the room carrying a tray loaded with four mugs of steaming tea and a plate of enormous white chocolate chip cookies. "I found some of Shelley's cookies in the kitchen," she announced with glee. "Mr. Wheeland, have you been holding out on us?"

The old man mimed snapping his fingers with mock chagrin. "You've caught me."

They all chuckled. As she descended the stairs, Beverly said, "Caught you doing what?" She sounded alarmed, and they all laughed again.

"It was just a joke," Diane assured her. "You'd better get in here if you want to get a cookie. They're going fast."

Beverly smiled. "Ah, but I know where they make them. Who do you think brought those?"

Margaret patted the settee cushion beside her. "Come sit down. Your father hasn't heard about your mishap, and you have to tell Diane about the light."

"What mishap?" Mr. Wheeland looked concerned.

"I had a minor accident." Beverly went on to say that she'd had to move to the side of the road to avoid another driver and banged up her car a little bit. Margaret had come along and driven her home. Diane studied Beverly, suspecting that there was a great deal more to the "mishap" than Beverly wanted her father to know. First of all, her car apparently had to be towed, since Margaret gave her a ride. Second, her face was colorless, like someone who had had a shock or bad scare, and third, unless Diane was mistaken, her clothes had sported patches of airbag dust on them before she changed.

"The important part," Beverly was saying as Diane tuned back in, "is that the reason I was able to avoid serious injury is because I saw a flash from the lighthouse that drew my attention in that direction. Because I was looking that way, I saw the other car coming around the bend instantly and I was able to avoid it. If I'd been looking straight ahead, or in the rearview mirror, I might not have had that extra second to react."

Mr. Wheeland shook his head. "That could have been a terrible accident. I'm not sure I believed all these stories about the lighthouse saving people, but now I suppose I'll have to revise my thinking."

Diane laughed. "I love a person with an open mind." Her gaze found Beverly's. "What did the light look like?"

"It was a flash from the Fresnel light. Two flashes, actually. But closer together than they would be if it was a working light. These were only separated by a second or two."

"That light hasn't worked in decades," Mr. Wheeland said. "It was decommissioned years ago."

Diane nodded, sitting up straight in her excitement. It was another miracle! "And we saw for ourselves that the light couldn't be operated. It's missing the things that make the beacon move and flash."

Beverly smiled. "I know I saw a light flash. Twice." She smiled. "I know I used to scoff when you used the word 'miracle,' Diane, but that's exactly what I consider today's events. Without that light..." She grimaced. "It could have been much worse."

"That's exactly what I was thinking," Diane said, "another miraculous light saved us—well, you—from a disastrous occurrence."

Margaret smiled, a peaceful smile that indicated she had no doubt about what she was saying. "We've solved the mystery, haven't we?"

"Well, we figured out Mr. Maker's story," Beverly said. "Is that what you mean?"

The older woman shook her head. "Each of us has faith that there isn't an earthly origin for all of the lights we've seen. Each of us has experienced some sort of miracle because flashes of light attracted attention."

"You're right," Diane said. "I accept that we've had divine assistance in the form of the Orlean Point lighthouse." She smiled at Beverly. "We all do now."

"You know," Margaret said, "I heard the saddest thing today. We may not have that old lighthouse to save our hides one of these days."

"What do you mean?" Diane felt a surge of anxiety.

"Apparently there's a move afoot from a developer who wants to buy that land to put condos on it. He's already got an architect, and he plans to call it Light Pointe Place."

"Again?" Diane shook her head. "I had hoped after the attempt to turn it into an inn that people would forget about trying to make it something it isn't."

"I don't think they want to make it into anything," Margaret said. "They just want the land."

"But what about the lighthouse?" Beverly said, fearing she knew the answer.

Her father snorted. "I imagine that'll be the first thing they tear down. Doggone money-hungry rascals."

"No!" Diane stood and began to pace, her thoughts racing as she did so. "We can't let that happen."

"We don't exactly have the money to buy and stop them," Beverly said.

"I wonder how far they've gotten." Margaret's gaze followed Diane. "We need to find out if they've talked to the town council yet."

"You know," Diane said slowly, "the lighthouse is an important piece of Marble Cove's history. It would be a shame to lose it to a bunch of condos. I wonder if the historical society would be interested in preserving it."

"How do we even go about that?" Beverly asked.

Diane shrugged. "I don't know, but I bet I can find a lot of information online. There should be something on the Maine.gov site. And I can talk to someone at the historical society and town council too."

Beverly's eyebrows rose. "You're going to be busy. I wish I could help, but I really can't take off work right now."

"I can help some," Margaret volunteered. "The gallery was busier than I expected during December, but now that the new year's here, I really am only keeping it open part-time."

Diane said, "And I can go over to the town hall and the historical society tomorrow." The Marble Cove Historical Society was actually housed in a room of the library building, but it was accessed by its own separate door.

Margaret laughed. "Optimist. You walk into either one of those places and you won't be walking out again for quite a while."

"Wouldn't it be wonderful," Beverly said, "to have the lighthouse repaired, repainted, and restored to its original condition? It could be opened as a tourist attraction, with velvet ropes to keep the contents of the rooms off-limits."

"Anchor chain or rope from the docks might be more fitting," Diane pointed out. She snatched up her coat and headed for the door. "I'm going to start researching it right now." Then she remembered her friends. Turning, she walked back and placed a light hand on Beverly's shoulder. "I'm so glad you weren't harmed. God bless our guardian angel of the lighthouse."

CHAPTER FOUR

I'm going to mail the building permit today," Dan said to Shelley on Thursday morning. "It normally takes three to four weeks, but the woman I spoke with said they're slow right now, so they don't have a backlog." His eyes were bright. "I figure we should be able to get started around the first of February."

"That would be wonderful." Shelley was still icing her knee off and on, and it throbbed terribly. She tried to sound more enthusiastic and less miserable.

Dan glanced at her and grimaced. "I'm sorry. Here I am babbling on about the remodeling when you're hurting. What can I do?"

"Not a thing. I'm fine." She smiled at him. "Thanks for putting the kids to bed last night."

"You're welcome." He hovered over her. "Do you need more painkiller?"

She snorted. "Yes, but I've taken the maximum I can take right now. This will pass." She glanced up at him. "Stop worrying and tell me more about the project." The pair were remodeling their home kitchen to bring it up to code for restaurant use. Her arrangement with the Cove in which she baked for them in exchange for using their facilities had been helpful when she'd started her business, but now that the business was growing and her goodies were such a hit at the Cove, she spent far too many evenings away from her family. She couldn't wait to be able to bake in her own professional kitchen.

"The project." Dan shrugged as he took a seat at the end of the couch. "I don't want to buy materials until we're certain we can get the permit, so we can do everything we want."

They sat in silence for a moment. Shelley had a million thoughts vying for space in her mind. What was she going to do about Aiden's birthday? How was she going to manage having her mother-in-law around for days? What was she going to do about work? And her business plans? The list went on and on.

First things first, as her mother used to say. "We need to talk about Aiden's birthday."

Dan nodded.

"Tomorrow, we'll have a little family celebration for his real birthday."

"I can bake the cake tonight after he's asleep," Dan said, "and ice it tomorrow. And I'll run by the store and pick up Spider Man today."

Shelley smiled, trying to forget the vision of a cake with an image of their puppy Prize on it that she'd been mentally designing. To decorate a cake, she really had to work on her feet—it was just too difficult to get the proper angles working with icing when she was sitting. "He's going to be tickled by that." Her smile faded. "But his gifts still need to be wrapped. I can't do it, and you're going to have a terrible time getting away from him long enough to sneak in some wrapping."

Dan nodded wryly. Having his daddy home all day was such a novelty that the little boy was following him all over the house.

"I can wrap the gifts tonight after he's in bed." He grinned. "While the cake is baking and cooling. I'm going to be a regular domestic god by the time you're back on your feet."

Shelley had to chuckle.

"Let's start his morning off with a birthday breakfast tomorrow."

"Pancakes and strawberries are his favorites." Shelley said. She appreciated that Dan was really getting into the planning too, which usually was her realm. It was kind of fun to share ideas, she thought.

"Sounds good." Dan rose. "Tomorrow morning, you can direct the operation while I make the pancakes. I need to take Prize out one last time before I leave," Dan told her. "And then I'll get you settled on the couch."

"Oh, I think I can—"

"No." Dan rolled his eyes. "And you wonder why Aiden doesn't follow directions sometimes. You stink at listening to orders."

That made Shelley laugh. "I do not!"

"Yeah, you do." Dan took the stairs two at a time, returning a moment later with the little dog under one arm. He stroked a silky ear as he walked. "Back in a minute." The puppy was on her way to becoming a delightfully pleasant pet.

"It's still snowing," Dan reported, reentering the room. He was drying Prize with a towel, and the puppy was less than thrilled with his handling, squirming and whining. The moment he set her down, she raced back up the stairs, where Shelley knew they would find her playing in Aiden's room.

*   *   *

"Now remember, Adelaide, you're going to have to be an extra-special help to Shelley for the next few weeks." Margaret addressed her daughter as they slogged through knee-deep snow later that morning. It had snowed all night and was showing no signs of stopping.

"I will." Adelaide nodded earnestly, looking like a shapeless little lump in her layers of snow clothes. Margaret had often worried that her daughter would get frostbitten when she played outdoors, because she didn't seem to register pain as quickly as other children did, which was typical of people with Down syndrome. "I'm a good helper."

"I know you are." Margaret gave Adelaide's shoulder a brief, approving squeeze.

The moment she knocked, Margaret laughed at herself. Who was going to answer the door?

But a moment later, someone did answer the door.

"Well, good morning, Dan. I wasn't expecting to see you," Margaret said with a smile. "If you're home, Shelley probably doesn't need Adelaide today."

"Maybe not, but *I* can use her," Dan said. He motioned them in, and they started peeling off layers and wiggling out of boots as he continued to speak. "Aiden is driving me crazy. I usually play with him when I'm home on the weekends, and he just doesn't understand that I have things to do around the house, the baby to care for, errands to run, and meals to make today."

Margaret resisted the urge to mention the fact that at-home moms who "didn't work" managed to get all that done on a daily basis. "Have you taken some time off?"

Dan grinned. "Didn't have to today. In this weather, there won't be anything on the water. No unloading to do."

Margaret winced. She knew Dan was an hourly employee, and that couldn't be good for the Bauers' budget.

"It's okay, though," Dan said, as if he had read her thoughts. "Diane recommended me to someone she met at the library, and I've got a job putting up built-in bookcases and remodeling a closet. So if I can break away from here this afternoon, I can get started on that job earlier than I'd expected."

"That's great news. How's your patient doing today?"

"*Im*-patient," Dan said, shaking his head. "She'd clobber me if I was as ornery as she's been. This morning, I thought I might have to *tie her to the couch!*" He emphasized the last five words, shouting over his shoulder.

"Fat chance!" came Shelley's response, and Margaret could hear the smile in her voice. "Who's at the door?"

Dan stepped back to let Margaret precede him into the living room.

"Hi, honey. I come bearing a babysitter," Margaret said.

Shelley laughed. "You'll be Dan's hero." They watched as Adelaide went on into the kitchen, and a moment later, they heard Aiden shout, "Hey, hi, Adelaide! Wanna play Legos?"

"Whew." Dan mimed wiping his brow. "Now maybe I can get a few things done around here."

"That's usually my line," Shelley informed him. Turning to Margaret, she said, "I feel ridiculous, lying here while he runs himself ragged."

"I know." And she did. "Years ago, I fell from a ladder while I was painting our dining room. I cracked a bone in my leg. I thought I'd go crazy."

"What did you do?"

Margaret thought back to those frustrating days. "Goodness, I haven't thought of this in a long time. I had good friends from a young mothers' support group who came every day. It's the kind of thing you can never pay back, so you resolve to pay it forward." She beamed at Shelley. "And it looks like this is my chance. What needs to be done?"

Shelley lowered her voice. "Could you help me wrap Aiden's birthday gifts? I put it off until the last minute, figuring I'd have time to do it...but that plan went out the window. Dan said he'd do it tonight, but I know he's dreading wrestling with wrapping paper and tape."

"I just bet." Margaret chuckled. "I'll be happy to help you wrap. Just tell me where to find things."

"It's all up in my bedroom," Shelley said. "Dan can carry me up there, and we could close the door to keep Aiden from seeing us."

"Before we begin," Margaret said, "may I get online on your computer? I just remembered something I need to check on right away."

"Of course." Shelley gestured to the desk.

"I found out yesterday that one of my favorite artists is giving a lecture at Colby College. Tickets went on sale yesterday."

But a few moments later, Margaret stared at the monitor in disbelief. "Sold out? Are you kidding me? How can it be sold out? It's an art lecture, not a rock concert!"

Shelley stifled a smile, seeing the depths of her friend's disappointment. "This artist really means something to you."

Margaret nodded. "I can't even explain it so that you'd understand." She hesitated for a moment. "Have you ever seen something—a painting, a photo, a quilt—that just called to you because you found the color or the arrangement so pleasing?"

Shelley nodded slowly. "I used to have a sweater in the most gorgeous shades of misty blue and lavender that made me feel happy every time I wore it. I loved that sweater. I wore it until it literally fell apart." She laughed self-consciously. "That sounds silly."

"Not to me," Margaret told her. "That's exactly what art is about. Each of us has a visceral reaction to certain colors, shapes, scents, sounds..." She sighed. "The last time I heard her speak, Louellen had some interesting insights into the way artists tap into the things that appeal to them. I was hoping to hear more of her theories."

"I'm sorry," Shelley said. "I bet there are students who are required to go. Maybe that filled it."

"Maybe. How disappointing." Margaret slumped in the chair. "I guess it just wasn't meant to be."

Shelley didn't know what to say. "I guess not," didn't exactly sound sympathetic. "Perhaps another opportunity will come up," she offered. "Or maybe she's speaking somewhere else within driving distance."

"Maybe." Margaret sounded doubtful. She straightened and appeared to set aside her disappointment. "Let's get started on this wrapping adventure."

Chapter Five

Beverly stopped in to visit Shelley on Friday afternoon. "Wow," she said as she shook the snow from her fur-trimmed parka and handed it to Dan. "If it keeps snowing like this, we're going to be completely buried. I'm so glad I'm working from home today."

Dan nodded. "I've already shoveled three times, but I feel like I'm getting nowhere."

"Me too." She laughed and went into the living room, where Shelley was ensconced on the sofa, one leg extended and the knee covered by a sturdy brace. "How are you feeling?" she asked her friend.

"Useless." Shelley made a face. "It's a good thing I only have to be off my feet for three days."

"Look at it this way: if you have to be laid up, at least it's during a huge winter storm when nobody's going much of anyplace. It would be worse if it was the middle of the summer."

"I hadn't thought of that," Shelley said. "Although I have a suspicion that trying to negotiate ice and snow with crutches is going to be quite a feat when I start walking again." She smiled. "I'm so glad to see you."

"I came to help. What can I do?"

"Talk to me," Shelley pleaded. "Margaret came again this morning and helped with a few chores. Dan's been home looking after the kids and the house. And the girls in my Sunday school class are organizing meals for the next two weeks. I need some company."

"That's easy enough." Beverly sat down in Dan's recliner. "So how, exactly, did you do this?" She listened as Shelley recounted the fall, wincing as her imagination supplied vivid images. "Oh, that sounds horrible."

Shelley shrugged. "It wasn't great, but it could have been worse. I'm trying to look at the positive side of things. I'm taking a little vacation, and I didn't need surgery."

Beverly laughed. "That's a good idea. Who's doing the baking for the Cove?"

"Rusty is ordering from the place he used to use before I started baking. But it's a commercial supplier, and they don't do anything fancy or unique."

"Well, then he'll be really grateful when you're able to go back to work."

"I suppose that could be considered a silver lining," Shelley said, nodding. "He'll be thrilled when he can get my products again."

"As he should be. Your baked goods are outstanding." Beverly felt the urge to prop up Shelley's ego. She'd never met anyone as talented as Shelley who failed to recognize her own worth. When Shelley only nodded and smiled, clearly ill at ease, Beverly decided to change the subject. "I guess you heard about my close encounter on Wednesday?"

Shelley nodded. "Margaret told me. I can't believe we both had accidents on the same day. Oh, Beverly, thank heavens you weren't hit by that car." She shuddered.

Beverly nodded. "I'm thankful for that. My poor car was all torn up, but I was barely bruised." She grimaced. "Except for a bump on my forehead from that darned airbag. I like your positive thinking, though. I wasn't hurt. And my car can be repaired pretty easily, according to the guys down at the garage."

"That's a blessing too." Shelley leaned forward. "Margaret said you saw lights."

Beverly nodded. She repeated the story she'd told Diane and her father.

When she finished speaking, Shelley's eyes were glowing. "I'm so glad you weren't harmed. It really gives me the sense that God is using the lighthouse to save lives."

"And perhaps reclaim some," Beverly added.

Shelley cocked her head. "What do you mean?"

"Oh, I don't know." Beverly shrugged, tracing her finger along the piped edging of the chair's armrest. "My faith certainly has been changed—strengthened—since I met all of you, and we started seeing the lights."

"Mine too." Shelley nodded. "And the lives of enough other people have been touched by things that happened as a result of light sightings that surely we aren't the only ones who feel this way."

"*We* includes Diane and Margaret, I presume."

"Yes." Shelley didn't hesitate. "Speaking of Margaret, have you talked to her today?"

Beverly shook her head. "No. Why?"

"She used my computer to try to get a ticket to see some artist's lecture at Colby College—"

"Oh! Louellen Lumadue. She told me all about her show and lecture the other day. I hope it lives up to her expectations."

"That's not likely," Shelley told her. "The tickets were all sold out. She was terribly disappointed. I've been wondering if there is anything we can do to take her mind off it. Any ideas?"

"No," Beverly said slowly, thinking through the offer that had occurred to her. "But maybe something better."

"What?"

"I have a friend from college who's on the faculty at Colby. Why don't I contact her and see if there's any way to wrangle a ticket for Margaret?"

Shelley practically bounced in her seat. "That would be fabulous. Call her right now!"

Beverly grinned. Wouldn't it be fun to surprise Margaret? The older woman was one of the kindest people Beverly had ever met. She dug out her phone and left a voice mail for her friend Claudia to return the call. Perhaps they could do lunch. It had been too long since she'd seen her friend.

Shelley looked like she was going to explode with anticipation. "Oh, I hope she can help."

"So do I." The driving snow that sliced across the window behind Shelley's couch caught her eye. "Did Margaret actually open the gallery today?"

Shelley nodded. "She said she wanted to paint, so she might as well. I can't imagine there'll be anyone running around town shopping today."

Beverly shook her head with a rueful grin. "No way."

A knock on the front door startled them both.

"I can get that," Beverly called to Dan. Rising, she went to the door. Pulling it open, she was confronted with two figures almost completely coated in white: Diane and Margaret. "Well, hello. What are you two doing here?" Quickly she stepped aside and motioned them in, then firmly shut the door behind them. It was simply incredible to see how much snow was falling.

"I walked downtown and went by the gallery when I realized Margaret was open," Diane told them.

"She convinced me to come home with her," Margaret added. "We certainly got our heart rates up trudging through those drifts!"

"Are the sidewalks even cleared yet?" Beverly asked.

"Some are, some aren't," Diane answered. "Most people have made an effort to clear away at least some of it, because if they don't, it's going to be so deep that even snowblowers will have problems."

"Dan?" Shelley called.

Dan popped his head in from the kitchen, where he'd been entertaining the children. "What's up? Hello," he tacked on, smiling at Diane and Margaret. "Are you four having a lighthouse powwow again?"

"No. Diane said most people are clearing their sidewalks just to keep the snow from getting too deep. Have you done ours?"

Dan shook his head. "I thought when Emma goes down for her n-a-p and Aiden has quiet time in his room that I'd run out and do it. And then I'll go over to the new job for a few hours, if you'll have help."

"I can stick around for a while," Diane told him. She looked back at the others. "Actually, we do need to have a lighthouse discussion."

"To talk about my lights?" Beverly asked. "No," Diane said in answer to Beverly's question. "I found out something odd today." Her tone was puzzled.

"About the lighthouse?" Shelley asked. She winced as she shifted the ice pack on her knee.

Diane nodded. "I went down to the historical society to see if they could help us. I spoke with someone who told me he was pretty certain the lighthouse had been added to the National Register some years ago."

"Really?" Shelley frowned. "It sure doesn't look like it."

"I never heard anything about that," Margaret commented. "Seems like it would have been front-page news."

Beverly nodded.

"I thought the same thing." Diane looked around the group. "So I looked through the electronic files of more recent issues of the paper, but I didn't see anything there either."

Shelley tugged absently at a lock of her long blonde hair, worn down around her shoulders today. "That's weird. How do we find out if it is or if it isn't?"

Diane grinned. "You employ an investigative journalist-turned-novelist to track down the truth."

The other three laughed.

"Consider yourself employed," Margaret said to Diane.

CHAPTER SIX

Later Friday afternoon, Diane was happy to see that the snow had finally stopped. She was getting pretty tired of running out every few hours and clearing her sidewalks and small driveway. But if she hadn't, she'd never have been able to manage the shoveling.

A short time later, her breath puffing out great clouds of white as it froze in the air, she trudged through the snow along Main Street to the Marble Cove municipal building's annex. It had been a lovely Victorian home many years ago, and the exterior was painted a soft blue-gray with deep ocean blue and vanilla trim. Someone with an excellent eye for color had chosen the shades; in the summer, lovely annuals filled the blue window boxes attached to the front. It was one of the prettiest buildings in town.

Diane had never been inside before. Really, all she knew about it was that the key to the lighthouse was kept there.

When she stepped into the foyer, she saw that walls had been knocked out and rearranged to make a more officelike space. A sign near the staircase indicated that the mayor's office could be found upstairs.

There was a coatrack along one wall, and a sign saying Reception above a set of French doors to the left. On the right, a second set of French doors proclaimed that one could pay one's taxes and utility bills there.

Stepping into the reception room, Diane closed the door behind her and approached the desk.

"Hello!" A young woman dressed in a fluffy pink sweater, gray corduroys, and Ugg boots that were the exact same pink of the sweater turned away from a copier. "I'm Angela. How can I help you today?"

Diane smiled as she introduced herself. The girl was adorably perky. "I am looking into having the lighthouse placed on the National Register of Historic Places, and I was told that plans to do so may already be in the works or even completed. Is there someone I could talk to about that?"

The girl pursed her lips. "The town council members are based here, but they don't actually work here or anything, so they only check in once in a while." She tapped a pen against her lips. "I can look in the files, but I've never seen anything about that. 'Course I've only worked here for about two months, so it could have happened before that." She indicated a comfortable-looking chair in front of her desk. "Have a seat and I'll check."

Angela walked to a set of filing cabinets against one wall and yanked open a large drawer. From her chair, Diane could see her fingers dancing through myriad folders. Then she slammed that drawer shut and repeated the process with two others. Finally, she turned to Diane with a frown. "That would have been too easy. Let me do a search through the council minutes. How long ago do you think this happened?"

"I don't have any idea." Diane leaned forward. "I don't even know if it's true. But I was given the information by someone who's active in the historical society, so I think it's probably credible."

"They don't have any information there?" Angela slipped into her seat and began tapping away at the keyboard in front of her computer monitor.

"I didn't get that far because it was closed," Diane said, "but I don't think so. The man I spoke to seemed sure it had been put on the National Register already, but he didn't mention a specific time frame."

"Hmph." Angela's eyes swept the monitor. "This office needs a complete reorganization. Nothing is filed where it belongs, meeting minutes are missing— Well, hello, Mr. Quinn," she said without even taking a breath, as the door to the reception room opened again. "What are you doing out walking around town today? You'll break your neck."

"Nah." The speaker was a medium-height older man wrapped in layers of outerwear. He had sturdy, no-nonsense boots on his feet, and as he spoke, he raised one foot to show them the tread on the bottom of the boot. "These things are as good as snow tires." He shed his mittens, dropped the hood of his parka and took off a black watch cap to display short, silver hair. As he started to unbutton his coat, he glanced at Diane, and she saw that he had twinkling blue eyes.

"Diane, this Mr. Everett Quinn." Angela performed a quick introduction. "Mr. Quinn, Diane Spencer." Addressing Diane again, she said, "Mr. Quinn is on the town council."

"Ah." Diane's interest rose. "Perhaps you can help me."

"I'll do my best." He nodded as he took the chair nearest hers.

She explained what information she was seeking.

Everett Quinn's brow furrowed. "I remember somebody asking about this before. I believe they must have started the process, but I can't recall any more than that. I imagine it fizzled out. It's a lot of work to get a building accepted for historic preservation."

Diane dug in her pocket and produced one of the business cards that she'd recently had made. "If you remember anything else, please give me a call." She smiled. "I can't stand mysteries. I'm going to have to figure out if the lighthouse really is protected by a national organization. And if so, why it hasn't been restored."

Mr. Quinn peered at her business card. "A writer, eh?"

She nodded. "My first book comes out in April. I'm so excited I can't stand the wait."

"Wow," Angela said. "That's pretty cool."

"Cool indeed," Mr. Quinn affirmed, and Diane suspected from the way his dimples deepened that he didn't normally use such slang. "What's it about?"

She explained her lighthouse mystery to her interested audience of two, and they both promised to buy copies of the book when it came out. That made her smile. But walking home a short time later, she wasn't feeling quite so happy.

The revisions that her editor had requested on her first manuscript had been more extensive than Diane had ever imagined. She'd worked hard to get them completed and returned on time, and then she'd tried to get right to work on her next story…and she had no idea how to make her plot cooperate with the outline she had already submitted to her editor. She'd written and discarded an entire chapter already.

Arriving at home, she wasn't in the mood to try to plot a story. Instead, she got online and went to the home page of Maine's government. At Maine.gov, one could find out about elections and state news, find a state official, or seek the appropriate state agency. She went up to the "search" field and typed in "National Historic Register," and in seconds, she found what she needed. The Maine Historic Preservation Commission had a direct link to the National Register of Historic Places, which in turn had a place to learn more about the application process.

First, there had to be a determination of eligibility prepared by the landowner. Hmm. So there certainly should have been information in Angela's files about it, given that the light was owned by the town.

Second, a formal nomination had to be prepared, and it was strongly recommended that an architectural historian be hired for the job. There were certain nomination submission deadlines that had to be met. Then it was up to the Commission. If they thought the property should be preserved, it would be presented through a brief slide show and an overview of the property's significance at a meeting of the State Review Board. Then, if that board accepted it, the nomination would finally go before the National Park Service to be an accepted or declined entry into the National Register.

Diane leaned back in her office chair. Wow. If the nomination hadn't even been started yet, it was going to take significant time and energy to go through the process. And money.

Perhaps the Marble Cove Historical Society would spearhead the project. Of course, they would need a committee chair. Not that she wanted another task on her plate, but since she was self-employed and her hours were more flexible, it might be something she could take on.

It would take at least six months, and that was if everything went smoothly *and* they were able to find the funds for the nomination preparation.

Her gaze fell on a piece of paper on which she had hastily outlined her second book for the publisher so long ago. Glumly, she reflected that if her imagination and inspiration didn't kick in soon, she would have plenty of time to devote to the project.

She'd intended to use the lighthouse again as a springboard for a mystery that was very loosely connected to the first with key characters, but she was having a terrible time finding a fresh approach to her outline. Her first book had practically written itself—although obviously it hadn't since she'd had this mountain of revisions to tackle. How did authors plot book after book after book? She was having trouble finding one new idea compelling enough that readers would want to buy.

*   *   *

Beverly decided to attend church on Sunday morning. For several months, she'd been tossing around the idea of visiting a few to see if she felt comfortable at any of them, but today she'd chosen to return to Old First, where she'd attended Christmas services.

Each of her three friends on Newport Avenue attended church regularly. It wasn't that she felt pressured though. They spoke of their beliefs, but they had never made her feel that she was wrong to sleep in on Sunday mornings. It was more that questions seemed to be slowly opening up inside her, seeking... something. Answers. Information. She wasn't sure why, but she felt that she might be able to identify what was missing in her life by attending church, listening to the words of the faith-filled.

Each of her friends also had invited her to attend with them sometime over the past months. They hadn't been pushy; they had just let her know that if she preferred not to have to walk into a strange place alone, she was welcome to go along with them. She'd nearly taken one of them up on the invitation, but this morning, she had felt the need to find her own niche.

During the Christmas holidays, she and Jeff Mackenzie had attended Old First, one of the earliest churches to be founded in the area. The house of worship was a traditional Gothic revival structure with peaks spearing up from the roofline, and a tall bell tower to one side. It was a large church with a large and robust congregation filling the sanctuary enough that the voices raised in song didn't echo off the interior stone walls. There was a stunning pipe organ to the right of the altar, a choir loft to the left. Every seat in it was filled, and the choir director, a youngish woman named Maddie Bancroft, conducted with a verve and energy Beverly admired.

Reverend Locke, the senior pastor, had a descriptive and compelling speaking style. She had found his Sunday sermon inspiring, but as the service moved on, her attention began to wander during the offertory. There was a man seated about six rows in front of her from whom she couldn't take her eyes. The shape of his head, his haircut . . . from that angle he looked a great deal like Jeff, her—her what? Her friend, she told herself firmly. Sure, he'd kissed her beneath the mistletoe on Christmas Day, but that didn't mean they were exclusive. Or even dating, really.

But spending Christmas with someone was a special thing, wasn't it? She didn't know what to think. He'd texted her a few times since he'd left town, but they'd been friendly catch-up bits of information, not passionate declarations of intention. Which she didn't want anyway. Did she?

The man turned his head toward the woman seated next to him. In profile, he looked nothing like Jeff. Of course he didn't. Jeff lived in Portland. Even if she was considering leaping into the dating pool, it would be silly to enter a long-distance relationship.

Long distance. That thought brought her job to mind. Goodness, but she was tired of commuting to Augusta. Even though she'd managed to cut down on her time in the office, it wasn't really very convenient to work from Marble Cove. Working on budgetary matters sounded dry and boring, but if anyone knew how many meetings she attended in the course of a week!

She would leave her job with the state in a heartbeat if she only knew what she wanted to do and could find some type of work she enjoyed. It almost had to be in the business arena. Her skill set relied heavily on her understanding of corporate finances, working with budget analyses and policing departmental spending. But where in Marble Cove could she find something like that?

So what did she enjoy that she could turn into a job?

Playing piano, for one. She loved sitting down and letting her fingers fly over the keys, creating music for herself and others to enjoy. But she wasn't sure she had the temperament or patience needed to teach such a skill.

What else?

She drew a blank. How silly was that, that she couldn't even think of anything else she enjoyed? No, it wasn't silly, it was pathetic. When had she lost sight of things so basic as relaxation and pleasure?

More determined now, she cast her mind back and sifted through her memories. What did she truly enjoy?

Not just piano playing. Music. Singing. She had sung in a concert choir and another group that did show tunes years ago when she was in high school, and she had loved it. She also had sung in a women's chorus in college, but since then, she wasn't sure she'd sung anything except possibly "Happy Birthday" and Christmas carols.

Unobtrusively, she lifted two fingers. Piano and singing. That was a start. She loved to read too. Another finger joined the first two.

Cooking. Art. No, neither of those fascinated her. Organizing, she decided. She thought of the neatly labeled boxes in her father's attic, the newly cleaned drawers in his kitchen, the way she'd efficiently gone through her possessions after she decided to move to Marble Cove. No doubt about it, she had a flair for organizing. And numbers, of course. Since she was a very small child, she'd been good at math. If she'd ever gotten anything less than an "A" in a mathematics course, she couldn't remember it. To her, there was something intensely satisfying about numbers. Making budgets add up, seeing where excesses could be trimmed...even going over her checking account balance wasn't an awful task like it was for some people. She had to smile at herself. What a geek.

Okay, so that was five. What else? Running, but she couldn't exactly make money doing that. The organ began the music for the doxology, but part of her mind continued to work. Depression glass! Her mother had loved Depression glass. She had only collected one pattern, but they had gone to flea markets and yard sales when Beverly was a child, and she had learned to identify many others. She hadn't done that in a long time, but that was something she definitely enjoyed. Perhaps she would begin collecting a new pattern.

As the service concluded, and the organ began a postlude that displayed the organist's stellar command of the instrument, Beverly rose and started out with the rest of the crowd. A few faces looked familiar, but for the most part, she was among strangers. It had never bothered her before, but today, glancing around at all the smiling faces, warm greetings among friends, and enthusiastic handshaking, she felt very alone. Very isolated.

And whose fault is that? she asked herself. What was that old chestnut that her mother always said? *"If you want a friend, you have to be a friend."*

All right. She took a deep breath, ignored the butterflies in her stomach, and extended her hand to a woman beside her. "Hello, I'm Beverly Wheeland."

"Hello, Beverly, I'm Elsie Roux. Is this your first time visiting Old First?" Elsie was an attractive, youthful blonde. She had several children straggling behind her, and a firm grip on one small boy's hand. All the children were as blond as their mother.

Beverly thought of her Advent visits and decided they didn't really count. "Yes. It was a lovely service."

Elsie smiled. "Reverend Locke is a good speaker. He's a wonderful shepherd for our flock too. Anyone who has even a hint of trouble goes on his prayer list and receives a visit."

"How nice." Beverly was clicking through her mental files, trying to place Elsie's last name. She knew she'd heard it before. Then it came to her. "Roux. Are you related to Hank?" Hank Roux was the handyman who had helped fix the Shearwater Gallery after the roofer had broken his arm.

Elsie smiled and nodded. "Hank's my husband." She indicated the crew behind her. "These are some of our children: Jasper, Brendan, Carla, Mazy, and Eddie." Eddie was the little one whose hand she held, but Beverly had no idea which of the others went with which name. She smiled and gave the whole tribe a general nod. Then Elsie's words sank in. "*Some* of them. How many are there?"

Elsie laughed. "Eight altogether. Brendan's twin Brian was the acolyte today, so he's off putting away his robe. And my oldest girl Christine went to the nursery to get Teresa, the baby."

Beverly shook her head. "You're a brave woman, Elsie."

The blonde chuckled. "It's all in your outlook. I love kids. What do you do, Beverly?"

"I'm a budget analyst for the state." Oh, it sounded so dry and boring.

She spoke with Elsie for several more minutes before the line to greet the pastor dwindled. Beverly thanked Reverend Locke, who welcomed her warmly, and exited the church, pulling her stylish woolen cloche hat firmly down over her ears after adjusting its satin bow.

"Beverly Wheeland?" The sound of her name halted her. Looking around, she spied an older couple threading through other congregants. "I thought that was you." The woman steamed up and stuck out her hand. "Frances Bauer, and my husband Ralph. I believe we've met before."

"Oh yes. Hello, Mrs. Bauer, Mr. Bauer. I'm sorry I didn't recognize you."

"That's all right," Frances said. "It's hard to recognize anybody when we're all bundled up like this. Are you joining Old First?"

"I don't know. I've just started attending, but I like it."

"Old First has some wonderful folks. My whole family goes here, except for my son Hal, who doesn't live close, and Dan's family." She shook her head. "Shelley said she preferred a more contemporary feel, whatever that means. But if it makes her happy, that's fine with me." Although clearly it wasn't. "We've got to get moving. The whole group's coming over for Sunday dinner, and we're going to celebrate Aiden's birthday today. Hard to believe he's four already! It was so nice seeing you, Beverly. I'm sure we'll meet again real soon."

As Frances Bauer marched away with her husband quietly following along, Beverly stood looking after them. Gracious. Mrs. Bauer certainly could keep a conversation going...without anyone else even contributing. Beverly smiled as she walked to her car, navigating through the paths made in the large snowbanks that had been pushed to the edges of the parking lot. Frances was about as different from Shelley as two people could be. No wonder they mixed about as well as oil and water. They said men married their mothers, but in this case, Beverly suspected Dan had chosen a woman who *didn't* resemble his mother in any way.

CHAPTER SEVEN

Shelley was bored. Or, if not exactly bored, certainly feeling useless. She was seated in Dan's parents' living room with her leg propped up, reduced to waiting for the meal to be served while Dan's mother and sisters bustled around in the kitchen getting it ready.

They hadn't attended church that morning. With her on crutches now, it seemed like far too much work to dress, drive, thump in and out of the sanctuary, and stand repeatedly.

"You doing okay?" Dan came into the room, one of his nephews clinging to his back like a monkey.

Shelley nodded. "Yes. But honestly, Dan, I could be out there helping. The doctor said that today I could start walking around, remember?"

"With crutches," Dan reminded her. "And he specifically said not to overdo it." He sent her a mock-stern look. "I suspect that your definition of 'overdoing' is far different from the doctor's."

As Dan finished speaking, his mother popped her head into the living room. "Shelley, I have eggs boiled and cooled, but I need someone to make deviled eggs. We can make a place for you at the table if you want to help."

"I'd be glad to!" Shelley knew her face looked far more enthusiastic than making deviled eggs would warrant under normal circumstances, but she didn't care.

Frances smiled. "Good. I figured you might be getting stir-crazy in here all alone."

As her mother-in-law's head vanished, Shelley was too surprised to reach for her crutches for a moment. Often, it seemed that Frances spent a lot of time criticizing, but Shelley appreciated that Frances had thought to include her.

In the kitchen, her sisters-in-law fussed over her, arranging a second chair so that she could prop her leg up on a pillow. She had to admit, it felt good to have it elevated.

"Do you want an ice bag?" Lilah asked. She was married to Dan's next older brother Hal, and was only a few years older than Shelley. Although they lived in Augusta, they tried to be there for Sunday lunch at least once a month.

Hal and Lilah had twin daughters, and her third child was due in May. Shelley often wondered how long it would be before Dan's mother began pressing Shelley and him to add to their brood. As if she didn't have enough.

"I'm good for now," Shelley told Lilah. "Thank you."

Frances thumped a bowl full of eggs, an empty dish, an egg tray, and a knife and fork in front of her. "Here you go."

Dan's sister Annie, wielding a large knife to slice potatoes for french fries, said, "I'm glad you felt good enough to join us."

"It's just a little tear in a ligament. I'll be fine in a few weeks."

"I'm glad. It could have been so much worse." Samantha, a year younger than Annie, shuddered.

"Yes, it could have been." Shelley shuddered too, able to imagine it all too well.

Frances clapped her hands. "Let's not have any more of this morbid talk. Shelley's going to be fine. Lilah, didn't you have an ultrasound done last week?" That question immediately turned the topic in another direction, and Shelley smiled at her mother-in-law, glad not to be the center of attention. Frances smiled back and winked.

An hour later, the meal had been served and devoured by the horde of locusts that was the Bauer family. Since it was Aiden's birthday, he sat at the head of the table, as the guest of honor at every Bauer birthday celebration did. He wore a yellow paper crown Dan's sister-in-law Patsy had made and decorated with glitter and a huge smile. "Time for cake and presents!" he crowed.

"Oh, we're skipping that this year," Dan's dad said.

Not fooled for a second, Aiden grinned. "*Pappeeee.* You're silly."

Just then, someone switched off the lights in the dining room, and Frances came out of the kitchen bearing a cake with five candles on it. There was always an extra candle for good luck, and Frances always made the birthday cake herself.

Aiden squealed and clapped, his eyes wide. Dan, standing behind Shelley, chuckled as he snapped pictures. "Can you blow 'em all out at once, buddy?"

Sucking in a huge breath, Aiden huffed and puffed and finally got the last flame extinguished. As the room burst into clapping and cheering and the lights came back on, Shelley looked around at Dan's big family and thanked God for every one of them. Her children were going to grow up with these traditions and the sense of security being a part of the Bauer clan would give them. They were loved by many, and they would know it.

She was loved by many, Shelley realized. Although she often didn't feel comfortable in their midst, these were her relatives as well as her children's, and they had accepted and welcomed her when she married Dan. Maybe she needed to step outside her comfort zone and work a little harder to accept them too.

"Attention, everybody. Attention."

Shelley tuned in to the voice raised above the babble. Her mother-in-law was standing, waving one arm in the air until the entire Bauer family was quiet.

"I just wanted to say that I won't be available for the next week or so to pick up the children, babysit, or whatever. Shelley's going to need an extra pair of hands, so I'll be busy taking care of Danny's family. So don't panic if I don't return your phone calls within five minutes. Annie," she added, staring meaningfully at Dan's second sister.

Everyone laughed, and Annie pretended to pout. Shelley stretched her lips into a smile, but inside, she was horrified. Since Dan had informed her after the fact of the invitation he'd extended, she'd expected Frances would stop by a bit more than usual. But underfoot for days on end? Their recent camaraderie forgotten, all Shelley could think was, *Oh no!*

*   *   *

On Tuesday, Beverly drove to Augusta to work, using her father's car. At lunchtime, rather than going to the staff lounge with her healthy packed lunch in her pretty lunch bag, she left the building and headed for an attractive seafood restaurant two blocks away on Water Street.

She arrived first, but before she was seated, she heard her name called. Turning, Beverly saw a slim figure in a cherry red suit clipping confidently toward her on pencil-thin red heels. The skirt was slim with a fashionable flare at the hemline, and a big Coach bag hung over her shoulder.

"Claudia!" Opening her arms, she gave her friend a warm hug. "How have you been?"

"Great! How about you?" Claudia Garner returned the enthusiastic hug. "How long has it been? I want to hear everything."

The hostess came to seat them then, and Beverly was glad for the break in the conversation. The last time she had seen Claudia was when her friend had attended the memorial service for Beverly's husband Will.

When they were seated, Claudia turned to her with a smile. "It's wonderful to see you. Did I hear you moved to the coast?"

Beverly nodded. She told her friend about her father's health ups and downs, about feeling she needed to be closer, and even about her thoughts on changing jobs. After the waitress took their order, Claudia, in turn, caught Beverly up on the doings of her own family, the passing of her husband's mother, and her breeding program with the Shetland sheepdogs she'd owned for many years.

The waitress returned with their first courses, steaming bowls of New England clam chowder filled with sweet Maine surfer clams in heavy cream and butter. It was a decadent delight, and Beverly promised herself an extra long walk later.

Their lunches arrived then, a crab cake Caesar salad for Beverly and lobster salad on a croissant for Claudia. As she neatly quartered her sandwich, Claudia asked, "So are you going to keep this job or look for something closer to home? That must be an awfully long commute."

Beverly nodded. "It is. I'm not planning to quit my job tomorrow or anything like that, but I have been kicking around the idea of a career change."

"Like what?"

"That's the problem." Beverly carefully forked up a large lump of crab. "I don't know. All I know is numbers. What would I do?"

"Accounting? I guess you'd have to go back to school and then take your test, though."

"Yeah. I'm not really interested in taking classes. I'm going to see if there are any firms in the area looking for budget analysts or finance managers, but there's not a lot of large industries around Marble Cove."

"Banking?" Claudia shook her head. "No. You'd never make anything near what you're making now."

"I don't really have to," Beverly said mildly. "Will and I were comfortably set, and I still haven't sold the house in Augusta."

"Didn't you have to buy another one?"

Beverly shook her head. "I moved into my father's house, actually."

Claudia shuddered. "I'd curl up into a little catatonic ball if anyone told me I had to live with my parents again."

"Father's not bad." Beverly had to grin at the image Claudia's words painted in her mind. "I was driving down there every weekend to check on him anyway, and with me there, he gets into less trouble."

"Is he having senility problems?"

Beverly hesitated. "Not really. His health is pretty good for his age. But he has diabetes, and sometimes the changes in his blood sugar can make him confused. And anytime he gets sick, his blood sugar goes wild. But overall, he's in very good shape and still pretty sharp."

"That's good. So back to your career…"

The two women chatted the whole way through the rest of their hour together, and then stood for a moment on the sidewalk afterward. "I'm so glad you called," Claudia said. "We shouldn't let so much time go by between our catch-ups."

"I know." Beverly nodded. "I have a confession to make. I didn't call just to catch up, although I *should* have. I have a question for you—a favor, if you will."

"Oh?" Claudia cocked her head, and the bell of her honey-blonde hair fell smoothly away from her jaw.

"My friend Margaret found out that an artist named Louellen Lumadue is going to be giving a lecture at Colby next week. She tried to get a ticket online, but they were sold out. Do you know of any way I could get one for her?"

"Oh, sure." Claudia waved a hand as if the request was no big deal. "They hold a certain number of tickets for every event for faculty and staff. Unless it's a highly regarded entertainer of some sort, they never get rid of them all." She grinned. "If you want to come by after work, I can pick one up for you this afternoon."

Beverly was astonished. "It's that easy?"

Claudia laughed. "It's that easy."

CHAPTER EIGHT

Beverly couldn't wait to see Margaret that evening. As soon as she got home from work, she called Shelley. "I got the ticket."

She yanked the phone away from her ear at the sound of Shelley's squeal of delight. "That's wonderful!"

"Is it all right if we come over to your house for a few minutes this evening so I can give it to her?"

"Oh, please," Shelley said, understanding that *we* referred to Diane, Margaret, and themselves. "Save me from myself. I'm so bored I could scream. My mother-in-law won't let me lift a finger. I can't wait to go back to work."

Beverly chuckled. "I'll tell the others. Seven thirty?"

"That's fine. Dan will put the kids to bed."

A couple hours later, Beverly realized she was the last to arrive at Shelley's. Margaret was hurrying through the door as she came up the front walk, and Diane was in the little foyer holding the door.

"Br-r-r! Is it ever cold out there," Beverly gasped. "I thought my face was going to freeze just walking fifty yards down the street."

"The thermometer outside my back door says nine degrees," Margaret reported. "And that's without wind chill."

"Ugh. It's a good thing I love this town and this area," Diane said, "because right now I'm awfully tempted to buy a house on a Caribbean island."

Beverly laughed. "You'd be back in two months."

"Yeah, but in two months, it would be a little warmer." Diane grinned. "Maybe."

"Hello," Shelley said as they all trooped into the living room. She was sitting in Dan's easy chair with her foot up on the footrest.

"How are you doing?" Margaret asked. "Ready to run a marathon yet?"

"Not quite yet." Shelley grinned. "But at least I'm allowed to be up and around on crutches now."

"I broke my ankle and had crutches when I was a kid," Diane told them. "Miserably uncomfortable things. Bruised my poor armpits so badly."

"These haven't been too bad yet," Shelley told her. "Maybe they've improved them a little in forty years."

Diane wrinkled her nose. "Brat." Then she laughed. "Closer to fifty, if you want the truth."

Margaret said, "I'm not even getting into this conversation," and everyone chuckled.

Beverly couldn't stand the suspense any longer. "I have a surprise," she announced.

The other three all looked at her.

"It's for Margaret."

"Oh, I bet I know!" Shelley clapped her hands.

"Spill," Diane demanded, while Margaret simply sat, her round face wearing a puzzled expression.

"A surprise for me?" she asked.

Beverly nodded. She fished an envelope from the pocket of her fleece vest and handed it to her friend. "Here you go."

Margaret turned the envelope over, examining both sides. She held it up to the light. "What is it?"

"Open it and see!" Shelley demanded. "You're as bad as my mother."

Margaret laughed. "All right." Carefully, she peeled the envelope open, not tearing a single bit of the flap. Inside was a folded piece of paper. Something fell out when she opened it. Reflexively, she grabbed for it, and when she caught it, she held it up to see what it was.

Her mouth dropped open. "This is a ticket to Louellen Lumadue's lecture! At Colby! Oh, Beverly, *thank you!*" She leaped up with more speed than grace and grabbed Beverly in a warm hug. "How on earth did you manage this?" She waved the ticket beneath Beverly's nose.

"I have my ways." Beverly relented when Margaret gave her a "get serious" look. "One of my old college pals is a professor at Colby. She's the one you really should be thanking."

"I will!" Margaret sat back down, eyes shining as she regarded the ticket. "Beverly, I can't thank you enough."

"Who's Louellen Lumadue?" Diane asked, and Beverly realized Diane hadn't been there when she'd discussed it with either Margaret or Shelley.

Margaret gave her a thumbnail version of the story. "So I got really excited when I saw that she would be the guest lecturer at Colby," she finished. "And then I found out the tickets were sold out. Boy, was I disappointed." She beamed at Beverly. "But not anymore, thanks to you!"

"Would anyone like cookies?" Shelley asked in the momentary silence that fell.

"None for me," Beverly declined. "I'm going to have supper with Father."

"Or me," Diane said. "My pants have been telling me to stop snacking so much."

"Or start walking more," Shelley told her, grinning.

"Exactly how do you have cookies on hand?" Margaret demanded. "You're supposed to be resting."

"I am," Shelley said. "Haven't you ever heard of frozen cookie dough?"

Everyone chuckled.

"Besides," Shelley went on, "I am able to be up and about for short periods each day now." She spread her hands. "Obviously. And I decided to use this time wisely. I promised myself I would try one recipe a day, and stay off my feet the rest of the time. That's still thirty-one new recipes this month."

"Thirty-one?" Diane looked a bit shell-shocked. "Are you going to need that many?"

"No. I imagine most of them will never see the light of day again, but I would like to add two or three to my standard list of offerings."

"So, essentially, you'll present your clients with a menu of options?"

"In some cases. I've already learned that there are clients at both ends of the spectrum. Some of them want to pick and choose from my offerings, while others have a specific idea in their head. For those kinds of clients, sometimes I have to research a bit to find exactly what will work. The only thing I won't do is work from someone else's recipe."

"I'm so proud of you, Shelley," Margaret declared. "Just last summer this idea was barely a glimmer, and now look at you. Six months later, you're a bona fide business owner."

"I have a long way to go, though."

"In what way?" Diane's tone was encouraging.

Shelley took a deep breath. "Well I already have several standard recipes that are always available. But I still need to work on additional, more spectacular offerings and perhaps some holiday specials."

"Valentine's Day is coming up," Diane said. "Have you got something in mind? Because you really should start advertising soon."

"Advertising?" Shelley shook her head. "My kitchen isn't even finished, and I'm already busy. I don't think I'm ready for that."

"Soon you'll need to be." Beverly had talked with Shelley about establishing goals, accounting practices, and inventory before, but Shelley had been so busy with special orders through the holiday season that they hadn't ever gotten back to those items.

"I hadn't thought about the business end of it. All I've been thinking about are cookies and how to package and price them. And getting the kitchen up to code." She laughed. "My head isn't big enough to hold more than that!"

"That's what business plans are for," Beverly told her. "While you're off your feet, this would be an excellent time to work on some of those elements." Diane loved that Shelley's business was becoming a reality, and she loved that her young friend was so excited about this. Shelley needed more confidence, and creating a business out of something she was so good at was sure to boost her self-esteem.

"Beverly's right," Diane said. "You need to start working on a business plan, Shelley."

"But I already have the business started. I've done quite a bit of planning."

"I think what Beverly and Diane mean"—Margaret took the cue from Diane—"is a list of goals for your first five years, some budget projections, a mission statement...I did all of this when I started the gallery, and I found it helped me clarify my thoughts a lot."

"A mission statement? It's just a cookie business."

"Maybe, but it still helps to be able to put into words exactly what you envision, and how big you want your business to be in five years, and how to plan to make that happen—"

"Okay." Shelley's forehead wrinkled. "I guess I don't really know what my mission statement is, except to bake cookies—"

"And sell them," Diane interrupted.

Shelley was looking a little overwhelmed. "This is actually a little scary. What if I can't do it?"

"Of course you can do it." Beverly cleared her throat. "You're already doing it quite successfully. Now we need to come up with a budget and some projections for how much you want to grow each year. Remember we talked about this a few weeks ago?"

"And then Christmas happened," Shelley said, a sudden grin breaking out.

"Right. But now we have the time, so let's do it."

"Go for it, Shelley. You've got an expert numbers person offering to help you. Quick! Grab her before she gets away." Diane had been ready to leap into the breach and offer to help, but she was relieved that Beverly's words got her off the hook. Beverly would be *so* much better at that type of thing.

"You know, Beverly," Margaret said, "there's a market for business consultants to help people like Shelley. It's a complicated process. If you're considering a job change, this might be something to explore."

"But I'm—"

"You'd be perfect!" Diane said. "Professional but approachable. You probably could rent office space here in Marble Cove for a very reasonable rate, and you could even do consultations through an online service."

"I have considered a job change," Beverly admitted. "But I haven't come to any conclusions." She held up a hand when Diane opened her mouth. "All of you know me by now; something like this would be a massive change in my life, something I have no intention of leaping into without thorough planning. So let's talk about something else for a while, shall we?" She smiled to soften her words.

Diane cleared her throat. "Since we're all here, shall I tell you what I've found out about the lighthouse being registered with the National Register of Historic Places?"

"Yes." Shelley leaned forward.

"Not anything new. But I know there's some information out there. It's just a matter of finding it."

"If anyone can, you'd be that person," Margaret said. "What are you going to do next?"

"I'll keep asking questions. And I'm also going to contact the National Register to see if I can find out if it's already been registered."

Beverly was smiling again, a wider, less inhibited smile than she usually had on her face.

"What are you smiling at?" Diane asked.

"You." Beverly's voice was full of glee. "The National Register isn't going to know what hit them."

CHAPTER NINE

The wind was blowing off the ocean, practically pushing Beverly along as she made her way home from Shelley's house a short while later. Pulling her hood tight around her face, Beverly staggered every few steps as gusts of wind repeatedly gave her a shove. Snow was now drifted over her nicely shoveled walk, and she plowed through it with annoyance. On the porch, she stomped and knocked her boots together to rid them of extra snow before she opened the front door. Ah, warm air. Finally. Stepping onto the rubber-backed mat she'd placed near the door, she called, "I'm back, Father."

As she hung up her coat and placed her boots on the boot rack where the melting snow wouldn't damage the floor, her father appeared in the door that led to the living room.

"I made dinner," he told her.

"You made dinner?" She repeated it cautiously, wondering exactly what was in store for her. "I would have done that. I just lost track of time at Shelley's house."

"It's all right. I just reheated the meat loaf you made on Sunday, got some of those tubes of biscuits out of the fridge, and opened a can of peas."

Relieved, she smiled at him. "Sounds good." Now that she was thawing out, she could smell the meat loaf. She sent up a small prayer of thanks that nothing appeared to have gotten burned.

"It's just about ready," he said. "I was going to eat without you if you didn't get here soon."

She chuckled. "Would have served me right."

Together, they walked into the kitchen. Beverly checked the rolls and meat loaf in the oven and gave the peas a quick stir. Then she set two places at the table. This was one of the best things about living with another person. Mealtimes were so much more enjoyable when there was someone else to talk to. Goodness, she was glad she had decided to move in with her father. Now if only she could find a job around here. Her friends' comments teased at her mind. Could she really make a career out of helping people start businesses?

They took seats at the old oak table and bowed their heads. Her father gave a simple blessing. Would it be appropriate, she wondered, to pray for help finding a job? That sounded rather selfish, she thought. Maybe "for guidance in figuring out the right new career" would be more acceptable.

Beverly began to slide slices of meat loaf onto her father's plate. "I'm thinking about looking for a job closer to home."

Her father accepted the plate and set it down. "You'd quit your job with the state?"

"Yes." She nodded. "I enjoy it, but I'm not exactly passionate about analyzing budgets and statistics. Making recommendations for ways to cut spending doesn't always make me the most popular person on the planet." Her tone was wry.

Her father chuckled. "I imagine not." He spooned some peas onto his plate, his face sobering. "Do you have another career in mind?"

"Not really. I'd rather not have to go back to school if I can avoid it." Beverly hesitated. "Margaret did have an idea just today, though, that got me thinking."

"Oh?"

"You know I've been helping Shelley Bauer get her baking business off the ground, right? I've really enjoyed the process, Father. I think I'd like to explore the idea of becoming a consultant for small business owners." Enthusiasm began to rise as she voiced the nebulous idea. "I could specialize in helping people start their own businesses, but I could also help companies streamline their budgets and find more productive practices."

"So how would you go about becoming a business consultant? Would you set up an office in town?"

Beverly laughed. "I don't know. I haven't begun to think about that. Honestly, I really only began considering it today when I realized how much I've enjoyed helping Shelley."

"You'll have to do some market research, see if there's a need for someone to do that kind of thing in Marble Cove."

She nodded. "But I could work online with people in other locations too. I can't think of any reason why a business consultant couldn't do a great deal of work from a distance."

"I guess you'd better get busy researching. That will give you a better feel for it," he observed. "You'll know more clearly if it's something you think you'd want to make a career out of." His eyes sparkled. "If you decide you want to do this, maybe I can help you with the planning stages. I have a million questions, and all of them are things you'd have to answer for yourself."

Beverly was surprised by her father's enthusiasm. "Thank you. That would be great to be able to share ideas with you." And it would. She loved her father, but there was no denying she and her mother had been very close. Almost exclusively so. For the first time, she wondered if her father had felt left out of their tight little circle.

After supper, she cleaned up the dishes. On her way to her bedroom, she stuck her head into the library, where her father sat in his soft leather chair, a book before him. "What are you reading?" she asked.

He chuckled. "Jules Verne. *Twenty Thousand Leagues Under the Sea*. I think I was in high school the last time I read this. He was quite thorough in his descriptions. One might almost call him verbose."

She laughed, recalling some of the tedious description in that story. "I'm going to tell Diane you called Jules Verne verbose. She'll be appalled."

He snorted. "She'll probably agree with me. How is she doing?"

"This snow has kept everyone indoors," she reflected. "But she seems fine."

"Working on a new book?"

"I think so. You'll have to ask her. Maybe she can come over for dinner one night soon."

"I'd like that."

As Beverly went upstairs, she made herself a mental note to ask Diane to dinner. She and her father had a wonderful rapport and could talk about literature and writing for hours.

In her room, she went to the desk she'd placed against one wall and withdrew a notepad and pen. Crossing to her bed, she propped herself cozily among the pillows, braced the paper on her knee and wrote *Starting Up a Consulting Business.* She took a deep breath. Was she really brave enough to just quit a good job on a whim?

It wasn't just a whim though, as evidenced by what she was doing right now. She would consider everything carefully and then make a decision.

Attracting Clients, she wrote. And then *Start-up Costs.* Moving on, she made herself a list of everything she could think of that she would have to do before she could really open the doors of a new business. *Office Space. Supplies & Equipment. IRS Regulations & Requirements. Services Offered. Package Deals.*

She felt a rush of excitement. This could be fun! What would it be like to look forward to going to work each day? Oh, she didn't dread going to work or anything like that, but... if she was honest, it was just a job. She worked hard at it because it was her nature to push herself, to excel. But the mere fact that she could think about quitting without hyperventilating was like a neon sign flashing in the night.

★   ★   ★

Margaret still was floating on air on Thursday. She was going to the Lumadue lecture! As she walked to the gallery, she squinted even behind the sunglasses she wore to protect her eyes from the glare the bright sunshine was creating as it bounced off the snow.

The first thing she did when she arrived was remove her boots and slip her feet into warm slipper socks. Then she started a pot of coffee, unlocked the front door, and picked up a feather duster—dusting was just one of the tasks that needed to be done every so often. She had to do it much more frequently in the summer because of the tourist traffic.

She glanced up in surprise as the door of the gallery opened, the bell over the door alerting her to an incoming visitor. "Oh, good morning. It's just you."

"Just me?" Beverly repeated, smiling. She took off her heavy coat—how on earth did the woman manage to look so stylish while bundled to the gills?—and carefully draped it over the back of one of the chairs Margaret's husband Allan made and sold. "When did I turn into an old standby?"

Margaret chuckled. "You know what I meant." She lifted one foot out to the side so Beverly could see her informal footwear. "If you were a real customer, I'd have to scramble behind the counter and put my shoes on."

"Ah. I see. Well, in that case, I'm glad I'm 'just me.'"

"There's coffee in the back." Margaret waved the feather duster in the general direction. "What brings you this way first thing in the morning?"

"No coffee, thanks. I'm trying to cut back on my caffeine. What brings me this way is that little abstract sculpture over there on that table. I've been drooling over it for weeks. I kept thinking someone would buy it and remove the temptation, but I can't stand it anymore. It has to be mine."

Margaret walked across the room with her friend to the sculpture she so admired. Making a lightning-quick decision, she said, "It so happens there's a twenty-five percent discount on this particular piece this morning." She checked the tag, reduced the asking price by twenty-five percent, and quoted Beverly the new lower price. It would mean that the gallery wouldn't make a commission, although it wouldn't cut into the artist's share, and she was fine with that.

Beverly looked stunned. "Margaret, you can't just do that on a whim! If you gave all your friends a discount, you'd never make any profit." She shook her head. "No, I'm paying full price."

She reached into her handbag for her wallet. But Margaret put a hand on her arm. "I don't discount things for everyone," she told Beverly. "You did me an enormous favor when you went out of your way to get me a ticket to Louellen's lecture. I'd like to thank you in a small way."

Beverly's shoulders dropped, and she blew out a breath of frustration in the middle of pulling out her wallet. "Margaret, you don't have to thank me."

"I know I don't *have* to. It was a very sweet thing for you to do. So let me acknowledge it just a little bit. All right?"

"All right. Thank you." Beverly smiled at her as Margaret removed the little sculpture from the display and carried it toward the counter. "But promise me you don't give away your commission on things on a regular basis."

Margaret raised three fingers in an imitation of the Boy Scout pledge. "I promise." Then she grinned. "You sound an awful lot like someone who could be starting her own business as a business consultant."

Beverly made a dismissive motion. "Having my own business is just a pipe dream, something I'm sort of tossing around."

"Yes, but—"

"Don't ask me a lot of questions yet," Beverly pleaded. "I'm only considering some ideas at this point. Chances are it'll come to nothing, and I'll stay right where I am."

In a pig's eye, Margaret thought to herself. She was pleased that Beverly had opened up even this much. She sensed Beverly was struggling with something very personal. She decided to add Beverly to the prayer list she kept each day, one containing a number of people who especially needed God's care and attention.

★   ★   ★

Early Thursday afternoon, the Bauers' doorbell rang. Shelley was already seated in the recliner where Dan and his mother insisted she rest much of the time.

She'd felt grumpy and out of sorts for the past few days. Frances Bauer had come to help every morning, and she'd stayed until dinnertime or later. Having Dan's mother around nonstop made Shelley extremely self-conscious; it was difficult for her to relax in her own home, and although Dan did try to run interference, he was rarely home to do so.

She planned to start back to work at the Cove as soon as she felt comfortable enough on the crutches to manage without help. The owner had been wonderfully understanding about the injury and had put up a sign saying that the Lighthouse Sweet Shoppe's desserts were temporarily unavailable and would be returning as soon as possible.

When Dan answered the door, she heard several feminine voices. At first, she assumed it was her neighborhood friends. But a moment later, she recognized a speaker and realized it was some of the women from her Sunday school class. Quickly, she sat up straighter and tugged at her sweater to smooth it.

"Shelley!"

"Hey, we missed you on Sunday."

"Gracious, girlfriend, what have you done to yourself?"

Three of her church friends spilled into the room, another young woman in tow.

Amanda Hawley held out a covered basket. "We heard you had to be off your feet for a little while, so each of us made a casserole for you."

"That way," added Bessie Burrell, "you won't have to be on your feet so much to get dinner made for your family."

Charmaine Glovinger drew the stranger forward with a gentle hand on her elbow. "Shelley, this is Allie Fox. Allie just moved to Marble Cove, and she came to visit our class last week."

Shelley smiled and held out her hand. "Welcome to town, Allie."

"Thank you. I appreciate you letting me barge in." Allie giggled, an odd, nervous titter that quickly subsided. She was small, with brown hair and brown eyes. She shook Shelley's hand tentatively and then held up a wrapped loaf. "This is cinnamon-raisin bread."

"Oh, I love cinnamon-raisin bread," Shelley said. Although Allie was probably close to her own age, she seemed very young and unsure of herself.

"Amanda said you had children. My little boy loves this bread. He'll eat three pieces at a time if I let him." The words were rushed together and once they were out, Allie giggled again. She appeared to be paying intense attention to the conversation; she reminded Shelley of a little brown bird cocking its head this way and that.

"I have a little boy who just turned four a few days ago, and a little girl, sixteen months old."

"Oh, my son will be four in September. Maybe we can have a playdate sometime. For them, not us. We can just talk." Again, she giggled for a moment and then fell silent.

"So how long are you going to be off your feet?" Charmaine gestured at Shelley's leg in the knee brace. "And what did you do to it?"

Shelley began to tell them about the accident, but her mother-in-law popped her head into the room. "Hello, girls. I'm Dan's mother, Frances."

Introductions were performed all around. Then Frances looked at the casseroles and bread. "Is that for Dan and Shelley? How thoughtful. I can take care of those while you visit." So saying, she picked up two of the casserole containers and headed for the kitchen, then returned moments later for the third casserole and Allie's bread.

Shelley resumed speaking. "So then my neighbor Diane came over—"

"I bet you'd like something to drink." Frances again, popping her head around the corner like a jack-in-the-box that wouldn't stay shut. "Hot chocolate, tea, coffee, some kind of juice...?"

"Oh, nothing for me. We aren't staying but a minute," Amanda replied.

The others concurred, and Frances nodded and withdrew.

"So Dan took me to the ER, where they decided I had a partial tear of a ligament in my knee." She went on to tell them about the MRI and the rest of the experience.

"Ow. Sounds painful. I get wigged out when I even bruise my knees," Bessie said, grinning.

"Here we go!" Frances sang the words as she marched into the living room with a tray containing a plate of cookies, four small cups, and a pitcher of ice water. "I thought you'd better have a little something to drink with these cookies. Enjoy." She set down the tray and sailed back to the kitchen.

Bessie, whose expressions broadcast every thought she had, looked at Shelley with very wide eyes. She looked from Shelley to the doorway and back again, shaking her head.

Shelley nodded, lifted her hands in a yes-she's-always-like-that, what-are-ya-gonna-do gesture.

Amanda gamely picked up the pitcher and poured glasses of water. "Have a cookie."

Shelley picked one up. "Don't mind if I do, thanks."

There was a burst of laughter, during which Shelley could hear Allie's odd little giggle. "Did you make these?" Bessie asked.

Shelley nodded. "Sort of. I had dough frozen, and Frances baked a batch."

"These are terrific," Allie told her.

Shelley smiled. "Thank you."

"Aren't you having your kitchen remodeled soon?" Charmaine asked.

"Next month." Shelley beamed. "I'm so excited I can't stand it!"

Her friends stayed for a few more minutes, during which they polished off the plate of cookies Frances had brought out.

As they rose to leave, Allie shot her a hesitant smile. "I'd love to visit again, if you wouldn't mind," she said.

"Of course I wouldn't mind," Shelley told her. "Bring your son. He and my Aiden can play together."

"And we'll just talk." Allie tittered, but then her expression dimmed. "It's been lonely since we moved here."

Moments after they had departed, Frances came in to pick up the empty plate and drinks. "I knew they needed drinks," she said, eyeing the empty pitcher.

Shelley resisted the urge to tell her that it was rude to force drinks on people who already had declined. "I think I'd like to have one of those casseroles for dinner. Amanda's chicken one sounded tasty."

"Why don't you let me make you some spaghetti?" Frances asked. "I already put those things in the freezer. I figured you'd need them more after you start working again."

"In the freezer? The bread too?" She couldn't keep the dismay from her voice.

"Well, of course." Frances sounded as if that was the only logical choice.

"Could you get it out right now, please?" Shelley asked tightly. "I'd like to offer it to Aiden for breakfast tomorrow."

Frances sighed. "All right, but I think you should keep all those things for when I'm not around."

As Frances exited the room once more, Shelley scrubbed both hands over her face, stifling the urge to scream. She was going to have to get up and start doing for herself again, or Dan's mother would make her insane.

CHAPTER TEN

Diane hung up the telephone Thursday afternoon and sighed. "I guess I'll just have to wait for Mr. Benton to call me." She spoke to Rocky. "Yes, I agree. It *is* frustrating."

Rocky cocked his head and regarded her with one raised eyebrow, making her laugh.

Jules Benton was the president of the Marble Cove town council. She had gotten his number from Angela, the receptionist with whom she'd spoken last Friday, and she'd already left him two messages, which he hadn't yet returned. Perhaps she would look up his address, just in case it was along a route she normally traveled. One never knew...she could get lucky, and he could be out shoveling snow.

She was curled up on the comfortable oyster white couch in her living room with a plethora of paperwork spread out around her. Earlier that morning, she had printed the National Register's information about how to nominate a site for their consideration. There was so much information required...and she also had to find a reputable architectural historian who might consider checking out the lighthouse for a reduced fee.

"Want to go for a walk?" she asked Rocky.

At the sound of his favorite word, the dog scrambled to his feet and barked once.

Diane laughed. "Okay. Let me get my snow gear on."

Rising, she got her camera and went to the closet to pull out her snow pants. She hadn't worn them skiing in years, but they'd certainly come in handy this winter slogging around on Marble Cove's side streets. She stomped her feet into sturdy waterproof boots and donned her favorite insulated coat before placing her camera in a roomy inside pocket. Next, she wrapped a scarf around her neck and face, tugged a fleece trooper hat with earflaps on and added her Gore-Tex insulated mittens with flip-tops. She needed to be able to free her fingers to take photographs.

Snapping on Rocky's leash, she said, "Whew. It's work getting ready to go outside," and then opened the door.

It was a short walk down Newport Street to Main, where she made steady progress toward the municipal building annex. In less than ten minutes, she once again entered the receptionist's office.

"Hi, Diane." Angela, the young woman to whom she'd spoken before, hailed her from behind her desk. "Aw, who's this?" She rose and came around the desk to let Rocky sniff her hand, then rubbed him behind his ears.

Diane introduced the dog and told Angela his story.

"Looks like you got lucky, buddy," Angela told Rocky. "Found yourself a pretty sweet deal, didn't you?" She smiled and stooped, pressing a kiss to the top of his head. Then she rose and went back around the desk. She was chewing gum, and she blew an enormous bubble as she picked up a hefty skeleton key on a labeled key ring. "Here you go, but I'll need it back as soon as possible. I had to get special approval to let you take it without an escort by a town official."

"Thank you." Diane accepted the key. "I'll be very careful with it. And I appreciate your help."

Angela nodded. "I looked again for that paperwork you asked about, but no luck. Sorry."

"That's all right. Thanks for checking." Diane made a beeline for the door, conscious of the fact that not everyone would appreciate a dog in the office as much as Angela. "I'll see you in a bit."

Outside again, she pulled her sunglasses from her pocket and put them back on, then turned toward the lighthouse. The promenade had been cleared of snow, but she soon saw that getting to the lighthouse itself was going to be some serious exercise. Not a single footprint marred the pristine surface of the snow that blanketed the dunes.

She stopped and regarded the beach. Hmm. Now how was she going to find the path? People were routinely cautioned to stay off the dunes and even though it was winter, she imagined damage still could be done to the fragile ecosystem. Squinting her eyes, she thought she saw the barest hint of an indentation, almost a ripple leading from the edge of the dunes out to the lighthouse. Was that the path?

She hiked closer, letting Rocky bound ahead of her to break a path. It did indeed appear to be the path, and they slowly made their way out to Orlean Point, where the lighthouse stood, a lonely sentinel surrounded by snow. Every so often, she stopped and snapped photographs. If she combined these with some of the many she had taken in other seasons, she was certain she could compile a nice set to enhance the nomination.

She paused and took exterior photographs from several angles, then unlocked the door and entered. Flash settings were required inside. There was barely enough natural light from the few small windows to see. Not that there was much to see, in any case. The building had been empty for many years, the thick coat of dust everywhere attesting to that. She debated ascending to the top, where the light had been, but she had taken photographs of that once before when she and her friends had finally been permitted to glimpse the inside, and she knew she could use those for this project.

An hour later, she was back on the promenade with Rocky, who appeared to have gotten enough exercise to subdue his natural energy. She was exhausted and wanted nothing more than to go home and rest.

As she trudged up Main Street, she heard someone call her name. Turning, she saw Beverly striding toward her. Even dressed for winter, the woman was a fashion plate. Her friend wore tall boots and a calf-length fitted coat. A long scarf wound around her neck, the ends tossed carelessly over one shoulder.

"Hello," she called. "Are you headed home?"

Diane nodded. "Yes. You?"

Beverly also nodded. "Want some company?" She took a deep breath. "I'd like to talk to you about my career and some things I've been thinking about."

Instantly diverted, Diane felt her exhaustion fall away. "Would you like to come over for some hot chocolate or coffee?" She smiled.

"Sure, why not," Beverly agreed.

Before they knew it they had walked up Newport Avenue and were in front of Diane's house. Rocky bounded ahead of them up the walk and stood, his tail wagging impatiently, until Diane opened the door. They all hurried inside and the two women divested themselves of their numerous outer garments, while Rocky circled twice, lay down on his bed, and closed his eyes.

"What were you doing?" Beverly asked. "You were bundled to the gills."

"Taking pictures of the lighthouse," Diane said. "If I have to start this nomination all over again, I need to submit interior and exterior photographs along with all the other information."

Beverly chuckled. "You've got enough photographs of that lighthouse by now to produce your own coffee table book. If you weren't too busy with your new novel, I mean."

Diane sighed. "I'm not busy at all at the moment."

Beverly arched her eyebrows.

"It's not coming as easily as the first one did. I'm having trouble finding the right approach to the plot, finding something that readers will really enjoy."

"It'll come to you," her friend said confidently.

Diane smiled, grateful for the vote of confidence, although she wasn't nearly as sure as Beverly. "What about you?" she asked.

"Me?"

"Your job search."

Beverly nodded. "Right, well, I've just started thinking about it, and I don't make big decisions quickly, so it may be a while before I really make a move. But I have been seriously considering the consulting business so I can stay in Marble Cove and keep an eye on Father."

Beverly's cell phone rang. "Excuse me," she said. "Speaking of, I should check in case it's Father." She glanced at the screen. "Oh, it's Shelley." Her tone was puzzled. "I wonder what she needs. Excuse me a moment, please."

Diane nodded, and Beverly walked over to stand at the window as she spoke to their young friend.

"...come over and go over it with you," Beverly was saying. "You'll have to do budget projections for at least three years, I believe. We can look at the regulations."

Diane wasn't intentionally eavesdropping, but the cottage was so small that even in the kitchen she could hear Beverly's end of the conversation.

"...need your EIN for that. And your bank account numbers too...yes...sure...two o'clock..."

Just as Beverly ended the phone call and turned to walk back to her seat, Diane eyed Beverly. "Looks like you've already started consulting."

"You know, you're right," Beverly said. "Maybe I have."

CHAPTER ELEVEN

S helley was hobbling around getting dinner on the table when Dan got home Friday evening. He'd called to tell her he was running a little late, which worked out just fine since she was too. Everything took so much longer on crutches!

"Hey, honey." Dan staggered through the back door, weighed down with several huge books, folders of various sizes and what looked like thick magazines. She clomped over to shut the door behind him and stared in dismay as he dumped his armload all over the counter.

"Hi," she said. "What on earth are you doing, and can you find a better place for those things?" She pointed at the variety of printed materials.

"They are in the right place," he assured her, hanging up his coat before giving her a kiss. "These are catalogs of kitchen stuff that we need to look through this weekend. Paint, appliances, plumbing, and lighting fixtures. You name it, I got it."

Shelley's eyes widened. "That's exciting. Let's eat quick so we can get started!"

Dan chuckled at her enthusiasm as he went to round up Aiden. Emma had been playing with some measuring cups, a plastic bowl and a wooden spoon Shelley had given her, and she scrambled to her feet when Shelley said, "Let's wash our hands, Em."

Frances had placed a folding stool near the sink so that she wouldn't have to lift the children up. Shelley let Emma use it now, thinking that this was one of her mother-in-law's better ideas. Thank goodness her days of needing a keeper were over. She couldn't move fast, but she could move again, so she'd thanked Frances and assured her she could cope.

"I'll still come over once or twice a week and clean," Frances had told her. "You don't want to be stressing that knee and maybe injuring it again."

Shelley didn't think that was likely, but she was so glad to get her mother-in-law out of her house that she would have agreed to anything at that point.

Dan and Aiden came into the kitchen as she finished drying Emma's little hands. Aiden scrambled into a chair while Dan lifted Emma into her seat and buckled it.

It was probably the fastest meal Shelley had ever eaten. She and Dan were done in record time. While both children were finishing, Dan brought her a variety of countertop samples and a large fold-out display that held every paint color under the sun. "We probably should choose a paint color first," he said, "and then the countertop."

But Shelley already had her eye on a granite sampler. "I'd rather choose the counters first. It would be easier to match the paint to that than the other way around."

"Okay." Dan raised his eyebrows. "That's granite." He indicated the box of stone she had chosen. "Granite is expensive."

"I know—oh, look at that! But Dan, granite is by far the best choice. Quartz is also really scorch-proof and stain resistant, but it's more likely to chip along the edges. I've already researched this. *Consumer Reports* says granite is the best for areas that get a lot of use, and my counters are going to be used constantly."

"Don't forget we're on a budget." Dan's voice was tight. "My dad's paying for this."

"I'm willing to compromise on most things," she told him. "We don't have to have top-of-the-line lighting fixtures or wildly expensive faucets, but the counter is one of the most important parts of my kitchen." She perused the chunks of granite. Her gaze lingered for a moment on a beautiful pinky-rose piece, and she ran a finger over it.

Dan said, "No way."

"I know. I want something more neutral. But it's very pretty." She moved on. "I thought granite is all unique. Don't we have to see the pieces?"

Dan indicated the box. "These are samples of what the company has in stock right now. If we choose it tonight, then I can order it tomorrow, and we're assured of getting exactly what we want."

Shelley nodded, still absorbed in the countertops. "Aren't some of these more expensive than others?"

"A little," Dan said. "But I asked the guy to give me the box with the most reasonable prices. For granite, that is."

"Oh, good." Shelley fingered a white piece of stone with shades of gray and dramatic gray veins. "This is really pretty. It's from Brazil." She picked up another and placed it beside the first. "And this is pretty, although it's very different. It doesn't have those huge veins in it, and it's more speckled than swirled. I think I like this one better. It's from India."

"That has pink in it," Dan pointed out.

Shelley flipped it over and read, "'Light cream-colored stone featuring gray tones, pink highlights and black specks mixed with gentle rosy swirls.' It's only got a tiny bit of pink in it, Dan."

"It's still pink. I was thinking more of something like this." Dan slid another piece in front of her, cream with many bold swirls and specks of gold, orange, brown and gray. Shelley thought it was absolutely hideous.

"I couldn't possibly cook in a kitchen with that," she said. "It's too busy. *And* the colors are appalling."

"Let's both choose another one," Dan proposed.

She didn't want to; she'd found one she really, really liked. But to please him, she perused the selections again.

"Check this out." Dan held up another one. "It's darker, so it wouldn't show stains—"

"Dan, if we keep it properly sealed, there won't *be* any stains."

"Well, anyway, I like this one." He flipped it over. "Teal green with neon green, white and black veining."

Shelley tried to be open-minded. She really did. But it was unbelievably awful. "It's interesting," she finally said.

"But I'm not fond of green. And I really want something very light, so the space looks big and friendly."

"Friendly." Dan pushed his chair back and folded his arms. "Do you have another choice?"

She went back to poring over the granite samples. "This is nice," she finally said. "It says it's a light bluish stone with lavender and white veining."

Dan didn't say anything.

"Do you have an opinion on this?" she asked him, annoyed with how bullheaded he was being. She half-suspected he was choosing ugly stones so that when he finally chose something reasonable, she'd be so relieved she'd agree. "Dan!" she said sharply when he still didn't say anything. "Do you like this or not?"

"Not," he fired back, his voice rising. "That has pink in it too. And purple. I don't want a pink and purple kitchen."

Shelley opened her mouth, but before she could speak, Aiden jumped into the breach. "Daddy! Don't yell at my mama." He began to cry. "You shouldn't yell at Mama."

Emma, probably also upset by everyone else's agitation, also began to howl.

Dan threw up his hands and rose.

"Don't you dare leave," Shelley said in a low voice as she awkwardly hoisted herself to her feet and started around the table.

Dan froze. He'd walked out and left her with upset children once before. He put Aiden on his lap while Shelley picked up Emma and patted her back, ignoring the crutch that clattered to the floor.

Dan sighed. "I'm sorry, buddy. You are absolutely right. I shouldn't yell at Mama." Aiden had burrowed against him, but the little blond head shook vigorously from side to side. "Sometimes Mama and I disagree, and we yell," Dan went on. "But we'll try harder not to yell when we don't agree on something from now on. Okay?"

"Okay." The word was muffled in the front of Dan's casual sport shirt.

Dan looked over their son's head at Shelley. "I'm sorry," he said, meeting her gaze squarely. "You're the one who's going to be spending your days in this room; you should choose what you like."

Shelley was stupefied. "I should?" She had expected the battle to resume the moment the kids were put to bed.

Dan nodded. "I don't hate pink, as long as we can temper it a little bit with some more neutral shades."

"We can do that," she said. "You can show me what flooring and paint you think would look good with that first selection." She smiled. "I won't force purple on you."

"Thank you." Dan grinned back. He held out a hand and squeezed hers when she accepted it. Then he leaned back so he could see Aiden's face. "You ready for a bath, bud?"

"Yeah!" He hopped down and sped from the room.

Dan rose more slowly. "Wish me luck."

Shelley smiled, setting Emma down so she could follow her brother. "Why don't I help? Two sets of parental eyes are much better than just one."

★   ★   ★

The week had passed far too slowly to suit Margaret, and she was ecstatic when Saturday finally arrived and she headed to Louellen Lumadue's lecture.

But an hour later, Margaret was too disappointed for words. What a waste of a Saturday afternoon! She couldn't believe she'd asked Allan and Adelaide to mind the gallery so she could come to this.

She was sitting in a lecture hall at Colby College listening to Louellen Lumadue deliver a lecture on color usage to represent cultural or religious concepts, complete with slides. It could have been wonderful. Should have been wonderful. Or, at least, acceptable.

When she first began to paint, Margaret had greatly admired Lumadue's use of color. Much like Jude LeBlanc, another artist whose seascapes she admired, Lumadue was a genius with color. Margaret had expected to come away from today's talk inspired and excited to try some new techniques.

Instead, the artist had presented such a flat, uninspiring lecture that half the students had drifted out early, and the ones remaining only did so because their professors were there taking attendance. Although she wouldn't be surprised if some of them had snuck out too.

The one saving grace had been a slide show of Louellen's work. Margaret could clearly see the power and impact her work had. And one of Margaret's personal favorites of Lumadue's was included, a painting that incorporated a hidden image. Interesting, though, that while her use of color was still effective, she'd stopped using any hidden imagery, and much of her recent work appeared to have a darker edge than her early canvasses.

The lecture ended, and people sprinted for the exits with unseemly haste. Lumadue appeared not to notice, just stuffed her notes in a briefcase and went to unhook her laptop from the college's equipment. Not a single person approached her except for one woman who presumably had been the coordinator of the event. And even she didn't stay long.

Margaret made her way to the front of the room. "Ms. Lumadue?"

Louellen Lumadue straightened to her full height and looked down at Margaret. She was unusually tall for a woman, but as slender as a reed. Her hair was a light, unremarkable brown, and she wore it scraped back into a sloppy braid that reached the center of her back. "What?" The tone would have made a less confident person shrink six inches.

Margaret simply stood and smiled at her. "You aren't going to remember me, but I heard you speak some years ago. You were so compelling that you piqued my interest in painting, and I've been painting ever since. In fact, I own a small gallery on the coast in the town of Marble Cove."

Louellen looked into Margaret's face then, her hands still on her briefcase. Finally, she said, "I hope you're making a living at it."

"Oh yes. Summer's easier, of course, when we have tourists everywhere. And we had a strong holiday season, so I'm hopeful."

Lumadue nodded. She was so markedly unenthusiastic that Margaret felt even more deflated than she had after the lecture.

"Well," Margaret said briskly, "thank you for the lecture."

"Even though it was terrible?" There was almost a challenge in the woman's voice.

Margaret hesitated. It seemed rude to agree. "The first lecture I ever heard you give was a little more compelling than today's."

Louellen snorted, smiling a little. "That was quite tactful."

Emboldened by the fracture in the woman's off-putting demeanor, Margaret said, "I was pleased to see that you included one of your hidden imagery pieces in the slide show. I remember that entire series. It's my personal favorite of your body of work."

Louellen's hands froze in the act of closing the latch on her large satchel. She seemed to be trying to compose herself. Margaret was flabbergasted. What had she said?

"Thank you," Louellen said quietly. Sincerely.

"Thank *you*," Margaret replied. "I think of those paintings quite often. They were so inspired. I love that seascape you have in the slide show, where the conch shell can just be discerned in the waves, but probably my absolute favorite is that stunning autumn woodland scene where the merest suggestion of a stag with a magnificent set of antlers catches the eye in the bark of a tree—"

"That was a long time ago." Louellen's voice was brusque again. "Those weren't particularly well received, although thank heavens they sold really well. I've gone in an entirely different direction since that period."

"Yes, there's a different energy to your more recent work." Margaret wasn't about to admit that she had preferred the earlier method.

Louellen shrugged. "I can tell you don't care for it. That's all right. I'm not crazy about a lot of it myself."

"Then why...?"

"The bottom line," the artist said, "is that I paint and lecture to pay the bills. Some people teach, some people build houses, some people write computer programs. We're all just trying to earn a living. It's my work."

Margaret shook her head. "There's much more to my painting than that. I hope you find the joy in your art again."

The tall woman laughed cynically. "Thanks, but I'm not holding my breath."

CHAPTER TWELVE

Late on Saturday afternoon, Beverly went out to sweep off the walk. It had snowed a little bit again, and she liked to keep the sidewalks clear. She was just closing the front door when a tall, lean man left old Mr. Calder's house and walked to a silver SUV parked along the street.

She shut the door and rushed to one of the windows in the front parlor. The lights were off in here; no one could see her. She felt silly, skulking about, but she wanted to see who the man was getting into that car.

As she watched, the visitor folded himself into the driver's seat long enough to turn on the engine. Then he got out again and retrieved a long-handled scraper with a brush attached and began removing the light snow from his vehicle's windows.

Dennis! Dennis Calder was her neighbor's grandson. He lived across town, but he checked in on his grandfather regularly. With Beverly's work schedule, she rarely caught a glimpse of him. He'd done some work at the State House in Augusta several years ago, and their paths had occasionally crossed in the corridors. Now he was some kind of business consultant, and she'd heard he traveled a good deal.

She'd always thought there was interest in his eyes, and at Diane's party last summer—the party she'd skipped—he'd asked Diane about her. He was someone she'd thought about more than once when she considered beginning to date again. She watched him move confidently around the SUV until he got back into the driver's seat and pulled away.

As he turned the corner onto Main and disappeared, Margaret's van turned onto Newport Street. Her friend drove slowly down to the other end of the street and pulled into her driveway. Today had been the day of that artist's lecture at Colby College, Beverly suddenly remembered. Oh, she hoped it had been as delightful as Margaret had expected.

She stuck her head into the living room where her father sat reading. "I'm going to run down to Margaret's for a few minutes," she told him. "I'll be back in a bit, and we'll have supper."

Her father nodded. "I'll be the one here holding down this chair."

She laughed as she stomped into her La Canadienne boots with the lower heel, pushing her pencil leg jeans down inside them. Then she struggled into her coat and tugged a white angora cloche hat with a large hand-felted white flower over her dark hair. She grabbed a matching scarf and mittens and was out the door.

It only took a minute or so to get to Margaret's, and she hurried up the curving walkway to the porch and knocked on the front door. Margaret's yard, so gorgeous in spring and summer, was nothing but a sea of white with lots of oddly shaped bumps and lumps protruding.

She heard footsteps, and a moment later, the front door opened. "Well, hello, Beverly." Allan Hoskins beamed at her. Beverly imagined he'd been a handsome man in his youth, because he was still attractive. Balding, he had deep dimples visible in his cheeks even with his neat white beard. He wore a black knitted sweater with jeans and wool-lined leather slippers. He held the door wider. "Come on in."

"Hello, Allan," she responded. "Thanks." She looked back toward the kitchen at the rear of the home. "I did see Margaret come in, didn't I?"

Allan's smile faded. "Yes. She's in the kitchen. Go on back."

Beverly proceeded to the kitchen, while Allan went back to the dark green recliner where he'd been reading a magazine. One of the cats came and wound around her legs. She was pretty certain that one was Oreo; it was the only black-and-white one Adelaide owned. Another, a brown tabby, gave her a long, intense stare out of wide yellow eyes and then returned its attention to its food bowl. Beverly felt as if she'd just been dismissed as unimportant. The thought made her smile. She'd never had a cat and didn't really understand the creatures.

Margaret had just retrieved a cup of herbal tea from the microwave. She looked startled to see Beverly. "Hi. Is everything all right?"

Beverly tilted her head. She supposed just showing up at dusk on a winter evening was out of character for her. "Hi. Everything's fine. I just came to see how the lecture was."

An odd expression crossed Margaret's face. Finally, she smiled and shook her head. "After you went to so much trouble to get me that ticket, I feel like I should lie and tell you it was fantastic. But the truth is, that was one of the worst art presentations I have ever heard." She gestured to her mug. "Want some tea?"

"I'd love some." Beverly couldn't believe it. For a moment, she was actually speechless as Margaret took out a cup and made her some hot tea.

She sank into one of the modern Scandinavian-style chairs at the table, the whole set made by Allan. Finally, she found her voice. "What made it so bad?"

Margaret shook her head again. "She had no sparkle, no zest, no apparent interest at all in the topic. She just flipped through a bunch of slides and delivered her lecture in what I can only say was practically a monotone." A spoon clinked as she stirred the tea. Returning to the table, she set a mug, a spoon, and a red sugar bowl shaped like a strawberry in front of Beverly.

"Do you think she was ill or something?"

"I don't believe so." Margaret took her seat again. "I approached her afterward to tell her that she had been my inspiration to begin painting, and she was extremely curt, almost rude. She actually said the only reason she paints is to make a living."

Both women were silent for a moment.

Beverly mulled over the surprising information. "Something must have happened to make her like this, don't you think? People don't change that radically without some signal event."

"You could be right. At first I was annoyed and upset that I had wasted an entire afternoon on that lecture," Margaret said. "But on the drive home, I started feeling more and more saddened. I can't imagine ever losing the joy in my art to that extent. It's one thing to experience a block or get stalled, but I honestly think if she could never pick up a brush again, it wouldn't even bother her."

"That's too bad. I hate to see talent wasted."

"So do I. I prayed about it on the way back to Marble Cove."

Beverly didn't have anything to say in response to that. Yes, she recently had begun attending church. She did believe in the presence of a higher power. But her burgeoning faith was still so new and personal that she scarcely knew how to talk about it.

When Beverly didn't respond, Margaret went on as though she'd never paused. "I've decided to invite Louellen to have a show here at the Shearwater Gallery."

"But I thought you said she wasn't enthusiastic about her work anymore."

"She isn't, but there was something—something so sad about her." Margaret chewed her lip. "She did such extraordinary work for a period of her life, but she seems to have deliberately turned away from it. I want to know more about what happened. No, I *need* to know what changed her focus."

"What if she says no? It doesn't sound as if she's all that thrilled about her art these days."

The older woman arched her eyebrows. "She's not going to turn down an opportunity to make money, especially during the slow season. Right? So perhaps I can use this chance to show her the beauty in her work."

Margaret's telephone rang, halting her words. "Excuse me," she said. Beverly heard other feet thudding through the house, and then Adelaide came barreling into the room, holding the phone. "Mom, it's for you."

"Thank you, dear." Margaret took the telephone.

Adelaide saw Beverly. "Hi! How are you?" She immediately came over with her arms outstretched for a hug. Beverly smiled and gave her a big hug. The young woman loved hugs, although Margaret had worked long and hard to make her understand that one shook hands with people one didn't know. Hugs were reserved for friends.

"How are you doing?" Beverly asked.

"Fine! Saw a kitty today. Out-thide." Adelaide wasn't hard to understand if Beverly listened carefully. "I want to feed it, but Mom said no. Too many cats now."

Beverly grimaced. "You have such a kind heart, Adelaide, but maybe your mom is right. You've got three kitties already."

"But it's cold. That kitty needs help."

"It must have a warm place to stay," Beverly reasoned. "It wouldn't be alive if it didn't have shelter, as cold out as it is."

"Hey!" Adelaide said, her brown eyes lighting up. "I'll catch it. You can have it. You need a kitty."

"Oh no," Beverly said. "I don't. I don't know anything about cats."

"You can learn."

"Beverly?" Margaret interrupted their conversation, and Beverly turned to her, thankful for the timely save.

"Yes?"

"It's Shelley. She's starting work again Monday evening, and she needs a ride home from the Cove when she's done baking. I have a Bible study that night. Would you be able to do it?"

"Sure." Beverly smiled. "It's the Martin Luther King holiday Monday, so I'm free all day long. Does she need me for anything else?"

Margaret conferred with Shelley, then shook her head. "No. She says thank you, though. She'll be done by eight."

*　　*　　*

Diane attended church on Sunday morning at the Marble Cove Community Church, which she'd been going to since the previous summer. During Pastor Carl's announcements before the worship service began, he held up a small booklet.

"This booklet tells the story of our church and includes some fascinating history. It's priced very modestly, and the proceeds go to the fund for the sanctuary renovation." The church had just begun a capital campaign to add air conditioning and better lighting and do some cosmetic interior work: fresh paint, new carpet, and curtains. "It's a lovely way to support our church, so be sure to stop in the vestibule on your way out to pick up your copy."

After the service, Diane purchased one of the booklets. The church was preparing to celebrate its twenty-fifth anniversary in the autumn, and there were some special activities in the works.

Leafing through the little booklet, she saw that it contained photographs, biographies, and stories of the various church groups and their ministries. Unfortunately, it had not been edited or proofread with care. She would have written—

Suddenly, she had a thought. What if she wrote a similar but bigger booklet about the lighthouse? Funds were going to be needed to restore some of the building, and a booklet like this could really show people the importance of making a donation. They could also donate the proceeds from the booklet, although that obviously wasn't going to be enough to pay for very much.

The idea was exciting. As soon as she got this little mystery about the National Register figured out, she would start on that. She already had quite a bit of information; it would be largely the oldest historical facts she'd need to research and expand.

And oh! Margaret could do some illustrations. It would be wonderful to have some visuals: a ship foundering on the rocks, a swimmer pulling someone from the sea, a sailor on the deck of a ship pointing at the light he'd just seen...and photographs also could be interspersed throughout. She had some marvelous shots from different angles, taken in different seasons. She even had some of the interior in its current state of disrepair. They would be a nice contrast to some taken at a future date when it had been restored. And perhaps she could get Edward Maker's permission to use one or two taken when his family lived there, if any existed.

As she began the short walk home, she glanced at the readout on her cell phone. Twelve thirty. Margaret probably was home from church by now. Diane was pretty certain her church's services began earlier than did those at MCCC.

She dialed, and Margaret's phone rang twice.

"Hi, Diane."

She could hear the smile in her friend's voice. Margaret had obviously checked her caller ID. "Hi, yourself. How was church?"

"Good. Millie Percell was back—remember I told you about her fall?" One of the other women in Margaret's congregation had fallen down a flight of stairs and suffered a broken hip. She'd been in rehab for several months, and she was still on Margaret's prayer list.

"That's wonderful. How is she doing?"

Margaret caught her up on Millie's latest health report, and then she said, "Would you like to join us for Sunday dinner? We'll be sitting down in about ten minutes."

"Oh, thanks." Diane was touched by the offer. Margaret worked hard to make sure Diane didn't feel alone in her new community. "But I'm going to go home and work this afternoon. Margaret, I had this idea..." Quickly, she explained about her church's booklet and how it had given birth to the idea of one about the lighthouse. "So I'd like you to think about doing a few illustrations," Diane said. "Just three or four, perhaps. And we can talk more about it. You don't have to answer me now."

"Oh yes, I do," Margaret said. "I think it's a great idea, and I'd love to help."

"Fantastic!" Diane concluded the conversation with a promise to get together and discuss the project soon.

Walking briskly, she turned onto Liberty Avenue on her way to Main Street. Something teased at her mind, and she recalled that the town council president, Jules Benton, lived on Liberty. She located the nearest house number. The Benton residence should be about three more doors down. Should she knock on the door? It seemed rude to do so on Sunday, right after church, somehow. She could come back another day if he didn't return her call soon.

The second the thought concluded, a blue Ford Taurus pulled into the driveway at the side of the Bentons' home. Stunned by her good fortune, Diane walked more briskly.

A man got out of the car and came around to the passenger side. When he opened the door, a woman stepped out.

"Mr. Benton?" Diane called.

The man's head swiveled her way. "Hello," he said, but it was clear that he had no idea to whom he spoke.

She hurried forward with a hand outstretched. "I'm Diane Spencer. I called your office a couple of times to try to speak with you, but it seems I've missed you every time." Unspoken was *"and you never called me back."*

"Oh yes. Ms. Spencer." Benton didn't approach, and Diane saw that he was supporting the woman whom he had just helped from the car. She carried a cane and clearly wasn't exceptionally steady on her feet. "I'll, um, have to give you a call this week. I'm afraid I'm a little tied up at the moment."

"I could wait," she offered.

"No, no, don't do that." He sounded harried. "I have to help my wife change out of her church clothes and get us some lunch." He cleared his throat. "But thank you for introducing yourself. I'll be in touch."

"Of course. Thank you." There wasn't much else she could do besides give in gracefully, so she waved and went on her way.

CHAPTER THIRTEEN

Shelley couldn't wait to get back to work on Monday evening. Finally, almost two weeks after she'd fallen, she unlocked the door of the little restaurant again.

She flipped the light switch beside the door and walked across the pine floors to the kitchen. After turning on those lights, she stuck her head back out of the kitchen and turned off the main lights again at the switch on the near wall.

Ahh. Her haven. Sometimes she felt almost guilty for the pleasure she took in these quiet evenings. She made her way across the kitchen carefully, stopping to set on the butcher block island the bags of baking needs she'd brought. The floor was clean, but slippery enough that the single crutch she used now slid easily out from beneath her weight if her concentration lapsed.

She opened the door of the cabinet that Rusty Garrison, the manager of the Cove, had for her own supplies. Rusty always left a note taped to the door when he had a specific request. Tonight the note read: *Glad to have you back. People have been begging for your blueberry crumb cake, if you feel like making it again soon. R.*

Her heart gave a happy little bump. It was the most wonderful feeling to know that people liked her baking! Tonight she intended to make fruit tarts that could be kept in the refrigerator until tomorrow, as well as a dark chocolate cake with a buttercream icing.

She turned to go preheat the oven—and her knee gave a vicious throb when she placed all her weight on it without thinking. Sucking in an involuntary breath, she grabbed the crutch from where she'd leaned it against the counter. This was going to take longer than she'd planned, she feared. She usually flitted back and forth between counter, oven, and refrigerator countless times while she baked. She was going to have to consciously try to limit her activity, which meant planning her steps ahead of time...She sighed and moved more carefully toward the oven.

She had hoped to be able to make the lighthouse cookies that a small gift shop in town purchased, but as the evening wore on, a glance at the clock on the wall told her that would have to wait for another time. Beverly had agreed to pick her up, and Shelley had told her eight o'clock would be fine.

Sighing deeply, she hurriedly arranged kiwi, strawberries, and blueberries in rings on the cream cheese filling she'd spread on the fluted tart shells. Piling plump red raspberries in the center, she grabbed the lime glaze that had cooled enough to brush over each finished tart and then placed them in the refrigerator. She left a note on the counter telling Rusty to have Brenna get them out fifteen minutes before serving them and to place a dollop of whipped cream "artfully" on each one. She knew that would make him grin.

Finally, she iced the cake in a beautiful rippled pattern and set a large bell over the entire cake plate. Then she washed and dried the few things she'd used, gathered all her supplies, and headed for the door. Before she turned off the light, she glanced back.

Maybe she hadn't accomplished everything she wanted, but the cake made a stunning centerpiece on the butcher block island.

Beverly's sporty rental was parked right in front of the coffee shop on the quiet Main Street. Reminding herself to take her time, Shelley negotiated the slippery sidewalk to where Beverly had thoughtfully pulled up next to a cleared spot between the streetside snowbanks.

"I'm so sorry I kept you waiting," she said breathlessly as she placed her bags and crutch behind the passenger seat before sliding in beside Beverly.

"I just got here a few minutes ago." Beverly held up a Kindle e-reader. "And I brought a book, so you really didn't have to rush."

"Thank you," Shelley said.

"So how did your first evening back go?"

"Slowly." She didn't want to whine, but it was a close call. "I'm moving a little slower than I'd like, but it will get better soon."

"You will," affirmed her friend. "And really, it could have been much worse. You could have broken a bone or be looking at knee surgery and months of rehab."

"You're right." Shelley sobered. She really did have a lot to be thankful for, beginning with those blessings. Even her mother-in-law, who could be bossy and overbearing, was a blessing. In disguise sometimes, she thought wryly, but a blessing nonetheless. Deciding a change of subject was in order, she said, "It really was great to work again. I've been thinking about my long-term business goals, like you suggested."

"Yes?" Beverly encouraged.

Shelley took a deep breath. "I wrote down a few things. I want to grow, but I don't want to grow too much, if that makes sense. How do I say in my goals that I don't want to be *too* successful?"

Beverly chuckled. "I can see why you would struggle with that."

"I'm a little overwhelmed," Shelley confessed. "Would you consider going over it with me?"

"I'd be happy to," Beverly said. "In fact, I'd be thrilled! In a small way, your business sort of feels like something I helped hatch."

Shelley laughed. "I don't know if I'd ever have had the courage to do this without you, Diane, and Margaret to cheer me on, so I guess that's absolutely true."

"Is there a time that would suit you?" Beverly asked. "Your life is so much busier than mine that we'd better try to find a time that works for you first."

"How about right now?" Shelley proposed impulsively. "Although it's probably too late for you."

Beverly glanced at the time displayed on the dashboard. "No, as long as we wrap it up by ten, that should be fine. I'll call my father and let him know I'm going to be out for a while."

★　★　★

The first thing Beverly showed Shelley was the Finance Authority of Maine's Web site detailing how to start a small business. There were some good suggestions on how to decide what your goals were, and how to clearly write them.

"I hadn't seen this before," Shelley admitted. "I was looking at some very general how-to sites." As she read over the information, something caught her attention. "I'm not planning to borrow money if I can avoid it," she told Beverly. "A lot of this stuff talks about preparing to get a bank loan, and I'm not planning on that."

"How are you going to pay for your supplies and equipment?" Beverly looked concerned.

"I have my equipment already." She smiled. "And Dan and his father are doing the construction of our kitchen."

"But you'll still need materials, new appliances, and all those things."

"Dan and I got a small home improvement loan from Orlean Citizens Bank."

"Ah." Beverly's eyebrows rose. "So you're not as clueless as you'd like me to believe."

"Oh, but I am!" Shelley giggled. "I didn't know anything about all this paperwork I needed to fill out to get a business started until I began working with you. Who knows what else I may have missed?"

"All right." Beverly smiled. "So what does your loan include?"

Shelley took a deep breath. "Dan and I did an estimate of all the materials we'd need. He and his dad did the stuff for the actual kitchen, I did the appliances and things I knew I'd need. I figured out about how much I thought I could make in a month, accounting for the differences during the high season, and the bank manager said it looked doable. So he did."

"So you already have budget projections?"

"Sort of. But not as detailed as I think we need for this goal planning stuff."

"Do you have a bank account yet?"

Shelley bit her lip. "Not a separate business one. Is that a huge mistake?"

"Not at all." Beverly realized she was going to have to handle this carefully in order not to crush Shelley's fragile confidence. "I'm just asking so we can check things off our list, so to speak. You're doing everything you need to do."

Her cell phone rang. She sighed. "I need to check that. It could be my father. Excuse me." Fishing around in her handbag slung over the back of the kitchen chair in which she sat, she withdrew her phone. The display read *Jeff Mackenzie*. "Oh!" She rose. "Give me just a minute."

Walking into the living room, she took the call. "Hello?"

"Hi, Beverly, it's Jeff."

Butterflies in flight beat their wings in her stomach. "Hi, Jeff. How are you?"

"I'm good. I'm, ah, going to be in town on Saturday, and I'd like to take you out to dinner. Are you free?"

"Yes, I am. I'd like that, Jeff." She realized she was standing in the middle of Shelley's living room with a stupid smile on her face.

"Great. I'll pick you up around six thirty, all right?"

"All right. How shall I dress?"

He laughed. "I'm a guy. I don't know the terminology. How about we agree on casual, but not too casual."

She chuckled too. "All right. That works for me."

They spoke for a few more minutes, talking about what they'd been doing. Beverly didn't tell him about her accident.

Finally, remembering that she needed to get back to her work with Shelley, she concluded the call. "See you Saturday evening."

"I'll look forward to it," Jeff said.

Beverly turned off the phone and walked back into the kitchen.

As she took her seat, Shelley glanced up. "Everything okay with your dad?"

"It wasn't my father. It was Jeff."

"Oh! And...?"

"He's going to be in town this weekend, and he invited me to dinner on Saturday evening." She feared she was blushing, and she busied herself looking through some of the paperwork lying before them. Really, it was just dinner, nothing to get excited about.

Shelley's eyes widened, and she said, "*Oooh*, that sounds promising. He's a cutie." She smiled slyly. "Isn't he?"

"Yes," Beverly admitted. "He is."

"You like him, right?"

"He's a very nice man," she agreed. "Now why don't we look at this—"

"Do you think it could get serious?"

"It's just a casual date, Shelley," she said firmly. "Don't read too much into this. It's not like he asked me to marry him."

"Well, no, but you *have* gone out with him several times now."

Beverly shook her head at her young friend's irrepressible inquisition. "I've gone out on repeat occasions with many of my friends. I'm not looking for anything more. You know that."

Shelley nodded. "I know. I'm only asking because I'd like to see you happy."

"I am happy. I have a very fulfilling life. Even more so in the past year since I got to know you, Diane, and Margaret." She tapped the paper in front of her. "Now let's take a look at these goals you've written down."

CHAPTER FOURTEEN

Diane closed her front door, leaving Rocky snoozing on the hearth rug, and walked over to Shelley's on Tuesday morning. It was single-digits chilly, as usual, but the sun was shining brightly, making the snow sparkle.

She knocked on the front door and waited patiently until Shelley could get there.

"Good morning," she said brightly when Shelley opened the door.

"Good morning." Shelley smiled. "You're out and about bright and early."

"I'm heading for the grocery store, and I wondered if there was anything you needed. I figured grocery shopping might be a bit of an ordeal at the moment."

"You figured right." Shelley sighed, turning around awkwardly with the crutch she still used beneath one arm. "Everything's an ordeal. I can't wait until I can get rid of this stuff." She indicated both the crutch and the bulky knee brace that she wore over her slim jeans. "It'll be nice to have my house to myself again. Not that I don't appreciate everything Dan's mother has done, but..."

Diane chuckled. "I understand."

Shelley shook her head. "She even told Adelaide that she didn't need to come over today, that she could handle the kids without help." Her tone was indignant. "Poor Adelaide was crushed."

Diane winced. "Maybe she just wanted them all to herself. She doesn't see all that much of Aiden and Emma, does she?"

"No." Shelley looked guilty. "I mean, we go over for family lunch every Sunday after church, but it's a madhouse with so many people there. So I guess that the only time she really gets to see much of the kids is when she comes over here." She gestured. "Come on into the kitchen. The kids are coloring, and I don't want to leave them alone too long. Crayons and freedom equals disaster."

Diane laughed. Oh, she remembered those days.

"Miss Diane!" Aiden came to the kitchen doorway. "Hi! Come see my picture."

"All right." She grinned. "I've been summoned," she said over her shoulder, as Aiden raced forward and took her hand to drag her toward the kitchen.

"See?" he said. He climbed onto his chair at the table, where Shelley had given him paper and crayons. "It's my house."

"My house!" echoed Emma, sitting opposite him, although she was strapped into her high chair. She also had paper and crayons, and she was industriously scribbling away.

"These are lovely pictures," Diane said, including Emma in her smile. "So this is your house, Aiden?"

He nodded vigorously. "An' my mama, an' my daddy, an' my Emma, an' my Prize. An' me."

Diane took in the picture. Indeed, there was a rather oblong "house" with a pointed roof. Inside were four stick figures. Two large, one small, and one with four legs that she assumed was Prize. Outside the house was the fourth figure, tiny in comparison even to the "Emma" one.

"Which one is you?" she asked, just to be sure she hadn't confused Prize and Aiden. It would make much more sense if Prize was the figure outside.

But Aiden pointed to that one. "There's me." He looked up at her guilelessly, beaming. "Do you like it?"

Diane knelt beside his chair and hugged him. "It's a wonderful picture, Aiden. You're quite an artist."

"I'm an artist!" he shouted. He fought his way free of her arms, jumped from the chair with a high-pitched squeal, and raced into the living room.

"Aiden," Shelley called after him. "Inside voice, please." She shook her head, smiling at Diane. "Little boys are so different from little girls."

Diane nodded. "He has lots of energy." She picked up the picture he'd drawn, frowning as she looked at it. "Aiden must not have felt like part of the family when he drew this."

"What? Why?" Shelley came to peer over her shoulder, and Diane held up the sketch.

"This is Aiden." She pointed to the tiny person outside the house—the house in which the other three family members and even the dog were gathered together.

"My heavens." Shelley sounded distressed. "I see what you mean." She turned and looked toward the room into which her son had vanished. "Why on earth would he have drawn something like this?"

Diane shrugged. "Who knows? I wouldn't attach too much importance to it. Children's perceptions change from minute to minute sometimes." And she was sincerely sorry she'd even mentioned it. The last thing Shelley needed was something else to worry about.

The back door opened then, and Shelley grabbed the sketch, turning and hiding it in a kitchen drawer.

"Good morning!" sang a cheery voice.

"Mee-mee-mee-mee." Emma loudly welcomed her grandmother with vigorous bounces in her seat. "Get down, Meemee?"

"Of course you can get down." Frances Bauer shrugged off her coat and tossed it over a chair, then walked over to unbuckle the strap of the little one's seat. "Good morning, Shelley. Hello, Diane, how are you today?" She beamed.

Diane smiled back. She knew Frances sometimes got on Shelley's last nerve, but she rather liked the woman. What you saw was what you got. She was generally cheerful and pleasant, and she worked harder than any two other people put together. She adored her family and was more than happy to talk about her gazillion grandchildren at the drop of a pin.

"I'm well, Frances. How are you?"

"Oh, I'm fine. Getting to spend so much time with Shelley and the kids has made this dreary old month a lot brighter, let me tell you." Frances snuggled Emma, pressing her nose into the crease of the toddler's chubby neck. "I'm going to have me a piece of Emma pie."

The little girl shrieked and giggled, and when Frances set her on the floor, she raced away as fast as her little legs would go.

"So what's on the agenda for this morning, Shelley?" Matter-of-factly, Frances went to the sink and began to clean up the morning's dishes that Shelley hadn't gotten to yet.

Shelley flushed. "Oh, stop. I can do that," she told her mother-in-law.

Frances waved a hand dismissively. "That's why I came over, dear. If you don't have a list for me, I thought I'd do a little laundry and maybe wash this kitchen floor." She made a face as she surveyed the worn vinyl. "I bet you can't wait until the new kitchen is done."

"I can't," Shelley admitted. "It'll be wonderful to be able to make all my recipes right here at home instead of having to work at the Cove."

"What do you need for your baking today?" Frances asked. "I can get it out for you before I start the laundry."

"Oh, that's all right—"

"It won't take but a minute. It'll take you twice as long dragging that leg around." Frances went to the cabinets. "Flour? Sugar? Vanilla?"

With her back to her mother-in-law, Shelley closed her eyes for a moment. Diane suspected she was praying for patience, but when her friend's eyes opened, Diane saw the tell-tale gleam of a tear. A movement caught the corner of her eye, and she realized Aiden was quietly standing in the doorway watching his mother.

"I'd better go." Diane gave Shelley a hug. "I'm glad you're getting around so well. It won't be any time at all until you're well." *Subtext: until you can do things for yourself again.*

Shelley sent her a wan smile. "Thanks. Don't worry about the groceries. If I need anything for tomorrow, Dan can pick it up on his way home today."

As she exited Shelley's home, Diane sent up a little prayer. *Dear Lord, please give Shelley patience to deal with her mother-in-law. And You could give Frances a little tact too. A little would go a loooong way.*

★   ★   ★

It was a brisk, invigorating walk downtown to Margaret's gallery. Diane didn't really need to get groceries; she'd mostly said that in case Shelley indeed did need something. But she knew the younger woman would never ask her to go shopping unless she already had a trip planned.

Diane felt a little guilty as she strolled along. She'd taken a walk downtown yesterday, and for days before that. There always seemed to be something compelling she had to get done before she could sit down and work on her new book. But she *did* have a lot of balls in the air, and juggling them all required her attention.

The ball she was handling today was the lighthouse history booklet she'd proposed. She and Margaret were getting together to discuss some of the details.

As she approached the door of the Shearwater Gallery, she recognized a man walking down the street toward her. "Good morning, Mr. Benton."

"Good morning." The town council president looked a little puzzled; she was almost certain he had no idea who she was.

She put out her gloved hand. "Diane Spencer. We met on Sunday outside your house?"

"Oh yes. Ms. Spencer." Benton shook her hand quickly and withdrew it. She suspected he would have kept walking if she hadn't stepped right into his path.

"When would be a good time for us to meet?" she asked him. "I'd like to talk with you about getting the lighthouse onto the National Register of Historic Places."

"Oh, right, right." Benton nodded. And said not another word.

Diane tried again. "Are you going to be in your office today? I could stop by in a short while."

"Ah, I'm not going to the office," Benton said. "I'm, ah, taking my wife to Augusta, so I won't be available today. Perhaps another time."

"How about tomorrow?"

The man looked supremely uncomfortable. "I really can't say without, ah, checking my calendar. Why don't you give the office a call soon?"

Diane didn't like to think ill of people, but if she was a betting woman, she'd bet Jules Benton was telling a big, fat fib. For some reason, he didn't want to talk to her about the lighthouse being listed on the National Register. So was it her, was it the lighthouse, or was it the thought of the registry listing that had him sidestepping her request?

"All right," she said. "I will call your office tomorrow. And if you're not in, I'll call you at home. Or perhaps I'll just stop by."

Satisfied with the way Benton's forehead wrinkled with worry, Diane sailed past him and entered the gallery, sending the little bell above the door jingling.

"Good morning," Margaret called from the back.

"Morning." Diane angled toward the back of the gallery, where she could see that Margaret already was perched on a stool working on a painting. "What are you working on now?"

Margaret turned to smile at her. "Winter on the promenade."

Diane chuckled. "Appropriate. At least you have plenty of inspiration for your subject matter."

"I stopped by the Cove and got a couple of Shelley's fruit tarts this morning. Want to help me taste test them?"

"Sure." Diane kept her face straight. "We'd really be doing Shelley a service. She needs to know if these recipes are worth making again."

Margaret grinned. "Absolutely."

"While we're munching, let's talk about this booklet." Diane fished a folded piece of paper from her pocket. "I made a list of things I'd like to include. The basic history, of course, but also a couple of the most dramatic rescues, a list of shipwrecks with cargo and survivors, brief biographies of the keepers, physical statistics like what it's made of and how tall it is, stuff like that. Oh, and the decommissioning."

"You'll have to be a little careful when you address Mr. Maker's father's stint as light keeper."

"I know." Diane thought sadly of the guilt the old man had carried around for so many years. "I would never include anything that would hurt him."

"Are you going to put in our miracles?"

"Absolutely. Not just ours, but a whole section devoted to the unexplained things that have happened through the years. And also, maybe a few vignettes or interviews with long-time residents, families who have lived here for generations, about what the light means to them."

"Oh, this is exciting!" Margaret laid down her brush and laced her fingers together, bending them backward to stretch them out. "I started working on a few drawings, but it's been a while since I worked in pen and ink." She screwed up her face, implying that her efforts hadn't turned out so well.

"May I see them?"

Margaret laughed and shrugged. "Why not? But I warn you, they're not very good." She slid off the stool and beckoned to Diane to follow her back to the office, where she lifted a folder off her desk and extended it to Diane.

Taking the file, Diane flipped it open and began to lay the sketches out on the desk. The first sketch showed a ship in distress in the distance, half sunken beneath the waves. In the foreground, a person in the water frantically clung to a floating barrel and waved a hand for help. It was an excellent beginning, although the person's features were a bit odd. Diane could see why Margaret wouldn't be happy with it.

She shivered. "This makes it seem so real to me. I can't imagine how terrified and helpless I'd feel in a raging sea like this with the only security sinking beneath my feet."

She turned to the next page and continued on through the folder. People on a beach launching a boat into the waves, with another sinking ship in the distance...a view of the beach from a stranded ship, with a sturdy rope angling from the beach to the deck...a woman in a long dress and apron standing on the promontory in front of the light, looking out to sea, while children played nearby..."Margaret, these are exactly what I was envisioning."

"Well, they're not what *I* was envisioning," Margaret said with a wry twist of her lips. "I seem to remember being better than that once upon a time."

"It'll come back with practice," Diane assured her.

"I hope so." Margaret looked chagrinned.

A thought struck Diane. "You should make these into note cards."

"Maybe." Margaret looked at the sketches, considering. "That's a good idea...*if* I can do a better job than this."

"I've taken a good many photographs of the lighthouse, so we can use some of those also. I even went inside again and took photos of it the way it is now, but it would be wonderful if I could find some from when it was a working light."

"They might have something at the historical society or the library. There's got to be more information at the library than we found."

"We were only looking for that one specific period," Diane pointed out. "So you're probably right."

As Margaret put the sketches back in the folder, she said, "I've decided to invite Louellen Lumadue to have a showing here."

"Really? I thought she was rude and rather obnoxious to you."

"She was." Margaret smiled. "But I can't help thinking that there's some way to help her regain her love for her craft. So I'm going to see if I can contact her and invite her to lunch. Once she's here and sees the gallery, I hope I can convince her to show."

"Margaret..." Diane was troubled. "You may not be able to fix this—to fix *her.*"

"I know." Margaret shrugged. "And if I can't, I can't. But I feel I have to try." She went to the small kitchen area she'd set up in the office and opened the little refrigerator. "Would you like a tart?"

"You bet." Diane grinned and nodded.

It didn't take them long to decide that there was not a single thing Shelley could do to improve upon the fruit tarts.

Shortly afterward, Diane took her leave and headed back out into the bright, frigid morning. She was ready to turn onto Newport Street and head home when she decided to drop by the municipal building annex again. It might be best to leave an official message with Angela, the receptionist, requesting a meeting with Mr. Benton.

Bypassing Newport, she walked briskly on and entered the municipal building annex.

"Good morning, Angela," she said as she opened the door to the reception room. "I'd like to leave a message for—"

At that instant, she realized there was another person in the room. He'd been standing out of sight of the doors, and he'd been so quiet she might not have noticed him if it hadn't been for Angela's gaze sliding past her shoulder.

She turned with a smile that turned into surprise as she recognized Mr. Benton, still wearing his hat and coat as if he, too, had just come in. "Oh, goodness. I didn't expect to find you here," she said sweetly. "I thought your wife had a doctor's appointment."

"It, ah, it was changed," Benton said. His shoulders drooped a little bit. "Why don't you come into my office for a minute?"

As Diane followed the council president into his inner sanctum, Angela rolled her eyes at his back. She gave Diane a discreet thumbs-up.

Mr. Benton's office wasn't impressive, as inner sanctums went. Clearly, it wasn't used a lot. The walls were painted a bland ecru with a border of scrollwork in ecru and black running around the ceiling. There was a rather battered-looking desk with a black office chair behind it, and two chairs, also black, arranged before it.

Along one wall was a bank of filing cabinets and a coat tree. On the opposite wall beside the window was a small table holding a coffeemaker, a stack of Styrofoam cups, and accessories. There was a blind at the window, but no curtains. One picture occupied the wall behind the desk. It was a picture of the Orlean Point lighthouse at dusk back before it was decommissioned, artistically rendered with its beam shining out across the water.

Benton took off his heavy coat and methodically hung it on a hook of the coat tree. He removed his black fleece cap and did the same. Diane was surprised to see he was balding. She didn't really know why she'd expected him to have hair, but it changed his look significantly. He had a very low forehead and bushy black-gray eyebrows with ears that stuck out like jug handles.

"Have a seat," Mr. Benton invited. He went behind the desk and parked himself in the big black chair. "So you are interested in—what, exactly?"

Diane perched on the edge of one of the faux-leather chairs. "I'd like to know who, exactly, owns the lighthouse."

"The Town of Marble Cove," he answered promptly. It was probably the first thing he'd said to her without stumbling over his words.

"And is there any truth to the rumor that developers are interested in tearing it down and putting condos on the point?"

"Not yet." Benton sighed. He spread both hands flat on the desk. "We have been approached about it. At the last council meeting, we had a presentation from a developer who has a plan for that piece of land."

"Light Pointe Place."

"Yes." He looked resigned. "No secrets in this town, are there?"

Diane merely smiled.

"We didn't make any decision, nor did we promise the man anything. It was just a proposal, not a formal request."

"Yet."

"Yet."

"But the council did discuss it?"

He nodded. "A little bit. Just in a hypothetical context, since we weren't being asked to make any decisions."

Diane took a deep breath, biting back the impulsive protests that wanted to burst forth. Instead, she asked, "Is the town desperately in need of the money a sale like that would bring? And have you considered the potential drawbacks of getting rid of the lighthouse, which is a large part of Marble Cove's charm?"

The councilman gave her a small smile. "Ms. Spencer, town governments are *always* in need of money. And yes, we did talk a bit about the lighthouse." His smile softened. "I got down on one knee and proposed to my wife on the promenade with that old light in the background almost forty years ago."

"Really? What a lovely, romantic way to propose." And wouldn't it also be lovely to add to the historical booklet?

She cleared her throat and resumed her questions. "Has anyone ever talked about getting the lighthouse on the National Register of Historic Places?"

He shrugged. "There's nothing in the minutes about it from the past couple of years."

"I'd like to look into it and possibly spearhead a nomination committee. Someone needs to do something to save that building. It's a historic treasure."

He smoothed a hand self-consciously over the thin strands of hair carefully combed across the top of his head from a side part. "Ayuh."

"I would really hate to see it replaced by condos, and I'm sure that would upset a great many other people, both locals and tourists who come here year after year."

He nodded. "It might."

But when there's money involved, what the people want isn't always a prime consideration, she thought with rare cynicism. "So you wouldn't object to letting me attend a council meeting with a proposal for a nomination to the National Register?"

"Guess not." Benton stared absently at the picture of the lighthouse on the wall. "Let me know when you want to be on the agenda."

"All right. I'll get on it right away." She stood and held out a hand. "Thank you."

The man also rose and accepted her offered hand. "You're welcome."

"I'll let you know when I've got the nomination under way."

Benton waved a hand as he went to open the door for her. "No rush. The town hasn't done anything with it in decades. Don't guess we'll be doing anything about it anytime soon."

CHAPTER FIFTEEN

S helley's new friend Allie came by the following day with
her son Bryce.

For once, Shelley beat Frances to the door. It was a
ridiculous and petty thing to be pleased about, and she
stopped with her hand on the doorknob, acknowledging the
defensiveness she so often felt. *Lord, please give me patience,
and help me to appreciate all my mother-in-law's good qualities.*

"It's nice to see you again," Shelley said as she admitted
the young woman and her little boy. Aiden streaked in from the
kitchen as Allie was grabbing Bryce's coat before he tossed it
on the floor.

"It's nice to see you too," Allie said. She gave a quick
smile and produced that nervous giggle again. How could
Shelley have forgotten that giggle? And why did she have the
urge to mother this girl? Allie wasn't much younger than she.
"Looks like the boys are going to have fun," she observed as
their sons chattered for a moment before Aiden drew Bryce
up the stairs to his room. They had met at Sunday school
last week, so there was no awkwardness.

"Incoming," Shelley called up the stairs to Frances, who
had come by bright and early to change the sheets on the

beds and do "a little cleaning." To Shelley, a little cleaning was picking up the trail of belongings that Aiden and Dan seemed to shed with every step they took, and trying to keep dirty dishes off the counter and in the dishwasher. To Frances, a little cleaning was vacuuming, mopping, and dusting.

"Thanks." Frances appeared at the top of the steps. She smiled when she spotted Allie. "Hello, dear. I believe we met before."

"Yes, we did. Nice to see you again." Allie's giggle was in full force this morning.

Shelley got Allie some coffee and banana-nut bread that she'd made yesterday after Frances left at lunchtime, and they settled at the kitchen table.

"So tell me about yourself," Shelley invited.

Allie shrugged. "Not much to tell. Bryce and I moved here in November."

No husband? But Shelley didn't say it aloud. "It's a nice community. And Light the Way is a wonderful church. How did you come to attend there?"

"Just good luck." Allie giggled, although there really wasn't anything to giggle about. "We've only gone twice, but I really like it. I started looking for a church after Christmas, and that was the second one we visited. I wanted to get Bryce started going to Sunday school. I thought it would be a good way for him to make friends."

Shelley nodded. "Aiden told me last week there was a new boy in his class." She gestured at her leg. "I only went to the service. I'm constantly surprised by how long it takes me to do things while I'm letting this knee heal."

Frances came through the room with a basket of dirty sheets, headed for the washer and dryer in the basement. "The boys are playing very nicely together," she told them.

"Would you like to join us?" Shelley asked. Frances raced around like a tornado when she was at the house.

"No, no, you go ahead and visit while I throw these in the washer. Then I'd better get back up there just to make sure everything's going all right."

"Your mother-in-law is awesome," Allie said in a whisper as Frances departed. "Does she help you every day?"

"Heavens, no." From the way Allie giggled, Shelley feared her denial had been a bit too forceful. "She's just been coming over while I'm recuperating. Another two weeks and I should be able to do everything myself again."

"Still, it's really nice to have family to count on," Allie said wistfully.

"You have no family close by?" Shelley jumped on the opportunity to learn more about the lonely young woman. "I don't, either. But most of Dan's family lives in Maine, and most of them are right around here."

"I'm from Virginia." Allie took a sip of her coffee. "My parents both passed away right after I graduated from high school. I have one brother who still lives down there, but we aren't close." She looked down at the table, tracing the pattern on the vinyl table cover carefully. "And I'm sure you're wondering about Bryce's father."

"Well, a little." Shelley hated seeming intrusive, but she *was* curious, and she sensed Allie needed to talk. "But don't feel you have to tell me." She smiled, and Allie tittered in that nervous fashion.

"There's not much to tell. He's a soldier. We met and got married pretty quickly when he was home after a deployment. He told me he didn't want kids. Shortly after that, I found out I was pregnant. I didn't tell him. I guess I just didn't want to face it." A tear slipped down her cheek, and Shelley silently got up and brought a box of tissues to the table.

"Thanks," Allie whispered. She cleared her throat. "We never, ever talked about it. I kept telling myself it would work out, it would be fine. He was shipped out again, and when I gave birth I called him to tell him the news, but he didn't want any part of it.

"He asked if I was giving the baby up for adoption, and I said no. So when he returned from his deployment, he moved his stuff out of our apartment one day while the baby and I were out. The next thing I got was an express mail packet of divorce papers."

She sighed. "And I can't complain, because I knew he never wanted children. But sometimes I can't help thinking that if only he knew what he was missing... I mean, he's never even met Bryce."

"I'm so sorry," Shelley said.

"Me too," Allie said, "but more for Bryce than for myself. Someday he's going to ask about his father—he already has said a few things. What am I going to say?" She winced. "'Your daddy doesn't want you' sounds pretty horrible."

"Wow. I see your point." Shelley tried to imagine herself in that situation with Aiden, the age he was. He'd have a million questions. "Does he know anything?"

Allie nodded. She was calm, but her fingers were systematically shredding the tissue into teeny-tiny pieces. "He knows his daddy is a soldier and that he had to go far away. So far, he hasn't asked when he's coming back. But he will."

"Yes, I imagine he will." Shelley sighed. "It's not going to be easy, but you can make yourselves a good life here in Marble Cove. Light the Way is a wonderfully supportive church family."

Allie brightened. "It seems to be." She gave a fatalistic shrug. "It happened, and I can't change it. I wouldn't *want* to change it, because otherwise I wouldn't have Bryce. And he's awesome." She giggled, but Shelley barely noticed it.

"That he is."

★   ★   ★

Diane had invited Shelley, Margaret, and Beverly for dinner Wednesday evening. It was partly because she just wanted to visit with them all together, and partly because she wanted to share what little she'd learned about the lighthouse nomination with them.

They all were due to arrive at six.

At noon, she made sourdough bread dough with some starter a friend at her church had given her. After letting it rise near her fireplace for two hours, she punched down the dough and kneaded it, dividing the dough into quarters when she had finished. She kneaded each of the pieces until it was round again, formed each one into a ball, and placed them all on a baking sheet, leaving as much room between them as she could.

Then the dough balls went back on the hearth to rise a second time until they doubled. Finally, she slid the baking sheet into her preheated oven and baked the dough for forty-five minutes. When they were finished, they smelled delicious.

Next she took a serrated knife and cut off the top third. Making a slice down to, but not through, the crust on the bottom, she gently used her fingers to pry the dough from the inside of the ball, turning it into a bread bowl.

At five minutes of six, she filled the water glasses and set a crystal pitcher of ice water on the table. She had made a pretty cranberry-orange compote that she set in the center of the table, and placed small bowls of baby greens on the counter next to the saucepan holding the dressing.

The table looked pretty. She had used her favorite Villeroy & Boch china and the crocheted tablecloth had been her grandmother's. She used the dimmer switch to lessen the brightness of the minichandelier lighting over the table just as the doorbell rang.

When she opened the door, Rocky nosed his way forward to be sure he approved of her guests. Margaret laughingly kneed him out of the way. "Back up, boy, invalid coming through!"

"Gee, thanks," Shelley said. She was using both crutches in deference to the slippery sidewalks, and Margaret had a firm grip on her arm. Beverly was right behind them, carrying a cake box that looked suspiciously like one of Shelley's. Rocky backed up obligingly at Diane's command, and the three women entered the cozy cottage. Coats, hats, scarves, and gloves were shed.

"Let's go straight to the table," Diane said. "I had a ball cooking today, and I can't wait to feed you."

"I brought a little something in case you didn't have dessert," Shelley informed her.

Diane grinned. "I didn't make a real dessert because I knew you'd bring something far better than anything I could make."

"Will red velvet cake hit the spot?" Shelley asked.

"*Oooh*," Diane moaned. "It's one of my personal favorites."

"There goes the diet," Margaret said, "and I don't even care."

Beverly laughed as she followed Diane into the kitchen. "So what did you spend all this time making today?"

Diane waved at the table as she went to assemble the salads. "Have a seat, ladies. Your first course consists of baby greens drizzled with a warm Gorgonzola cheese dressing and topped with crumbled bacon and chopped almonds."

"Oh my." Shelley eased herself into a chair with her braced leg extending out to one side. "This is beautiful, Diane." She laid her napkin in her lap.

"And so easy," Diane said, her eyes twinkling. She brought the salads to the table and set one at each place.

They said a brief silent prayer of thanks and then started their meal.

"So Shelley," Margaret said, "how is that knee doing?"

Shelley sighed. "It's healing. Too slowly for my liking, but it's definitely getting better."

"I was afraid you'd be working at the Cove and unable to join us." Diane smiled at her youngest friend.

"No, after working Monday and Tuesday evenings, I decided I really needed to rest my leg tonight. I probably will work tomorrow if I can." She grimaced. "It's been a frustrating week. I'm moving slower than normal, and I haven't gotten as much baking done as I'd like. Today I had to wait until my mother-in-law left to make the cake. I was afraid it wasn't going to be cool in time to ice it, so I set it outside the door for a few minutes. But then I had to stand out there with it to make sure no hungry stray critters discovered it."

Everyone laughed. Beverly said, "Diane, I want this recipe. I've been cooking more now that I'm not just cooking for one, and I know my father would love this dressing."

As they finished their salads, Diane collected their plates and carried them to the sink. Then she turned to the bread bowls she had already plated. She had made a broccoli-cheddar soup which she carefully ladled into the bowls before presenting them to the diners.

"Oh my heavens," Margaret said. "Do you know how much I love these things? Anytime we drive to Augusta, I always make Allan stop at that Panera Bread near the interstate."

"I know the one you mean," Beverly said. "I adore that restaurant. Mostly because of these," she said, looking with undisguised pleasure at the bread bowl Diane set before her.

Diane resumed her seat, serving herself last. "That," she said, gesturing at the dish in the center of the table, "is cranberry-orange compote. Please serve yourself."

Everyone dug in, and after some exclamations over the excellence of the soup and bread, Margaret said, "Have you learned any more about the historic designation for the lighthouse, Diane?"

"Not a lot." Diane thought back to her frustrating conversation with the council president yesterday after she left the gallery. Recounting the tale for her friends, she said, "So I don't know much more than I did. Tomorrow my project is going to be seeing what I can learn online. The National Register of Historic Places has a great Web site. I haven't had a lot of time to look at it, but I'm hoping that I can find some information about the lighthouse there."

"Why would the council president be so reluctant to even talk about the lighthouse's historic registration?" Beverly shook her head. "Seems like he outght to be able to see its potential."

Margaret raised a hand, rubbing her thumb and fingers together to indicate money. "I suspect it has to do with finances. Marble Cove struggles to maintain the cobblestones and pretty streetlights and the rest of the ambience that makes downtown a draw for tourists. Pouring money into restoration of the lighthouse would mean shorting some other parts of the budget."

"I wonder if they'd be amenable to the idea if the lighthouse was an income-producing attraction."

"Like what?" Shelley asked. "You mean charge people to tour the lighthouse?"

"Exactly." Diane thought for a moment, trying to organize all the ideas that were flying around in her mind.

"Remember what I said about restoring it and cordoning off the living areas so people could see but not touch?" Beverly reminded them. "We could make that a reality."

"Tourists could climb up inside the tower and get the view from the walkway." Diane began listing things on her fingers. "There could be tour guides in period costumes to talk about it and answer questions."

"I believe one of the light keepers used to hand carve decoys," Margaret told them. "That might make a nice display inside too."

"What about a sextant?" Beverly asked. "And maps...maybe a small display on early navigation."

"You know," Margaret said thoughtfully, "I bet a lot of the families that have been here for generations have artifacts from some of the shipwrecks. Perhaps we could put out an appeal for those. Buttons, metal dishes, anything that hasn't rotted away that came from a wrecked ship."

"And photos," Diane said. "I know there are some photos of shipwrecks from the early twentieth century."

"Outside, there could be an area with a restored lifeboat," Shelley said. "If it was properly treated, the weather wouldn't hurt it."

"And other Maine coastal items such as lobster pots and clam rakes. People who don't live near the sea think that stuff is fascinating." Shelley giggled.

"Old ships' anchors," Diane said. "Anchor chain. Salvaged bells. Barrels used for water." She clapped her hands. "This could be a wonderful exhibit!"

"So there'd be a fee for entry?" Beverly frowned. "We might do better if we just asked for a donation. Sometimes people part with fives, tens and twenties more easily when it's a donation."

"But a donation for what?" Shelley asked.

"The Orlean Point Light maintenance fund," Margaret suggested. Then she looked at Diane. "Tell them about the booklet."

"All right." Diane explained her idea about writing a historical pamphlet illustrated with her photos and Margaret's artwork.

"But that's only if I can stop drawing faces that look like cartoons," Margaret said. She shook her head. "I was never terrific at portraiture, but I can't believe how much trouble I'm having with a few pen-and-ink sketches."

"Draw them without faces," Shelley suggested.

Everyone looked at her, and she turned pink with embarrassment. "I don't mean without *any* faces," she added. "Use a different angle that doesn't require you to draw their faces."

Margaret rose from her seat opposite Shelley, came around the table, and smacked a loud kiss on her friend's cheek. "You're brilliant!" she said, as Diane and Beverly chuckled.

"I could oversee the initial printing process," Beverly said. "You know, get quotes and do that kind of legwork."

"What could I do?" Shelley asked.

"You could help me," Diane said. "This booklet is going to be full of facts and figures that will need to be double-checked for accuracy, typed into documents, and then proofread once they're entered. I know it's not glamorous—"

"It's perfect," Shelley said. "It's something I can do at home."

"In between baking, keeping a home, chasing two small children, and training a puppy." Diane grimaced. "Makes me tired just thinking about it."

CHAPTER SIXTEEN

Margaret was taking Louellen Lumadue to Captain Calhoun's Crab and Lobster House. She had called immediately after her conversation with Diane on Tuesday and invited her to lunch. They had settled on Thursday.

Diane had agreed to mind the gallery, and she arrived at exactly the same time Louellen did.

Margaret introduced the two women and then said to Diane, "Thanks for your help."

Diane grinned and held up her laptop. "No problem. I can work here as easily as I can at home, and I doubt we'll be swamped with tourists this afternoon. Go have fun."

Louellen smiled as Margaret led the way out the front door. Captain Calhoun's was just down the block from the Shearwater Gallery within easy walking distance. "What does your friend do that she can work on her computer? Accounting?"

Margaret shook her head. "No, Diane's a writer. Her first book comes out in April."

Louellen inclined her head. "How nice. I've always thought it would be far more difficult to write than to paint, even though they're both classified as artistic endeavors."

"I agree," Margaret said with feeling. "When I paint or sketch, I can often see what I want the completed piece to look like in my mind. I can't imagine how one would do that with a story."

"I guess that's why people plot and plan out stories. But I'm far too organic for that. I often start a piece without a clear idea of where it's going. I let the art lead me where it wants me to go."

Margaret considered that. "I think my art would lead me right to a blank canvas."

Louellen laughed.

"I'm serious. I can't imagine starting a painting without knowing what I intend to paint. To me, that's as difficult as writing a book."

The two women pushed into the restaurant, where they were greeted and seated without delay. "No wait this time of year," Margaret said.

"But I bet it's a madhouse in the summer." Louellen looked around at the cozy restaurant with a fire burning in the enormous hearth on the back wall.

"It can get pretty busy," Margaret agreed.

The waitress approached with menus.

"What does this place do best?" Louellen asked. "I can't decide. It all looks so good."

"The lobster roll in a New England-style hot dog bun is delicious," Margaret told her. "So is the Caesar salad with crab cake. It's lump crab meat, and it's terrific." She smiled. "Honestly, I don't think there's a dud on the menu. Everything they make gets praise."

"The lobster roll sounds good." Louellen closed her menu and handed it back to the waitress.

"I'll have the crab cake. Water for each of us, please, and I'd like some decaf."

"I'd like coffee too, but bring me high-test," Louellen told the waitress. She smiled at Margaret. "Since I have to drive back after this."

"I hope you'll come back to the gallery for a few minutes. I'd like to show you some of the things we have on consignment." She hesitated. "I'd like to show your work as well, Louellen. But I'd want to have a formal exhibit."

Louellen held up a hand in a "stop" gesture. "Whoa. I appreciate the offer, but I don't really do exhibitions anymore. I'd be happy to show my work in your gallery, but I don't want to interact with the public."

"Why ever not? Generally people at exhibitions are quite pleasant."

Louellen made a face. "I wish I could say I've grown a thicker skin over the years, but the opposite seems to be true. I can't take the wannabe critics who tell me what I could do to improve my work."

"But aren't there so many more who like your work, who collect it, who compliment your skills? Couldn't you focus on those and shut out the complainers?" Margaret had run into a few armchair critics herself, but it was just a small part of the oddities that came with a creative career.

"Maybe, if I tried. But honestly, I'd rather just put in my nine-to-five and then shut the door on the studio at the end of a workday."

"You never get ideas from things that happen in your life?" She couldn't even imagine "turning off" her creativity. All day every day, some chance thing gave her a new idea, a different angle, a fresh color palette.

"I do," Louellen said. "That's not the kind of thing you can stop, but I do like to relax and forget about it if I can."

Margaret supposed she could understand that. Last night, sitting around Diane's table with her friends, she hadn't been thinking much at all about her work. "Well," she finally said, "I'd be happy to show some of your work even without doing a 'meet the artist' party. I could put up a small display somewhere in a dark corner where no one is likely to notice it—"

Louellen laughed. "You are persistent, aren't you?"

Margaret smiled. "Only about things that are important to me."

There was a moment of silence. Then Louellen leaned forward. "Why am I important to you? Or why is my work so important?"

Margaret shrugged. "You and your work are part of my journey. Who I am as an artist reflects what I've seen and learned and studied throughout my life. Very early on, you caught my eye, compelled me to look more deeply. Like in your hidden imagery series. I—"

"I don't want to talk about those paintings." If Louellen's voice had been angry or cool, Margaret might have argued. But the vulnerable note arrowed straight to Margaret's heart.

"The criticism of that series affected you deeply, didn't it?"

Louellen was silent for a long time. "Do you have a piece or series that's particularly dear to your heart?"

Margaret nodded.

"And has it been well received?"

Again Margaret nodded, but more slowly.

"Imagine that you'd labored over your vision until you looked at it and thought it was absolutely perfect. Not one more brushstroke. But then someone comes along— someone who is purported to be a knowledgeable art critic— and absolutely savages your masterpiece. How would you feel?"

"I'd be shattered," Margaret said quietly. "Devastated."

Louellen nodded. "Yes. That's exactly how it feels." Her eyes were dull. "I couldn't do another painting with a hidden image in it. I literally could not fathom picking up a brush with that intent."

"So you changed focus."

"Yes. And I stepped back from my art. It's not as important to me anymore. People can say what they want. I'm not going to let it bother me."

Seeing her opening, Margaret slipped inside. "So there's no reason why you should mind if the Shearwater Gallery does a modest exhibit of a few pieces of your choosing?"

Caught off guard, Louellen opened and closed her mouth, then shook her head, smiling wryly. "You may be the most persistent person I've ever met." She shrugged.

"All right. If you want to do a showing so badly, I'll bring you a few things. But absolutely positively no big splash, no speech."

"No big splash," Margaret promised. "No speech. Just a few spaces on a wall devoted to your work."

Louellen sighed. "All right. You win. I'll do your showing."

★   ★   ★

"Hello, Standish and Lane Consulting. How may I help you?"

Beverly took a deep breath. "Good morning. My name is Beverly Wheeland from Marble Cove. I'm not seeking a consultant, but I'm considering a career change to business consulting, and I wondered if one of the partners would be willing to speak with me about his or her experiences in today's economy."

"Hello, Beverly. I'm Julia Standish. I started the company about fifteen years ago and took on a partner five years ago. I'd be happy to try to answer your questions."

"Thank you." A flood of relief filled Beverly. She hadn't been sure how other consultants would feel about speaking with someone who, essentially, wanted to take jobs from them. Although she had been very careful to choose other Maine firms that were nowhere close to Marble Cove, so she hoped they wouldn't feel threatened. Still, with so much Internet business out there today, they might well mind more competition no matter where she was located.

"You want to fire your questions at me?" Julia Standish asked.

Beverly chuckled. "All right. First, are you able to make a reasonable income that supports you? I don't mean a country-club lifestyle, but I also would prefer not to eat boxed mac and cheese for dinner every night either."

"That shouldn't be a problem." Julia's voice was warm with humor. "I'm able to make my mortgage and car payments, pay my bills and go out to dinner occasionally, and meet all my obligations—including a daughter in college, who seems to believe that I am a never-ending source of gas, tuition, and rent money."

Beverly's eyebrows rose. Standish and Lane must be doing all right then. "Has the economic downturn affected your business much?"

Julia paused. "It hasn't changed my income a terrible amount, if that's what you're asking. But one thing my partner and I have noticed is that our clientele is very different. She was independent too, before we merged, and we both have seen a shift from bigger corporate clients to small, home-based business folks who need help and advice."

"That's actually the market I'm most interested in working with," Beverly told her. "A friend of mine is starting a small business, and I've been helping her, which is what got me to considering this seriously."

"I'm not aware of a lot of other consultants along the coast there," Julia said. "Are you?"

"No. The closest ones I've seen were all in or near the cities."

"You might do quite well there," Julia mused. "People like personal treatment and face-to-face meetings. I travel two days a week to visit clients that are too far away to come in."

"I travel from Marble Cove to Augusta to work now," Beverly told her.

"Ugh. That's not a drive I'd enjoy, especially in the winter."

"Agreed." Beverly thought of those sickening moments when her car had spun off the road and crunched over the boulders. "Is there a part of the job you particularly enjoy? And conversely, what's the most frustrating part?"

"Hmm." If Beverly were in Julia's office, she imagined she might see the other woman leaning back in her chair as she thought about the question. "That's tough. The best part...well, I absolutely love seeing people succeed and know that I've helped them. And I love the actual consulting, teaching people how to set up and manage their businesses. The part I like the least, I suppose, is the infrequent stinker of a client who is never happy, doesn't follow your guidance, and then blames you when they fail."

"What did you do before you started consulting?" Beverly asked. That wasn't on her list of questions, but she was genuinely curious.

"I was an accountant," Julia answered promptly. "But I was really tired of working like a wild thing from January to April every year, and I realized I would enjoy more client contact."

"Yes, I think that I might like that as well. But how did you go about acquiring clients at first? It seems as though it may take awhile to build a client base that will sustain a reasonable income."

"Well, I was married at the time," Julia said, "so I had the luxury of backup if things didn't go well. And perhaps I was rash to just quit my job. But, oh, I was so *sick* of balancing books! I gave free seminars on starting up businesses, I wrote a column for a local newspaper aimed at small businesses, and of course I begged everyone who hired me, and was pleased, to recommend me to friends. I called everyone I could think of and told them about my new endeavor; I advertised free initial consultations and occasionally offered a few other services free."

"Gracious," Beverly said, "I believe the word 'determined' must have your name next to it in the dictionary."

When they concluded their conversation, Beverly thanked Julia profusely for her time. She hung up and then took a few moments to make orderly notes in a laptop document of all the ideas Julia had thrown at her.

Beverly felt optimistic as she walked to the kitchen to refill her water glass before calling the second consultant on her list. Julia Standish had certainly given her a lot to consider. A new career suddenly seemed much more concrete than it had before that phone call.

CHAPTER SEVENTEEN

Diane went to the library Friday morning to see what she could dig up about the history of the lighthouse.

Although the women had learned a bit about it when they were uncovering Edward Maker's secretive history before Christmas, they also had learned to their dismay that some of the records had been destroyed in a fire. What, if anything, Diane wondered, had been spared?

Diane hurried up the old stone steps of the Thorpe Free Library, worn in the center from decades of feet stepping in the exact same places. To the right of the door was a brass plaque proclaiming that the library had been named in honor of the man who'd once owned the old brick home, Henry J. Thorpe. On his death in 1851, he had bequeathed the house and what was apparently a prodigious collection of books at that time, to the town to be used for a public library. Some years later, Diane had learned, the beginnings of a historical collection had been created, and eventually the Marble Cove Historical Society had split off from the library and taken over the care of the collection, although it was still housed in the same building.

Stepping through the huge, heavy old front door, Diane closed it behind her and took a moment to hang her coat on the coat tree in the front foyer. She took a deep breath, savoring the "library" smell. It brought back wonderful memories from her childhood, when her mother used to take her to their local library once a week to exchange their books.

The circulation desk was just inside the first room on the right. "Hello, Gilda. How are you today?"

"Just fine, dear." The librarian, Diane knew, had been employed there for more than three decades, according to Margaret. Gilda looked to be about sixty-ish, with short, stylish silver hair and twinkling blue eyes that peeped over her reading glasses. She wore a thick Fair Isle wool sweater over a turtleneck to combat the chill that came in with each patron who opened the door. "What can I help you with today?"

"The lighthouse. I'm looking for any historical information you might have."

Gilda frowned thoughtfully. "Well, there are some things that recently were donated to the historical society that we took up to the Maine Room. A lot of it was part of the original bequest that came with the house. Somehow, the historical items were moved into storage and forgotten for many years."

"What was the bequest?"

"In 1851, a local resident named Henry Thorpe passed away. He left this house and a book collection—quite extensive at that time—to the town as the foundation for a free library."

Diane nodded. "Hence the name."

Gilda smiled. "Yes. Would you like the key to the Maine Room?"

When Diane nodded, the librarian said, "When you're finished, just replace anything you've used and lock the door again. You can bring me the key on your way out."

"Thank you." Diane headed up the stairs. There were two stories above the ground floor. The ground floor was devoted to children's fiction and contemporary adult fiction, and a microfiche area was in the basement. On the second floor, a wall had been knocked out between two bedrooms to hold the reference section. The two other bedrooms were the Maine Room and the adult nonfiction section, and the third floor contained classic literature and additional adult fiction.

The Maine Room was filled with the historical society's collection of local and state history, Diane knew. She'd never been in the room before, and she was curious about exactly what it might hold. After fitting the key into the lock, she pushed open the door and stepped inside.

A long reference table ran down the center of the room, with shelves on each wall and a section of stacks at the far end of the room. A card catalog to her right would help her locate the information she was seeking. Setting her bag on the table, she began looking for anything related to the lighthouse.

Three hours later, she had made progress, but she suddenly realized she felt distinctly light-headed. *Blood sugar,* she thought immediately. *How could I forget I need to eat?* Chagrinned, she dug out the package of dried fruit and the small container of cheese and crackers that she had placed in her purse to keep hypoglycemia at bay. The food only worked if she actually remembered to eat it, she thought, shaking her head at her own folly.

Minutes later, she was feeling renewed enough to go back to work. She had a list of light keepers dating back to the mid-1800s. She had found one book that said the lighthouse had been constructed after Henry J. Thorpe had left the bequest, but she wondered if that was really true or if that was mixed up with the library. Just how many public facilities and services could one man leave in his will for a town? On the other hand, she hadn't gotten the names of any light keepers going back any farther than that.

She also found a picture of a little boy in a cap and long coat. He stood at the edge of the beach and behind him were the bones of a ship of significant size that must have wrecked many years before. The caption beneath it read: "T. S. Longworthy in front of the *Charlotte Andressen,* Orlean Point Beach, 1892."

Longworthy was the name of the second light keeper on her list, although she thought perhaps there were some earlier ones she hadn't discovered yet. Perhaps this had been his son. She turned on her computer and signed into the library's free Wi-Fi service, then did an Internet search for

Charlotte Andressen. Immediately, she found the name in a list of known Maine shipwrecks: *HMS Charlotte Andressen foundered off Orlean Point, Marble Cove, ME, 1757*.

Her pulse sped up. 1757! She had no idea there were shipwreck records dating back that far. But this list contained records clear back to 1710. As she carefully perused the list, she found a 1714 wreck, also a British ship, and a 1733 French frigate that foundered there as well. Oddly, there were no wrecks after that 1757 one.

Next she did a search for Orlean Point, but there were no additional hits for shipwrecks off Marble Cove, although other areas up and down the Maine coastline saw their share.

That was weird, considering the light had probably not been constructed until the 1800s. Or at least, she hadn't found any evidence that it had. The first light keeper on her list, Donald Foley, couldn't possibly have been around in the late 1700s if little T. S. Longworthy's father had been the light keeper in 1892.

Renewing her efforts, she looked through what felt like dozens of additional sources in the Maine Room. There was an astonishing number of very old tomes, although that shouldn't be so remarkable if they were the remnants of the original Henry Thorpe collection.

When she finally finished, it was after one o'clock, and she was starving. Rocky would be quite desperate for a bit of exercise by now too. And she'd made a lot of progress. In addition to the list of light keepers, she had compiled a list—an extremely sparse list—of shipwrecks off the Orlean

Point coast. Even more interesting, there hadn't been a single loss of life since the *Charlotte Andressen* on the 24th of September 1757, in which 280 of the four hundred people on board had perished.

It made her wonder exactly when the lighthouse really had been built.

Gilda was still at the desk when Diane returned the key, but her face registered surprise. "Heavenly days! Have you been up there all this time?"

Diane nodded, chuckling. "Yes, and I got so caught up in my research I forgot to eat. My blood sugar sure let me know how unhappy it was."

"That's not good." The librarian tilted her head. "Are you feeling all right now?"

Diane nodded. "Yes. I had a small snack."

"Did you find what you were looking for?"

"Sort of. I'm trying to find out when the lighthouse was constructed. I can't find much information back beyond the mid-nineteenth century."

Gilda tapped a pencil against her lips. "A hundred and fifty or sixty years ago? That's a long time. But I wonder..." She reached for the telephone book beneath the desk. "I have one suggestion. There's a lady named Odessa Karpenko who is one hundred and seven years old. She has lived in Marble Cove almost all her life. I believe her parents emigrated from the Ukraine when she was an infant."

"One hundred and seven." Diane couldn't even imagine it. "Is she...would she be able to speak to me, do you think?"

Gilda nodded. "Oh yes. She's a little forgetful, but certainly not senile. She lives with her granddaughter's family. Would you like me to give you their number?"

Diane nodded. "Yes, please." The centenarian would have been born sometime around 1905. Perhaps she had heard some bits of local history that Diane herself hadn't been able to unearth yet.

★　　★　　★

Friday afternoon, Shelley's cell phone rang. "Hello?"

"Hi, Shelley, it's Frances."

"Hello, Frances."

"I just wanted to let you know I can't make it by this afternoon," her mother-in-law said.

"Oh, that's all right. I appreciate all you've done, but really, I'm doing much better, and I don't need—"

"Of course you do. If you don't rest that knee, young lady, it's not going to heal like it should, and then where will you be? I've blocked off my morning tomorrow to come and give you some help with laundry and cleaning."

Shelley opened her mouth, and then closed it again. What, really, could she say? "Thank you. I appreciate that."

When she hung up the phone, she let her head drop and squeezed her eyes shut, feeling the incipient tendrils of a headache curling around the edges of her brain.

Taking a deep breath, she opened her eyes again and tucked her phone into the pocket of her jeans. Looking around, she took in the disaster that was her kitchen. Oh heavens. She was going to have to clean up before Frances got here tomorrow to clean up! Otherwise, she'd hear endless comments about putting things away and picking things up.

She left the crutch propped against the wall where it had been since breakfast and began picking up dishes and dumping things into the dishwasher as fast as she humanly could. Finally, when there wasn't an extra inch of space to be seen in the machine, she dumped in the soap and turned it on to wash while she cleaned up the pots and pans and other things that couldn't be washed.

She thought of the living room, with its carpet practically buried under toys and newspapers and a dog bed that badly needed to be washed, and all the unmade beds upstairs. But first, the bathrooms simply had to be attended to. Maybe tonight Dan would be able to—

No, he wouldn't. Because tonight he'd promised Allan that he'd finish a table that was supposed to be shipped tomorrow. There was no way of knowing how late he'd be, but he often seemed to wriggle out of being around for bath time anyway. Although she supposed that wasn't really fair, because he'd been a great help since she'd hurt her knee.

She hobbled around the living room while Emma played happily on the floor with a Little Tikes kitchen set. It had been an incredible yard sale bargain—it had even come with the original dishes, a pan, a phone, and a coffeepot.

Aiden was upstairs in his room, playing with Prize. Finally, she got the living room picked up. She stripped the blanket and cover off Prize's dog bed and tossed it in the washer along with a load of rugs that were looking terribly dingy. Someone had told her that if she sprinkled baking soda over the inner foam core each time she put the cover on, it would help keep the dog bed from smelling bad, and unless she'd completely lost her sense of smell, it seemed to work.

The downstairs bathroom wasn't too difficult to clean, but she might have to leave the tub upstairs for Frances tomorrow, since there was no way she could kneel yet. Even if she took off the brace, it would probably kill her to bend this dratted knee.

Emma was rubbing at her eyes when Shelley came out of the bathroom, cleaning bucket in hand. Setting her supplies aside, Shelley crossed to the little kitchen set and picked up her daughter. "I see some sleepy eyes," she said, rubbing the warm little back. "You ready for a nap?"

In answer, Emma dropped her head onto her mother's shoulder. Shelley's heart filled with love as she felt a tiny arm encircle her neck. Slowly, she made her way up the stairs with her precious burden.

"Mama," Emma said sleepily around the thumb she had tucked in her mouth.

She changed Emma's diaper and then laid her in her crib, tucking the pink thermal blanket snugly around her daughter's shoulders. Quietly, she made her way from the room and pulled the door behind her.

Walking farther along the hall, she decided to check on Aiden. Perhaps he'd fallen asleep too. Dan had let him stay up a little later than normal last night.

Aiden's bedroom door was closed. Quietly, she turned the knob and began to open the door, hoping not to awaken him if he was, in fact, asleep.

The door opened about an inch and caught on something.

"Mama!" Aiden sounded startled and alarmed. "Don't open the door."

"Why not?" She pressed harder. It was probably Aiden's pajamas or some other clothing discarded where it shouldn't have been.

"Mama, no—!"

The door gave way. As it swung fully open, the sound of plastic pieces spilling across the floor was unmistakable. Legos, no doubt.

Shelley pushed the door back and stopped. Stared. "Aiden Daniel Bauer," she breathed. "What have you been doing?"

The shelves on which Aiden kept his toys were bare. *Completely empty.* Baskets of Legos and little Fisher-Price people and parts had been scattered across the room. A large box with a wooden train track, Thomas the Tank Engine and his friends, a kit full of foam pieces with which he built dinosaurs—even the shelf of his favorite books had been cleared off.

Shelley put a hand to her forehead, unable to believe her eyes. He'd been so quiet! "Look at this mess," she said when Aiden didn't answer. He stood, caught red-handed in the midst of major misbehavior, hanging his head.

"I was just playing, Mama," he said.

"No," she said, very precisely. "Just playing is what we do when we get out one or two toys and make them do things, or build things with them. *This* was not just playing." What on earth was she going to do? It would take half the day to clean up this mess.

And then the doorbell rang.

CHAPTER EIGHTEEN

At three thirty on Friday afternoon, Diane rang the doorbell of a sizable Cape Cod over on Compass Street. A woman around her own age promptly opened the door with a smile. "Hello. You must be Diane Spencer." She extended a hand. "I'm Eva Winslow. Please come in."

"Thank you." Diane shook the woman's hand and followed her hostess into the home. Half the main floor was a large great room. The kitchen, at the back, displayed gleaming black granite countertops and appliances, glass-fronted cabinets and an island with four barstools separating the kitchen space from the living area. *Shelley would love this*, she thought.

"My grandmother is thrilled to have a visitor," Eva told her. "Winter is hard for her because she can't get out much."

"Is she really a hundred and seven?" Diane could hardly fathom living more than a century.

Eva laughed. "She sure is. After her husband died, she lived alone until she was ninety-one. Then she lived with her youngest son, my mother's brother, until he passed away unexpectedly last year. My mother was her oldest child and there were three more girls, but they're all gone now." Her voice softened. "So she came to live with us."

"It's nice that she didn't have to go into a home," Diane said.

Eva shrugged. "There was no reason for that. She can still walk, she can still see. Her hearing's not great, but her mind is still pretty sharp." She went to one of the doors that led to the other half of the main floor and knocked.

"Come in," Diane heard an aged voice call.

Eva turned the knob and opened the door, beckoning Diane to follow.

Inside was a large and pleasant room that combined a bedroom and sitting area. Through a wide doorway, Diane saw a handicapped bathroom with a walk-in shower.

In a reclining rocker in the sitting area was an old lady. She wore a warm wool sweater buttoned neatly to the neck with a blouse collar above it. A thick ivory afghan covered her legs. The old woman's hair was clean and brushed into neat waves that barely covered her pink scalp. Her ears were large, and her nose seemed to dominate her small face. Thick glasses magnified her faded brown eyes, but they were warm and friendly, as was her smile.

"Baba," Eva said, "this is Diane Spencer, the lady who would like to talk to you about the lighthouse." She turned to Diane. "This is my grandmother, Odessa Karpenko."

The old lady held out a trembling hand. "Hello," she said.

Diane took the frail hand and very gently gave it a soft movement up and down. "It's nice to meet you, Mrs. Karpenko."

"Odessa," she said in heavily accented English. "You call me Odessa."

Charmed, Diane nodded. "If you'll call me Diane."

Eva pulled up a chair for Diane and another for herself. "Sometimes she prefers to speak in Russian," she said. "So I'll translate if that happens."

Diane found the old lady fascinating. She could have listened to her talk about her history all day, but she was conscious of the time. She imagined Mrs. Karpenko would tire quickly. After a bit, she managed to steer the conversation around to the lighthouse... and the floodgates opened.

Odessa spoke rapidly, her gaze on Diane. She switched back and forth between English and Russian, and Diane had to keep glancing at Eva for assistance.

"She says everybody knows there are angels that guard the lighthouse."

"Really?" That was the first time that Diane had heard that claim, and it took her breath away.

"She says the people in Marble Cove have always had visits from angels, even many years before the lighthouse was built."

"What do you mean," Diane asked Odessa, "when you say visits from angels?"

Odessa's wrinkled countenance lit up.

"Her mother used to tell her stories about the people who lived here many years before their family came. The others in town told her mother these stories... that angels saved a boy from the sea... they guided a fishing fleet back to the harbor in a fierce storm once...they brought rain to the community when there was a terrible drought and everyone else's crops were failing."

Diane scribbled as fast as she could, nodding. She glanced up and smiled warmly at the old woman.

"You see angels too?" Odessa asked.

Diane hesitated. "Lights," she finally said. "I never thought that they could be angels, but I suppose in some way, they must be, because they've saved the lives of several people whom I know and love."

Odessa was nodding vigorously. "Yes. Light angels," she said in her thick accent. She reached over and gently patted Diane's hand, and Diane felt that today she'd found another believer.

Then Odessa picked up where she had left off. Oh, how Diane wished she'd brought a tape recorder. She could hardly wait to tell her friends about Odessa's angels. Surely they must be similar, if not the same as the miraculous lights.

She wondered why there was no mention of the angelic claim elsewhere. She'd look again, but she hadn't seen anything about angels in her research earlier today.

"Did you ever meet the light keeper who was there when you were a little girl?" she asked, trying to get into some more concrete territory.

Odessa nodded. "Mr. Longworthy." She went into another spate of Russian, to which Eva listened attentively. "He was the light keeper then. She went to school with some of his children," Eva explained.

"Do you remember anything about the light keepers before Mr. Longworthy?"

Odessa nodded and began to speak again, and Eva translated. "There were at least two, she believes, before Longworthy, but she can't remember their names. But she knows that the first light keeper was there the night the light went out."

"The night the light went out?" Diane's ears perked up. "What does that mean?" Instantly she thought of Edward Maker's sad story, but just as quickly, she realized that Odessa must be speaking of an age many decades earlier. If there were two or more light keepers before Longworthy, then that put Odessa's story about the first light keeper back well over a century earlier.

Odessa's eyes lit up. She looked surprised that Diane didn't know what she was talking about.

"There was a great storm, and the light in the lighthouse blew out." Eva began to translate as Odessa chattered in Russian. "But there was a big fire in the town, and a ship was saved from foundering on the rocks because the captain saw the light from the fire." She listened intently and frowned. "She doesn't know the lightkeeper's name, but she says a...a church man—I think she means a minister? A pastor? named Jeremiah Thorpe led the rebuilding of the church."

Odessa nodded wisely. "God's will," she said solemnly. "Angels."

Diane understood what the old lady was trying to express. She smiled. "God sent his angels to save that ship in a very unusual way, you mean?"

Odessa nodded again. She talked and talked, and talked some more, with Diane asking questions along the way, until Eva finally interrupted gently to suggest they continue the discussion another day.

Thanking the pair for their assistance, Diane promised to visit Odessa again and took her leave, her head reeling with all she had learned.

★   ★   ★

Beverly looked at the sketches on Margaret's counter in silence.

Margaret chuckled. "It's all right. You can say it. They're still not good."

"They're still not as good as your usual work," Beverly said quietly. "They're still a lot better than anything I could do."

"Yes, but you just hit the nail on the head." Margaret began to gather up the sketches she'd been working on for the booklet. "They're not the quality I usually produce. And I can't put something like these out there with my name attached to them, even in a historical booklet."

Beverly nodded. "Why do you think you're having so much trouble with them?"

"I wish I knew. I haven't worked in pen and ink for years, but I honestly didn't expect it to be this difficult. It's an unforgiving medium. One mistake and you're starting over. But I've been practicing on scrap paper, and I was feeling pretty good about my efforts." She sighed. "Between that and the flat, uninspiring landscape I produced this week, it's enough to make me worry that I'm losing my touch."

"You're having trouble with your usual medium?" That sounded like there might be something more wrong than just a rusty technique.

When Margaret nodded, Beverly advanced her thought. "Is there anything bothering you that might be affecting your work?"

Margaret thought for a moment, her gaze unfocused and far away. "I've been a little stirred up after talking to Louellen Lumadue recently. Her attitude toward her art is that it's mostly just a job. A way to pay the bills. It's really been bothering me. I don't understand how anyone can do any kind of artistic endeavor without loving their work. I mean, look at Shelley."

"Shelley?"

"Shelley's an artist in a different medium." Margaret flung out her hands. "She experiments until she gets her intended result, and she uses flair and imagination to give them her signature, if you will."

"That's true." Beverly hadn't really thought of Shelley's baking that way. She would have to mention it to Shelley the next time they worked on her business goals together. Because Margaret was absolutely right. A true artist loved her work.

Beverly's cell phone rang. Pulling it from her handbag, she checked the readout. "It's Jeff," she said in surprise.

They had plans to have dinner together tomorrow evening, and she wondered if he was calling to cancel.

Holding up a finger for Margaret to give her a moment, she turned away and took the call. "Hello?"

"Hello, Beverly." Jeff's voice sounded warm and sincere. He wouldn't sound like that if he was ditching her, would he?

"Hi, Jeff. How are you?"

"I'm fine. Looking forward to seeing you tomorrow night. But I have a different reason for calling."

"Oh?"

"A friend of mine has an extra set of tickets to the symphony in Augusta. I wondered if you'd like to go with me." He gave her the date. "I would have waited until tomorrow evening to ask, but he wants an answer today."

Beverly frowned, taken aback. They hadn't even had dinner yet, and he was asking her for another date. "I suppose that would be nice," she said slowly.

Jeff was silent for a moment, as if he sensed her disquiet. "Great," he finally said.

They suffered through a stilted conversation before Beverly concluded the call a few minutes later.

When she didn't speak immediately, Margaret said, "Is everything all right?"

Beverly nodded. "Yes. I suppose so."

"I—" This time, it was Margaret's phone that interrupted them. "Excuse me a moment."

Beverly remained at the counter, pulling out the sketches to study them again as Margaret paced around with the phone at her ear. Studying the illustrations, she completely tuned out her friend's conversation.

But half her attention was on her own thoughts. It wasn't that she didn't like Jeff. She did. She just wasn't sure that she wanted to be rushed off her feet. And how silly was she, to be worrying about that? He'd told her himself the only reason he'd asked her immediately was because the tickets might not be available if he waited. But he could have simply accepted them and asked her later. Surely he could have found another date if she couldn't go. The implication that he wouldn't go if she couldn't was what bothered her, she finally realized. She wasn't ready for anyone to be thinking serious thoughts about her, nor was she ready for serious thoughts of a man in her life. Oh bother. Why couldn't dating be simple? Pushing the whole train of thought away, she gave her attention to the illustrations.

Finally, Margaret flipped the phone shut with a snap and came back to stand beside her.

"Hmph. I wasn't expecting that phone call."

"Oh?" Beverly glanced at her. "Is something wrong?"

"That was Louellen Lumadue." Margaret shook her head as if the exchange had left her bewildered. "Yesterday, I talked her into bringing me a couple of pieces to show. She was reluctant, but she finally agreed. I honestly thought she felt comfortable enough to let me hang a couple of her paintings. But now she says she made a mistake, that she doesn't want to bother."

"That's rather odd," Beverly said. "Isn't it? What artist doesn't want to show their work?"

"Exactly," Margaret said slowly. Then she shrugged. Grabbing the file of sketches, she started for the corner that contained her studio. "I've got to get back to work. It's unfortunate that she refused, but it's her loss."

CHAPTER NINETEEN

Shelley shook a finger at her son. "You stay right here and start picking up this mess, Aiden. Do you hear me?"

Her son nodded, his little lip quivering.

Shelley felt like a terrible person as she turned and hurried—as much as anyone with a stupid gimpy knee could hurry—to answer the doorbell that had just rung. She was so upset with Aiden. What had that child been thinking? Now she was going to have to get that whole mess put away before Frances arrived first thing in the morning, just looking for things out of place.

Something was bothering her son, she feared. She couldn't put a finger on it, but he seemed easily upset these days. Any other time, he would have scrambled around and philosophically started picking up.

She was in such a rush to get to the door that she nearly slipped and fell on the throw rug. Throwing out a hand, she caught herself on the back of a nearby chair. The motion bent her knee in an odd direction, and she gasped as a missile of pain burst through it.

The doorbell rang again.

"I'm coming," she called. Taking a deep breath, she carefully stepped over the rug and tugged open her front door.

On the stoop stood Allie, the new member of their Sunday school class.

Go away, Shelley wanted to say. *I'm too busy to chat today.* Instead, she relaxed her shoulders and smiled. "Hi, Allie. What's up?"

"I was driving by and thought I'd stop and see if you needed any help. I have my son in the car, so he could entertain Aiden." She gave one of her nervous giggles. "I figure you probably really need to sit down and take a break about now."

Shelley opened her mouth to say, *Thank you, but I'm fine,* but what came out was, "You're a lifesaver. I would really appreciate the help."

"Great!" Allie brightened. "Just let me get Bryce."

A few minutes later, Allie stood with Shelley in the doorway of Aiden's room. "Wow." She looked at Aiden. "Did you blow something up in here?"

Aiden shook his head. He knew he was in disgrace. Rushing to Shelley, he buried his face against her. "I'm sorry, Mama."

"Hey, Aiden, wanna play?" Bryce burst into the room. He apparently saw nothing wrong with the decorating scheme, because he immediately said, "Thomas! Hey, let's build a railroad."

Shelley smiled at his enthusiasm. *Thank You, Lord. You knew exactly how to help me not scream at my son.* She grabbed the bucket that had held all the train tracks, trains, and accessories, and said, "Great idea, Bryce. Let's put them all in here and you boys can take this down to the living room and set up."

In mere moments, the train set was picked up. Allie carried the bucket downstairs for the boys, while Shelley took a break and sat on Aiden's bed, resting her troublesome knee.

"You look like you hurt," Allie observed when she returned.

"I do," Shelley confessed. "I twisted it right before I answered the door."

"Ouch." Allie wrinkled her nose. "Why don't you just stay there and entertain me while I pick this stuff up? It won't take any time at all, and since I bent your ear the last time I was here, you can tell me your life story this time." She giggled.

"My life story's not very interesting," Shelley said. "Although I just recently started my baking company so I'm very proud of that." It was a thrill to say those words.

She explained about baking for the Cove, how Beverly was helping her to develop a business plan, and how Dan and his father were about to start on their new kitchen.

Allie's eyes were wide. "That's really exciting, Shelley. When do you think you're going to be able to get started on a larger scale?"

"I'm hoping to grow gradually," Shelley said. "Right now I sell some things to the shops downtown. I also have a growing local clientele, and as soon as my kitchen's done, the Cove also will be buying from me. But I'm working on ensuring that I have a steady base of income, if that makes sense."

"It absolutely makes sense." Allie shook her head admiringly. "You've got this all thought out."

"Hardly." Shelley snorted. "My friend Beverly is the one who helped me get all of my random thoughts into some kind of order. Now that she has, it seems as if I should have been able to figure all that out on my own. But without her, the whole concern about a steady income base might have just bothered me without my really knowing why. But now I have a much clearer idea of what I need to do to get from Point A to Point B, and guess what? I'm no longer feeling nearly as stressed or concerned."

The two women worked together on Aiden's room. When Emma woke up, they all trooped downstairs for a few more minutes of socializing. Just as Dan's truck pulled into the driveway, Allie said, "We've got to get going."

"Thank you so much," Shelley said. "That was a delightful surprise, and I can't tell you how much I appreciated the help."

"It was my pleasure," Allie said sincerely. She giggled a little. "I was afraid I might be too forward, just dropping by without an invitation."

"No, it was fine." Impulsively, Shelley reached out and hugged the younger woman. "Let's get together again next week. Check your schedule when you get home and call me."

"I'd like that." Allie's voice was quiet, and for an instant, Shelley felt the crushing loneliness her new friend carried inside her.

Lord, Shelley thought, *thank You for giving me the chance to be an instrument of Your work today. Help me remember to make an effort to be a welcoming presence in the lives of Allie and Bryce.* Then she thought of the woebegone look on Aiden's face earlier. *And give me patience, Lord, with my son.*

★   ★   ★

As soon as she got home, Diane called Shelley to ask if her friend could come over to Diane's home for a few minutes that evening. Unfortunately, Dan was helping Allan, so Shelley couldn't leave.

"That's fine," Diane said. "Would it work for the rest of us to come to you?"

"That would be great," Shelley said. "What's up?"

Diane chuckled. "If I tell you now, we won't have an excuse to get together."

That settled, she called Margaret and Beverly, and shortly after eight o'clock the four friends were sitting around Shelley's kitchen table with coffee or tea, according to their tastes, and a plate of Shelley's cookies: blueberry oat bars and chocolate-covered cherry cookies.

"My heavens," Margaret exclaimed as she bit into the chocolate cookie. "These are delicious, Shelley. Are these going to be one of your signature cookie selections?"

"These are fantastic too." Beverly nibbled at a bar cookie.

"I hadn't planned on that," Shelley told them. "But even if I have a standard group of selections, I want to have a whole menu of other possibilities, and these are good enough to keep, aren't they? If you guys like both of these, I'll use them somehow. They're both attractive and colorful."

"Speaking of things that are attractive and colorful," Margaret said, "I thought I had talked Louellen Lumadue into a small exhibit at the gallery, but she called and backed out."

"Did she give you a reason?" Diane wanted to know.

"Not really," Margaret said. "She just said she didn't want to bother."

"That," Diane stated, "is not a real reason, especially since she works full time to support herself with her art. You'd think she would jump at the chance to show her work."

"From things she said during our discussion," Margaret said, "I've gotten the impression that a lot of the work she does nowadays is contracted. Murals, certain scenes for interior decorators, things like that. So maybe she doesn't need the income and really just doesn't want to bother."

"There aren't many people who don't need more income," Shelley pointed out.

Margaret chuckled. "You've got that right."

"How badly do you want to show her work?" Diane asked.

Margaret thought for a moment. "I would really like to," she finally said. "Not just because the woman was an inspiration to my own career, but because I think she needs to do this. She actually seems to fear criticism so much that she's avoiding it by not showing her work."

"Why?"

"Some critic was unkind."

"But in your—*our*—type of work, that often occurs. Must have been some mighty strong criticism." Diane frowned thoughtfully. "Still, I think you should call her again. Refuse to take no for an answer."

"Do it right now!" Shelley urged.

"All right." Margaret rose and pulled her cell phone from the pocket of her warm corduroy trousers. "I will."

Walking into Shelley's living room, Margaret found Louellen's contact number and initiated the call. Filled with determination, she waited anxiously.

"Hello?"

"Louellen. This is Margaret Hoskins. I'm not taking no for an answer."

"I beg your pardon?"

"You need to bring me a few pieces of your work to show."

"Oh, but—"

"I have a feeling it's really important." And it was. Margaret had the strongest conviction that Louellen needed to do this. She'd learned from her experiences heeding her intuition in regard to the lighthouse that she shouldn't discount such feelings. Finally, she played her last card. "You were a pivotal part of my journey, remember? It would mean a lot to me to have you exhibit in my gallery."

There was silence from Louellen's end.

"Just a few pieces," Margaret insisted. "Your choice. It doesn't even have to be your recent work."

Finally, she heard an impatient exhale. "Oh, all right," Louellen said gracelessly. "I'll bring you three canvasses tomorrow. That's all."

"Thank you." Margaret concluded the call and hurried back to the kitchen. "She's going to do it!" she announced.

"Way to go," Diane said.

Margaret nodded. "Thanks for giving me that little push. She *needs* to do this, I feel sure of it." She sank into her chair. "Whew. I feel like I just climbed a mountain!"

"A mountain of negativity," Beverly tacked on. "I can't wait to see these paintings. I hope you can make her feel better somehow, Margaret."

★ ★ ★

"So why did you call this powwow, Diane?" Shelley asked, turning to their friend.

"I got a lot of new information about the lighthouse today. You've all lived here longer than I, and you may know something about it that you've forgotten."

Sharing her visit with Odessa Karpenko and her granddaughter, Diane highlighted the important points of Odessa's recollections. "So Odessa—Mrs. Karpenko— didn't know when the lighthouse was built. But it had to be there before 1781, because in 1781, the light went out during a bad storm and a church in Marble Cove burned to the ground."

"What church?" Shelley leaned forward.

"She didn't know the name," Diane said. "But the important part of the story is that on the night the church burned, there was a storm. *And* a window broke in the lantern room and the light was soaked and went out."

"Because back then, the light would have been a real fire, fueled by whale oil or kerosene." Beverly was uncharacteristically animated, wholly engrossed in the story.

"Right." Diane took a deep breath. "Before the light keeper could get the light burning again, a large ship saw the light from the fire and because of that, realized that they were off course. That fire saved the ship!"

"How do you know that?" Margaret asked.

"Odessa said the ship anchored in Marble Cove the next morning and went to find out what the fire was. A local minister named Jeremiah Thorpe told the people from the ship that it was God's will that the fire saved their ship. The passengers insisted on contributing to the rebuilding of the church."

"That's incredible," Shelley breathed.

"I know." Diane grinned. "When I started this research, I had no idea I'd find out anything so dramatic. What a great story to include in my booklet! I hope I can find more details about that night." *I might as well have a good time writing it, because I'm sure not having much luck writing anything else.* She suppressed the discouraging thought. She'd worry about it as soon as she finished this booklet.

"I can't believe that lighthouse has been standing since at least 1781," Beverly said. "I wonder when it was built."

Margaret was tapping her fingers on the table over and over again, deep in thought. "Thorpe. That name sounds familiar."

"It ought to," Shelley said. "Thorpe Library?"

"Yes, but there's something else..." She focused on Diane. "When did you say you were going to the historical society?"

"Tomorrow. Curiosity is eating me up!"

"I'll go with you. This is going to bug me now until I remember where I heard the name Thorpe before."

★   ★   ★

Frances arrived at Dan and Shelley's house before they even had finished breakfast on Saturday morning. When she heard her mother-in-law's car pull in, Shelley stopped with a bite of cereal halfway to her mouth for a moment. Her gaze slid to Dan's, and he smiled and shrugged. "She's determined to take care of you."

"She certainly is." She was always very careful about how she spoke of Frances in front of the children. "And she's done an amazing job this week."

"Good morning!" Frances all but sang the words as she sailed in the door. She had her coat off and put away and was bustling around the kitchen. "What are you making today, Shelley? If you give me a list of ingredients, I'll get everything ready again. That makes it so much easier for you."

It really didn't, because yesterday her mother-in-law had gotten out a number of bowls and baking items she hadn't needed, she'd set out margarine to melt instead of butter, and she'd gotten out brown sugar instead of granulated. Shelley had been on her feet as much as she normally was just getting everything the way she needed it to be. "Thank you, but my leg is feeling better today. I can manage that." Before Frances could argue, she said, "Aiden's in the living room, and I think he needs some help getting his DVD turned on. Could you help him?"

Frances turned and went into the living room. When she hit the doorway, she exclaimed, "My goodness gracious, this room looks like a war zone! I swear a bomb must have gone off in here last night." Tongue clucking, she hurried forward. "Shelley, where is your pride? If my house ever looked like this, I'd be mortified."

Shelley grimaced. She usually picked up after Dan and Aiden, but she just hadn't had time last evening and—

"Stop yelling at my mama!" Aiden's childish treble was shrill and angry.

There was a moment of shocked silence. Shelley put a hand to her mouth in horror. What had gotten into her son?

"Honey," she heard Frances say gently, "I wasn't yelling at her."

"You were too, and you have to stop. She's a good mama!"

"Yes, she is a good mama." Shelley got to the entry just in time to see Frances kneel in front of Aiden, wincing as her joints protested the motion. Dan, right behind Shelley, put a hand beneath her elbow. "I'm sorry, Aiden. I shouldn't say things about your mama's housekeeping, should I?" Aiden shook his head. "It's rude and thoughtless," she went on, "and I promise to try not to do it again."

She glanced up and saw Shelley standing there, and her face grew red. "Shelley, I apologize if my words seem thoughtless sometimes. Ralph always tells me I should keep my lips zipped until my first impulse to speak passes, because it's usually something I shouldn't have said anyway."

Shelley had to laugh. Ralph had hit the nail squarely on the head with that assessment.

Frances gave Aiden a hug and slowly rose to her feet. She came over to Shelley and hugged her, and Shelley was stunned to feel the older woman trembling with distress.

Frances drew back, still holding Shelley's shoulders. "You're a part of my family, honey, or I'd probably be more careful about the things I say. I'm sorry. My own kids know to just ignore me. I hope you know to do the same."

Releasing Shelley before the younger woman could respond, she bustled toward the stairs. "I'll go up and start making the beds. Dan, you help Shelley in this room, you hear?"

CHAPTER TWENTY

Margaret and Diane headed for the Thorpe Free Library and the Marble Cove Historical Society on Saturday morning. Allan had agreed to mind the gallery while Margaret accompanied Diane.

The two women made their way along the sidewalk carefully as they walked downtown. It had been shoveled clear of snow, but slippery spots abounded. Neither of them particularly wanted a broken bone to commemorate the winter.

The name *Jeremiah Thorpe* had continued to nag at Margaret throughout the rest of her evening. Even this morning she'd been turning it over in her mind. She'd heard a story with that name in it, she was certain, and it had nothing to do with the Henry Thorpe who'd founded the library or the story Diane had learned from Odessa Karpenko.

The library was just opening when they arrived. They said good morning to the librarian Gilda, but when Diane asked for the key, the silver-haired lady said, "Mr. Carney has beaten you to it. He's probably already got the door unlocked."

Gilda was right. As Margaret and Diane ascended the stairs, they saw light spill from the open doorway of the Maine Room. A man had unlocked the door and was entering, flipping on a light as he went.

Diane nudged Margaret with her elbow. "That's the man who was shoveling snow ... the man who told me he thought the lighthouse was on the National Register already."

"That's Floyd Carney," Margaret told her. "He's the president of the historical society. If anybody can help us, he can. I think he's lived in Marble Cove his whole life, and he loves local history."

As they entered the room, the man was removing his coat, revealing a warm flannel shirt with a turtleneck layered beneath it. "Morning, ladies," he said. "Can I help you? Oh, hi, Margaret."

Margaret took off the hat and unwound the scarf from around her neck, chuckling. "Hard to recognize folks this time of year when we're all bundled up, isn't it? Floyd, this is my neighbor, Diane Spencer."

Diane shook the man's hand, finding him to have a sure, firm grip. "It's nice to meet you, Floyd. Margaret tells me you've lived here a long time."

Floyd had very blue eyes and a luxurious head of pure white, curly hair. He was still quite charismatic, and she imagined he'd been a real lady-killer in his youth. "Lived here all my life."

"So you must know a lot about the lighthouse."

Margaret snickered to herself. Diane was like a dog worrying at a bone when it came to pursuing a lead.

Floyd's cheeks creased when he smiled, dimples that had dug deep over the years. "I guess so. What do you want to know?"

Diane pulled a notebook from the capacious bag she was carrying.

"Wait," Margaret said. "Before you two get completely immersed in research, I want to do some research of my own. Floyd, do you still have those boxes of unsorted things from the Carr estate in the storeroom?" She and Allan had helped Floyd and some other volunteers pick up a number of boxes of historical matter from the family of an old local couple who had both passed on.

Floyd nodded. "Keep meaning to get to them, but we just don't have enough help. Nothing's been organized, so you go ahead and dig to your heart's content."

"Thanks." She left Floyd and Diane engaged in animated conversation and made for the room downstairs at the back of the house. It had once been a dining room, and someone had placed a folding table in the middle of the room so that no one would walk through and bang into the low-hanging chandelier.

The boxes she remembered were stacked against one wall, and she pulled up a folding chair and opened the first one. "Thorpe," she muttered to herself. "I know I saw that name in one of these boxes." And she hoped no one else had gone digging since then, or the piece she'd seen on the top might not be there any longer. She decided first to take a quick glance at the top contents of each box, hoping to get lucky.

The first box appeared to hold a great deal of information about sporting events from the 1950s and '60s. The second had photographs, programs, and articles from the town's sesquicentennial celebration held in the 1950s to commemorate one hundred and fifty years since Marble Cove's incorporation as a town. She knew the community had been there a great deal longer, though.

She pulled out one booklet from a stack in that box, leafing through it. She'd idly glanced through a number of these things the day they'd picked the boxes up, and she was growing more and more certain she'd seen the Thorpe information in one of them.

The name *Thorpe* leaped out at her, and her heart beat a little faster. But it was only the story of Henry J. Thorpe's gift that led to the creation of the library.

Setting that box aside, she continued on. The third box held nothing interesting. The fourth and fifth had yearbooks from yesteryear. She'd enjoy looking through those someday, she thought with a grin, seeing some of her Marble Cove friends as they had appeared in their youth.

Opening the lid of the sixth box, she sucked in a breath. This was old stuff. *Really* old stuff. The box appeared to be filled with a collection of bound composition books. Opening one, she saw a handwritten title page: "Stories About Fishermen of Marble Cove" by Edith Mauer. Skimming it, she realized Edith Mauer must have only been a young girl when she wrote these. The heavily embellished writing of the day looked laborious, and the simple text had clearly been written by a student. Had these been a school project? She'd probably never know. And there were no dates in any that she'd seen yet. But they had to be very old; they would fall apart without very careful handling. In fact, she probably should tell Floyd to get these preserved as fast as he could.

She set it aside and carefully opened another. "Jeremiah Thorpe and the Night of the Great Fire" by Edith Mauer, 13 April 1827. Fire? Did the author mean the fire Diane had learned about that burned the church? Adrenaline surging, she flipped to the first page and began to read…and hit pay dirt. The name *Jeremiah Thorpe* practically leaped off the page at her. Sucking in a breath of excitement, she wiggled in her chair and made a little fist pump. "Thorpe—Yes!"

All she wanted to do was read the story about the fire, but she forced herself to set the book aside and keep looking. A moment later, her self-control was rewarded when she came across the title "My Grandfather, Rev. Thorpe" by Edith Mauer, 20 October 1825.

Reverend Thorpe? She'd never heard anything about Henry J. being a preacher. And besides, hadn't he been a bachelor?

Margaret carefully flipped the page with one finger.

Jeremiah Thorpe was my grandfather. He came from England on a ship. After his ship almost sank, he was thankful…

Margaret read through the entire composition. It was only a few pages long, but it certainly did answer a lot of questions. She dug through the box, but she only found two more items that appeared to have relevance for their search for information about the lighthouse.

Diane came into the room a few minutes later. "Find anything?"

Margaret nodded. "1762."

"What?" Diane looked confused.

"That's the year the lighthouse was built—1762."

Diane did a double-take. "Really? Where did you find that?"

Margaret held up the composition books. "I don't know where these had been hiding, or why they ended up with the Carr family, but just wait until you read them."

"Surely they don't date back to 1762," Diane said skeptically.

Margaret chuckled. "No, but the person who wrote them has written down stories she learned about the lighthouse. The author was the granddaughter of Jeremiah Thorpe, the preacher who spearheaded a group that built the lighthouse. Diane, he saw an unexplainable light, just like we did—only there was no lighthouse there when he saw it!"

"What?" Diane unfolded a chair leaning against the wall and sat down, taking the little book gently in her hands. Silence reigned in the former dining room as the two women devoured the information.

Finally, Diane looked up. "I think we should ask Floyd to photocopy these for us. The booklets will lay flat quite easily. I don't think it would harm them."

Margaret nodded. "Good idea. And there aren't that many pages. Let's do it."

"I can't wait to share this with Beverly and Shelley!"

When she returned to the Maine Room, Margaret turned to Floyd as she began to put on her coat and outdoor gear. "Floyd, have you ever heard the name Edith Mauer?"

Floyd frowned. "Not that I recall. Only Mauers I ever heard of were Mrs. Carr's family. She was a Mauer before she married."

Diane grinned at Margaret. "There's your connection."

After leaving the library, Margaret headed for the gallery. She had arranged to meet Louellen there at eleven, and she didn't want to be late.

There was no one waiting in front of the building, and she quickly unlocked the door and turned on the lights. Because temperature changes weren't good for artwork, she kept the thermostat at a moderate temperature year round, and it felt good to shuck off her coat again. As she finished putting on a pot of coffee, the bell over the gallery door jingled. Margaret turned to see Louellen struggle through the door, carrying a large paper-wrapped rectangle.

"Good morning! Can I help you bring things in?"

"'Morning." Louellen shook her head. "There are only two more smaller ones. I'll get them if you'll take this."

More than happy not to have to go back out into the frigid air, Margaret carefully seized the large canvas and carried it to the back of the shop, where she propped it against the counter. Her fingers were itching to rip off the paper, but she decided that would be too rude, so she waited, watching through the window as Louellen carried two smaller wrapped packages in from her SUV.

Setting them against the counter as well, Louellen shrugged off her coat and carelessly tossed it over one of Allan's chairs in a display grouping. Unceremoniously, she began to rip off the wrapping. "You can help," she said to Margaret.

Needing no encouragement, Margaret carefully began to unwrap the largest canvas. It was a seascape, a roiling sea in stunning vivid shades of blues and greens that Margaret knew she would recognize instantly as a Lumadue because of the sheer finesse with which the artist had applied the color. Propping the canvas again, she stepped away and studied it, then closed her eyes, steeping herself in the masterly management of the colors.

Then she realized there was no other sound in the gallery. She opened her eyes and glanced at Louellen to find the woman studying her with surprisingly vulnerable eyes.

"Oh!" Margaret said. "Louellen, this seascape is ... beyond stunning. I don't have words for it. But I love it. I truly do."

The set of the taller woman's shoulders visibly relaxed. "It's brand-new," she said. "I just started experimenting with this color layering technique a few months ago, and I'm pretty pleased with how it's turned out in the pieces where I've used it." She finished unwrapping the second painting and the third as she spoke. "For what my opinion is worth," she said.

Margaret heard the comment and realized that what she had taken for brusque disinterest at the lecture was really a poorly constructed wall of defense against comments that cut Louellen right to her artistic soul. Painting exposed one's deepest thoughts, in some ways. Margaret knew the feeling well—it was a risk to let other eyes see what you'd created. And having been judged lacking in the past, Louellen was probably terrified.

For the first time, Margaret wondered if she was doing the right thing, bullying the artist into showing her work. The next chance she got, she was going to look up critiques of Louellen's past works and see just what had been said to wound her so deeply.

As the other two paintings came into view, Margaret sucked in a breath of genuine admiration. "These are lovely," she blurted out.

But Louellen shook her head. "They're different. I was experimenting with a new technique."

Margaret wanted to gush over the paintings, to ask questions about technique and color choice, but she sensed Louellen retreating. Perhaps she'd pushed enough. Just getting her to bring these in had been quite a task. "I'm going to do a front window display with them," she told Louellen. "Right now!"

Louellen glanced at her watch. "I'm having lunch with a friend. I'll try to stop by and take a gander after lunch if I have time." Her tone sounded as if it wouldn't bother her a bit if she didn't, but Margaret knew better by now.

The moment Louellen left the shop, Margaret went into high gear. Twenty minutes later, she had what she thought was a striking display; she even ran outside to approve it from the view through the gallery window.

She had to run to the post office with a purchase a client had made through the Web site yesterday. Allan and Adelaide were supposed to join her for lunch, so she locked the gallery, hurried to the post office and then hurried right back.

*　　*　　*

Outside the library, Diane had parted ways with Margaret, who hurried down the sidewalk in the direction of the gallery. Her backpack containing the photocopied information Margaret had found felt like it was burning a hole right through her jacket. She couldn't wait to get home and read all of it in detail!

Her elation faded a little as she thought of the outline she was working from for her second novel . . . although working was a generous term, considering how little time she'd spent on it lately. Perhaps she would be able to use some of this research as a springboard to help her refine the plot.

A car passed her and pulled into a driveway close by. It was Mr. Calder's driveway. The driver's door opened, and a tall man got out. It looked like—

"Dennis!"

The man's head whipped around. "Beverly?"

"No." She smiled to herself, recalling this man's interest in her friend. "It's Diane Spencer. You came to my party last summer, remember?" She strode forward, extending her hand.

Dennis Calder, her elderly neighbor's grandson, shook her hand enthusiastically. "Of course I remember, Diane." He grinned ruefully. "It's hard to identify anyone when we're all bundled up like Eskimos."

She laughed. "I have the same problem from time to time. How have you been?"

"Good, good." He jerked a thumb over his shoulder. "I was just going in to check on my grandfather, maybe make him a grilled cheese sandwich and some hot soup for lunch if he'll let me."

"He's pretty independent, I recall."

Dennis rolled his eyes. "That's like saying Mount Rushmore is pretty big."

Diane laughed.

"Have you run into Beverly Wheeland lately?" Dennis asked.

Diane nodded. "I see her frequently. She moved in with her father a few months ago."

Dennis's face registered surprise. "You mean right over there?" He pointed at the Wheeland home directly across from his grandfather's.

Diane nodded. "The one and only."

He looked thoughtful. "Perhaps I'll stop by sometime when I'm visiting my granddad."

"I'm sure she'd enjoy seeing you."

"Is she—do you know if she's seeing anyone exclusively right now?" His handsome face flushed, but he regarded Diane steadily as he waited for her answer.

Diane shook her head. "Not that I know of."

Dennis nodded. "Tell her I said hello, will you please?"

Diane suspected that to Dennis, stopping by "sometime" probably meant in the next day or so. She'd better make sure Beverly knew about her old friend's interest. "Of course." She patted his arm. "It was nice to see you, Dennis. Stay warm."

CHAPTER TWENTY-ONE

When Margaret got back to the gallery, Allan had a bite of lunch waiting for her. Adelaide, who was with him, had been watching for her mother through the plate glass window. After taking a moment to admire the new display again, she entered the shop, where Adelaide was practically dancing a jig with excitement.

"Mom! Mom! I gotta show you som'pin'." Adelaide grabbed Margaret's hand before she could even get her coat off.

"Okay, honey. Just give me a minute." Margaret was laughing as she took off her coat. She glanced over her daughter's head at Allan with her eyebrows raised. *What's this about?*

Her spouse just grinned. *You'll see.*

"If it's a kitten, the answer is no," she said hastily, unable to imagine anything else that would get Adelaide so fired up.

The moment Margaret had hung up her coat, Adelaide grabbed her hand again. "Come see!" She towed Margaret toward the front of the store and actually climbed into the display window.

"Adelaide, wait." Margaret had placed Louellen's paintings in this window, and she was very pleased with the exact placement of the works. The last thing she wanted to do was bump into something. She had visions of a domino-like effect as one easel fell into the next.

"Come on, Mom. I'm being careful."

Margaret smiled. Of course she was. Since Adelaide was little, Margaret had been cautioning her to be careful around the easels. "All right." She used the stool her daughter had hauled over to step into the window. "What do you want to show me?"

"Angels!" Adelaide pointed to first one painting, then another and another.

"What?" Margaret glanced at the painting again, about to correct her. "Oh no, honey, these are..." She trailed off as she followed Adelaide's pointing finger. Adelaide outlined an arrangement of clouds in the sky that really did appear to be an angel.

Before she could tell her it probably was just coincidence, Adelaide pointed at another one. This time, the angel image subtly peeked from the leaves of a willow tree. And in the third painting, there did indeed appear to be an angel among the waves that crashed against a headland.

Margaret put a hand to her heart, and her mouth fell open. "Oh."

Behind her, Allan had come to stand near the window. "I know. It's rather astonishing when you first discern them, isn't it?"

"How did you find them?" She turned and looked at him.

"I didn't." He smiled and indicated their daughter, almost bouncing with childlike glee at the way she'd surprised her mother. "Adelaide did."

Goose bumps broke out on Margaret's arms beneath the warm sweater she wore. "Adelaide, did you know the angels were there?"

Adelaide shook her head. "I saw that one"—she pointed— "when I was outside. And then I saw the other ones. Aren't they pretty?"

Margaret nodded, hardly knowing what to say. "Very pretty." Angels. There was no mistaking it, now that she was looking, she thought with wonder. Each painting carried the undeniable image of an angel with huge feathered wings and a long, flowing robe. Each face was a mere suggestion, but portrayed utter peace. Margaret felt calmness and peacefulness rolling through her as she studied the images.

She fished her cell phone from her pocket and pulled up her contact list, dialing Louellen Lumadue's number.

"Hello?"

"Hi, Louellen, it's Margaret. I have a question about the paintings you brought in."

"Fire away."

"Did you paint them with any common theme in mind, other than landscapes?"

There was silence at the other end of the line. "Not really," Louellen said. "Why?"

"There appears to be a common theme hidden in them."

"No," Louellen said positively. "There's not. I told you I don't do that anymore. What is it you think you see?"

"Please stop by before you leave town this afternoon if you possibly can," was all Margaret could say.

Louellen made a sputtering sound. "Now you've aroused my curiosity! Why can't you just tell me?"

"I'd rather you see it for yourself." Margaret wanted to see Louellen's expression when she saw the angels. It still was hard to believe she hadn't painted them in purposely, but recalling Louellen's vehemence about the failure of her hidden imagery paintings, she was certain it hadn't been a conscious decision. Had a heavenly presence been guiding her hand?

She sat down with Allan and Adelaide in the back room and had lunch. Then her husband and daughter left for home.

Still thinking of Louellen and the angel paintings, Margaret realized she needed to know what kind of critical remarks had been made about the last series of hidden image paintings. Before she settled down in her studio corner to work on a canvas of her own, she got online and did a search for Louellen Lumadue hidden images.

Immediately, a lengthy list of Web site addresses popped up. Scanning them, she found one from *Kennebec Journal*. The writer began by extolling a grant the Maine Foundation for the Arts had received. Then it morphed into a review of three artists in three different mediums whose work had been exhibited by the MFA.

Her eyes quickly found the one about Louellen. It was horrible. "Lumadue's overdone studies of purported hidden imagery strain the bounds of imagination. Whatever this artist saw is lost on her viewing public." Margaret gasped. If she'd gotten a cut like that, she'd be devastated.

Unfortunately, she found two more bad critiques in other local news outlets. One merely called her work boring and quoted from *Kennebec Journal*'s poison penman.

But another was even worse.

She assumed the writer had quite a high opinion of his own judgment. One phrase in particular echoed in her mind: "...among the most trite, banal, and clichéd work it has ever been my misfortune to view..."

Margaret shoved away from the desk, too upset to read any more. No wonder Louellen wasn't keen on showing her work anymore. No wonder she'd gone the route of working by commission, which generally guaranteed the individual who hired her liked her work already. No wonder she pretended not to care!

Saddened for the woman with whom she had a budding friendship, Margaret was quiet while she turned to work on a painting of her own.

She didn't get it. That series of paintings had been terrific! Margaret prided herself on recognizing skill and flair, and Louellen had both. The only explanation was that after the one reviewer trashed the work, the others felt free to jump on the bandwagon. What had Louellen originally said about that series? *"Those weren't particularly well received, although thank heavens they sold really well.*" That single small addition to the sentence was important, Margaret thought. It meant that *someone*—probably a number of someones—had liked the hidden imagery. Louellen, though, appeared to have focused on those hateful words—well, really, who wouldn't?—and had completely forgotten about the great sales.

Around three o'clock, the bell over the door jangled impatiently. Startled, Margaret looked up just in time to see Louellen Lumadue striding toward her.

"All right, show me what you're talking about." Louellen looked seriously perturbed. "I couldn't think of another single thing until I figured it out. Where are the paintings?"

Grinning, Margaret gestured. Louellen really didn't appear to know about the angels. She was going to be so excited when she saw what she had done! "They're displayed in the front window. Let me grab my coat, and we'll walk outside so we can get the full effect."

Louellen snorted, something Margaret had noticed she did when she was trying to appear prickly, while Margaret grabbed her parka and then guided her guest outside.

The two women stood on the sidewalk and eyed the paintings in silence. "What?" Louellen demanded.

Margaret smiled. "Look at the bigger picture rather than detail." She pointed to the willow tree. "In the willow... what do you see?"

Louellen glared at the painting as if to force it to light up and show her its secret. She shook her head. "I don't see anything," she said stubbornly.

"Stand back a bit," Margaret encouraged her.

Louellen still shook her head. "Nothing there."

Exasperated, Margaret stepped forward and outlined the general shape of the angel in the willow bark. "See the angel?"

Louellen went very still. Rather than looking more closely, she closed her eyes. "Margaret, there are no images hidden in that willow bark." In a voice of exaggerated patience, she spoke slowly as if to a small child. "I know this because I painted them."

"Perhaps you did, but your subconscious must have been painting right along beside you when you did them."

"No," Louellen said in a challenging tone. "There are no hidden images in these paintings." Her mouth twisted. "Do you really think I would revisit one of the biggest failures of my career?"

"Those paintings were *not* bad work. You had some small-minded idiots who probably know very little about art criticism say nasty things."

"Looked it up, did you?" Louellen glared at Margaret. "Then you see why I have no intention of doing controversial work like that again ever in my life!" She pivoted and started for the door. "Let me know when you're done with these stupid paintings. I have no idea why I let you talk me into this anyway. These are some of the worst things I've ever done."

"Wait!" Margaret cried.

Louellen froze in her tracks, her hand on the doorknob.

"You said they sold well," Margaret reminded her. "That should tell you a lot."

"Like what?" It was half anguished plea, half snarl.

"People—*real* people—love the hidden imagery, Louellen. Your work sold well and fast because it appeals to people who want to hang it in their home so they can see it every day. People react to it like I did, remembering it for years. Isn't that a truer measure of success than some self-important critic's opinion?"

Louellen was silent.

Margaret saw that her eyes were filled with tears. Silently, she walked to the counter, grabbed a tissue and extended it to the taller woman.

"Thank you." It was a whisper. She took a deep, hitching breath, and Margaret could see her battle for control.

Finally, Louellen spoke. "Those harsh words have shaped more than a decade of my career. I decided that never again was I going to care deeply about what I was painting. It was easier to do trite, requested pieces that I knew the client wanted."

Margaret nodded encouragingly.

"I know you think you see something in the three paintings I brought you," Louellen told her. "But when I did the hidden image series, I knew exactly what I was doing. I didn't paint anything special into the current pieces." She shook her head to emphasize her words.

"Do you have any more recent work similar to these?"

Louellen cast Margaret an incredulous look. "If I did, do you really think I'd let anyone see them?" She turned and opened the door, shaking her head. She began to walk away slowly, as if each step was an effort.

Margaret hurried forward, catching the door just as it closed and ducking out long enough to call, "Think about what I said! The people who matter appreciate those pieces, just like I do."

But Louellen didn't stop. She hurried to her SUV and opened the door without looking back.

Margaret stood shivering on the sidewalk as the other artist's vehicle pulled away. *Lord, if You could fill Louellen with Your peace, it would be such a gift. Lift her unhappiness and help her take off her blinders. Let her see what beautiful things she has created and be willing to share them with the world.* She thought of the infinite comfort and kindness that the hidden angels in the newest paintings projected. If Louellen had that inside her, and she didn't even know it, who knew what she could do if she decided to tackle more hidden imagery?

★ ★ ★

Shelley usually worked at the Cove after hours when she could have the kitchen to herself. But this Saturday, Rusty had asked her to come during the afternoon because he wanted to paint the restaurant's kitchen, and he intended to start right after the close of business Saturday.

Headed homeward after finishing her baking, Shelley felt exhaustion dragging at her. She hadn't been sleeping well for worrying about when she could resume a normal work schedule. Every time she thought she was doing better and could set aside the knee brace, the abused joint let her know that was a bad idea. It was discouraging.

As she parked the car and carefully lifted herself to her feet, she remembered that Dan, who'd been home when she left, had planned to work in Allan's workshop for a while that afternoon. He'd invited his mother to come care for the children. And while Shelley had no worries about her mother-in-law's devotion to her grandchildren, she mentally braced herself for heaven-only-knew what criticism Frances was bound to utter.

When she entered the kitchen door, Frances was at the counter with Aiden on a stool beside her. Emma played on the floor nearby, building a tower with lightweight cardboard "bricks" that Aiden had gotten for Christmas one year.

When the initial flurry of greetings ended, Shelley hung up her coat and limped over to the counter. "What are you making?"

"I'm helping Meemaw with dinner," Aiden announced. "We're gonna have chicken and biscuits."

"Yum!" Shelley's response was heartfelt; her mother-in-law made some of the best chicken Shelley had ever eaten. "I love Meemaw's chicken and biscuits."

Frances turned with a smile. "Thank you, Shelley. Coming from you, that's a real compliment."

Shelley went upstairs to change clothes—she always smelled of bad food odors when she came home from the restaurant. As she slipped into a fresh blouse and tugged a thick, cable-knit sweater over her head, she saw a clothes basket on the floor near the door that she hadn't put there. What on earth had Frances been doing now? She was almost afraid to ask.

When she came back down, Aiden had climbed down from his stool and was helping Emma with her building.

"I did a load of the children's laundry for you," Frances told her. "I thought it would save you a trip up and down the steps. Everything is folded and set on their dressers. I wasn't sure how you liked it put away, so I thought I'd better let you do that."

Shelley immediately felt ashamed of her churlish reaction upstairs. "You're a godsend," she said, determined to get along with Dan's mother today.

Frances chuckled. "Hardly." She lowered her voice, as Shelley came to stand beside her and dry the dishes that were overflowing the top of the dish drainer. "I suspect most of the time I'm a terrible trial to you."

"Of course you're not." It was an automatic response.

"Oh, Shelley, you're sweet." Frances stopped washing dishes and turned to face her. "You just need to learn not to be so thin-skinned."

Shelley took a deep breath. Her hackles had risen at the last words, but she forced herself to reply calmly. "I know I'm too sensitive. My family was never as, as—"

"Opinionated and boisterous?"

"Well, yes, so it's taken me a while to grow used to the way this family behaves." She thought of the way Frances' own children rolled their eyes and laughed at some of her sweeping pronouncements. Her daughters simply acted amused and teased her.

"Nevertheless, if my ways bother Aiden, they probably bother other family members more than I thought. He's just the only one brave enough to tell me so." Dan's mother smiled and shrugged, eye twinkling, and Shelley saw Dan in that smile. "Feel free to call me on it when you hear me starting to offer opinions that aren't needed."

Shelley grinned and nodded. "Okay. You asked for it. But also, I will try to be less thin-skinned. I feel very lucky to be part of such a large, loving family. I can only hope Dan and I can do as good a job raising our children as you did."

Frances looked genuinely touched. "That might be the nicest thing anyone's ever said to me." She reached over and gave Shelley a hug. "Would you take it the wrong way if I told you to go sit down and let me set the table for you? You look like that knee is killing you."

Shelley laughed. "I won't, and it is. Just let me get an ice pack, and I'll get out of your way."

Chapter Twenty-Two

On Saturday evening, Jeff seated Beverly at a small Italian restaurant just outside of town. She'd been happy to see him at the door. Her uneasiness after the concert invitation subsided when he smiled at her as he was doing now. His hair gleamed with chestnut highlights, and his blue eyes were warm and admiring.

"You look beautiful tonight," he said. He reached across the table and took her hand, enfolding it in his much larger one. "Thank you for coming to dinner with me."

"Thank you for inviting me. Are you staying in town tonight?"

Jeff nodded. "I stayed at the Quarterdeck the last time I was here. It's a charming little place."

The Quarterdeck was a local bed-and-breakfast. Beverly had never been inside, but Diane had stayed there once or twice before she bought her home, and she'd said it was lovely. "I've heard it's very nice. I'm sure Josie appreciates any business that brings you to town during the off-season."

Jeff's dimples deepened. He dropped his gaze, a small smile playing about his lips. "Well, I have a confession to make. I don't really have any business in town. The only business I have is a date with a lady I like very much."

Beverly was flustered. She wasn't ready for a declaration like this. Was she? "Jeff, I'm flattered—"

"Uh-oh," he said, "a sentence that begins that way isn't usually a good thing. Can I take that last sentence back?"

Beverly regarded him, searching his eyes for signs of annoyance or hurt. He didn't appear to be upset. "I'm not sure you can. Let me just say I appreciate your interest, and I am enjoying your company. Let me also say I'm not ready for anything deep right now."

"Okay."

Beverly stared at him. "That's it? Okay?"

Jeff nodded. "Okay. I enjoy your company too. A lot."

As she searched her heart, she realized, to her surprise, that the guilt and sadness she'd felt after her husband's accidental death was starting to fade. She was beginning to forgive herself. And that made it easier to smile at Jeff and say, "I'm glad you're here. Would you like to go to church with me tomorrow? Perhaps we could get lunch and do something in the afternoon. Have you ever gone antiquing?"

Jeff's eyes lit up. "That would be great. And I love scouring flea markets, antique shops, and the occasional auction. I collect old fishing lures."

"Fishing lures?" Beverly tilted her head. "You mean like those little fly things that people tie?"

Jeff made a clucking noise with his tongue, shaking his head and chuckling. "Um, no. The ones I collect are wood, metal, and rubber. A lot of them are elaborately painted and have multiple hooks...and you really don't want to get me started on that. Do you collect something special?"

"Depression glass," Beverly said promptly. "My mother had a set, and I got hooked. I've got three different patterns that I particularly like." She looked down at their clasped hands. "I haven't had much time the past few years for leisure pursuits. Living in Augusta and driving over here every weekend to see my father took up most of my free time. But now that I'm living in Marble Cove, it's a little easier." She bit her lip. "I'm considering a career change, looking for something closer to home so I don't have to travel every week."

"A career change? Not just a job change?"

Beverly shook her head. "I'm a budget analyst for the state. There's not much call for that kind of thing in Marble Cove." She laughed. "And that's an understatement."

"So what do you think you'd like to do?"

She took a deep breath, a little surprised at herself for telling him all this. But why not? "You remember Shelley. I started helping my friend Shelley organize a new business here in town, and it occurred to me that I could become a business consultant. I probably could help companies reduce waste, but I think being a start-up consultant might be very rewarding."

"What would you do for clients that they can't do themselves?" Jeff sounded deeply interested.

Before she knew it, she began to tell him about the details of the things she had been doing for Shelley, about her interviews with some other consultants around the state, and about the skills she felt she could bring to the job. It was a safe topic that she could discuss at length without anything getting too personal.

And that's what she wanted right now.

★   ★   ★

"Come down to Margaret's gallery with me," Diane said. She was standing on Beverly's front porch on Monday afternoon, dressed in layer upon layer to combat the freezing temperatures.

Beverly eyed her friend. "Why?"

Diane laughed. "That is such a *Beverly* response. Do you ever do anything just because?"

"Of course I do," Beverly said indignantly. She thought for a moment. "Sometimes."

Diane laughed even harder. Finally, she recovered enough to say, "Well, in this instance, I have a very good reason for requesting your attendance. I want to share what I've learned about the lighthouse with everyone, and Shelley's going to be there at three o'clock."

"You could have just told me that from the beginning." The comment came over her shoulder, as the younger woman turned to the closet to start pulling on her outer layers. "I need to go out anyway to pick up my car from the body shop."

"It's fixed?" Diane asked.

"Good as new, or so they tell me."

While Beverly finished getting ready, Diane stuck her head into the living room, where she suspected she'd find Mr. Wheeland. "Hello, there," she said, smiling at the old man.

"Hello," he said, sitting up straighter in his chair as a smile lit his face. "What are you doing here?"

"I'm going to borrow your daughter," Diane said. "Just for an hour or so, if that's all right."

He waved a hand. "That's fine. I think she's getting sick of seeing this old mug anyway."

"Father! I am not." Beverly had come to the door, zipping her coat.

Diane and Mr. Wheeland exchanged an amused glance.

"Well," he amended, "I wouldn't blame you if you were."

She walked over and kissed him. "I'm not," she said decisively. "See you in a little while. I'll get dinner when I get back."

The two friends walked briskly downtown to the Shearwater Gallery. Shelley had arrived ahead of them, children in tow. The minute she got the last little arm free from its coat sleeve, both children went running in circles in the wide open space. At first, Shelley went after them, trying to keep them in sight around the open-ended display columns, but Margaret simply laughed. "Oh, let them go. They can't hurt anything."

"You don't know my son," Shelley said darkly. She walked to one table that held some fragile blown-glass sculptures, taking the lovely items and setting them back on Margaret's sturdy counter. "I think these are the only things, though, that could have been in real danger."

Beverly hung her coat over the back on one of Allan's chairs and sat, gracefully crossing one leg over the other. Diane wondered if her friend ever made a move that *wasn't* graceful. Then, realizing their time was limited and Margaret might want to get back to work, she said, "Margaret found some fascinating information at the historical society on Saturday. It's almost completely unknown, because even they didn't realize they had it."

"How is that possible?" Shelley asked. She had pulled a zipped bag of large, puffy chocolate-chip cookies from the bag attached to Emma's stroller.

"These items were in a group that came in after someone passed away," Diane explained. "But no one had ever gone through them."

She picked up a stapled sheaf of papers she had retrieved from her handbag. "So here's what I've learned."

"Inside voices," Shelley cautioned her children. She turned back to Diane. "Sorry."

Diane adjusted her reading glasses and began. "All this information comes from a series of composition books written in the 1820s by a young girl named Edith Mauer. She writes that Jeremiah Thorpe was her grandfather."

"Jeremiah?" Beverly shifted, her attention sharpening. "I thought his name was Henry."

"Henry was Jeremiah's grandson," Diane said. "He would have been a cousin to this little girl, I believe, although she doesn't ever mention Henry."

"Go on," Margaret urged.

Diane cleared her throat. "Jeremiah Thorpe was a minister, the leader of a small congregation that was aboard a ship that almost foundered off Orlean Point in August of 1761 in a bad storm. Jeremiah and his flock prayed loudly, so says Miss Mauer, and suddenly, a great light blazed on the shore, showing them where they were." She glanced up, noting her friends' rapt expressions. "Apparently, the ship was saved from ramming into the rocks because of a bright light coming from Marble Cove—what's now Marble Cove, of course—and when the captain saw it, he realized he was off course. Eventually, he was able to anchor in the cove, and once off the ship, Jeremiah Thorpe and his followers knelt and thanked God for the preservation of their lives. When they told their story and asked about the light, the people of the area were mystified. There was no way to produce any kind of bright light such as he described. Jeremiah believed that God was directly responsible for their salvation by creating a miraculous light, and he vowed to serve God for the remainder of his life, answering whatever summons was issued."

"Summons?" Beverly said. "That sounds a little melodramatic."

Diane nodded, smiling. "Don't forget these are the writings of an adolescent."

"Enough said." Margaret chuckled.

"If this is true," Beverly said, "we have to add it to the records you started of all the lights of unexplained origin that have saved people through the years."

"But how do we know this is true?" Shelley asked.

"We don't," Diane said. "But Edith wrote more than half a dozen of these little compositions, and all of them deal with the history of the town and the area. I think everything is presented as accurately as she heard it. Some of them are extremely interesting, and some of them are pretty bland. If they were fiction, wouldn't she have filled all of them with exciting occurrences?"

"Good point," Shelley conceded.

"Moving on," Diane continued. "Jeremiah Thorpe and the group with him settled in the area. There was a small settlement here already, but they added to it significantly. There were one hundred twelve of them, according to Edith's accounts. Jeremiah was serious about giving thanks for their lives, and the very next year, 1762, a lighthouse was erected on Orlean Point. Interestingly, I found shipwreck lists and records that indicate that the last wreck with fatalities occurred in the 1750s. After the lighthouse was built, there were very few wrecks and no recorded fatalities."

Margaret's eyebrows rose. "That's a pretty telling statistic. Reverend Thorpe must have had a direct pipeline to the Almighty."

Everyone chuckled, and Diane said, "You may be right, Margaret. According to Edith, Thorpe's church outgrew the first modest building in which they worshipped, and in 1775 they built a larger one, a wooden structure like the first. But in 1789, there was a fire, and the church burned."

"Oh, how awful," Shelley murmured.

"In some ways," Diane said, "but not so much in another. Edith writes that there was a horribly fierce storm that night, and that one of the windows of the lighthouse was broken and the light went out. The keeper eventually got it started again, but in the meantime, a ship off the coast misjudged its bearings just as the earlier ship had done, and was heading straight for Orlean Point. But the church was engulfed in fire at that point, and flames shot high into the air—and the ship's captain realized he was off course in time to make a correction. That ship, too, anchored in Marble Cove."

"What parallels!" Beverly's eyes were wide.

"Yes, but here's a significant deviation," Diane told her. "This ship wasn't carrying church people. This ship was carrying wealthy Canadians bound for the port of Halifax, which was already a thriving community. They were so grateful for their lives that they donated the money to build a new church on the same site. And in 1790, Jeremiah Thorpe's congregation built a new church of stone."

There was a short silence, broken finally by a happy shriek from one of the playing children.

"What an amazing story," Shelley said.

"What I think is amazing," Margaret added, "is that no one in Marble Cove knows this story!"

"I think I may know why," Diane said. "It appears that the Thorpe family died out in the 1800s. I looked up Edith Mauer. She was a Thorpe granddaughter born in 1815. And even though there were a lot of them, most of them left the area or died, according to the census records. Edith stayed here and had a family, and I guess these composition books stayed in the family and ended up in an attic that was cleaned out a few years ago."

"So maybe there *are* Thorpe descendants here in Marble Cove, and we don't even know it," Margaret mused. "They probably just have different last names."

"Well, thank goodness they sent the stuff to the historical society instead of pitching it," Beverly added, "or we might never have learned any of this."

Shelley gestured to the papers Diane still held. "So what church was it?"

Diane's face fell. "I don't know. Edith doesn't say. I don't even know if it's still standing."

"I bet it is," Margaret said. "I can think of a few churches in and around town that have a couple hundred years of history behind them."

"But if they don't know any of these details," Shelley said, "we'll probably never know which one it was."

"I guess we'll just have to keep looking," Diane said. "Great. The last thing I need is one more research project."

"What have you found out about the nomination for the National Register of Historic Places?" Beverly asked.

"Not much." Diane sounded disgusted. "Jules Benton is still ducking and weaving every time he lays eyes on me." She folded her arms, clearly frustrated. "I know that man knows more than he's told me about this whole business, and I'm going to pry it out of him if it's the last thing I do!"

CHAPTER TWENTY-THREE

The bell over the shop door jangled in the silence that followed Diane's declaration, and everyone jumped. Margaret peeked toward the front, and then she jumped up and hurried forward. "Louellen! Hello. I wasn't expecting you today."

"I wasn't expecting to come here today, and yet here I am. Help." Louellen was trying to edge another large wrapped canvas into the gallery while holding open the door with one foot. Margaret went to the rescue, and Louellen set the canvas against the nearest column.

Quickly, she made introductions to her friends.

Shelley, already corralling her children and wrestling Emma into her snowsuit, said, "It's nice to meet you, Louellen. I love your paintings, and because I do, I'm taking my hooligans out of here before they do any damage."

Everyone chuckled.

"Wise idea," Diane said. She caught Aiden and held out his coat. "Arms in, mister."

While Shelley and Diane took care of the children, Louellen said, "I have a couple more paintings in the car. Want to help me bring them in?"

"Sure." Margaret headed for the door. She was bursting with curiosity. After their last encounter, she hadn't expected to ever see Louellen again.

"I can help too," Beverly said.

The three women hurried out into the cold and retrieved the additional canvasses. While Louellen began to take off the paper, Diane and Beverly got their coats and took their leave as well.

Margaret turned back to Louellen after they'd left. "Is there some special reason you've brought in these canvasses?"

Louellen carefully removed the brown paper cover from the nearest painting. "You know, there is." She turned the unframed canvas around so that Margaret could see the front.

Margaret studied it carefully. It was a lovely study in shades of white and gray, depicting a stretch of the Maine shoreline in the dead of winter. And there ...! On the swirling white snow in the foreground was the distinct feathery outline of an angel. Louellen was already busy with the wrap over the next canvas. When she got both of the additional projects unwrapped and turned around to face Margaret, angels peeked out of each one.

Louellen shook her head as together they studied the paintings. "I owe you an apology, Margaret. I was certain you were wrong. But over the weekend I just couldn't stop thinking about what you said. I looked at some of my other recent paintings and started to study them." She paused and swallowed. "There are angels in all of them."

She turned to Margaret with wide, dazed eyes. "Angels. How did that happen? I didn't paint them. Did I?" She answered her own question. "But I must have."

"Would you like to look at the others again?" Margaret indicated the window display.

Louellen nodded, and the two of them climbed into the window. As Louellen scanned the other two paintings, Margaret could tell when she found the angels by her sharp intake of breath. She turned to Margaret. "How did you find them?"

"I didn't. My daughter noticed them first. I wondered if you had done it on purpose."

Louellen shook her head. "No. Angels aren't really my thing." She studied the paintings again and gave a short laugh. "Although apparently, they are."

"Why do you suppose you chose angels?"

The artist hesitated, sadness clouding her eyes. "My mother passed away not long before I painted the canvasses here. I was really struggling, and I read a book about angels that I found very comforting. It's possible that my subconscious influenced my painting."

It was indeed possible, Margaret believed. She felt even more strongly that a divine hand had been guiding Louellen's work during that period. "Certainly, there are artistic precedents for that, although this is different in intent, I believe, from surrealism."

Louellen laughed. "Yes. I wasn't deliberately channeling my subconscious. If that's where these angels came from, it's more like they were channeling me." She shook her head, wonder in her face. "This is the craziest thing I've ever done. I mean, yes, perhaps I was thinking of heaven and heavenly hosts when I was working, but I certainly didn't *intend* to paint angels into every picture!"

Margaret smiled gently. "Perhaps this was God's way of offering you comfort."

"That's a nice possibility." Louellen clasped her hands together. "Since I found the angels, I've been studying lesser-known but enduring artists, and it seems most of them are influenced by something in their lives, and often their styles and style changes reflect that."

Margaret nodded. "I can understand that." She considered her next words carefully. "You have an enthusiasm in your voice that would really resonate if you talked about this topic. Would you be interested in coming into the gallery some afternoon and speaking to a small group?"

Louellen had the grace to wince. "You mean compared to that abysmal lecture I gave at Colby?"

Margaret had to laugh. "Well, yes, now that you mention it."

Louellen shook her head. "That was a low point for me." She glanced at the "angel" paintings again. "I'd like to talk about these, I believe," she said slowly. "And it could help sell my work. Do you think anyone would come?"

"I can guarantee it," Margaret said. How, she had no idea, but surely she'd think of something.

Louellen hesitated a moment longer. "All right then. Let's do it!"

★   ★   ★

Shelley's doorbell rang Monday evening after dinner. Dan had gone out to his father's to help with something, and he'd taken Emma along. Aiden had balked at the last minute and wanted to stay with Shelley, so she gave him his bath early and told him he could play until time for stories.

That would be Beverly at the door. Her friend had agreed to come over tonight and look over the business planning information Shelley had compiled.

Carrying one of the baskets of laundry that always seemed to be magically refilling, she hurried toward the steps. Aiden came out of his room. "Who's at the door?"

"It's probably Miss Beverly," she told him. "Remember I told you she was coming over to have a grown-up talk with me?"

Aiden nodded. "I'll be good, Mama."

Shelley smiled. "I know you will, honey." She turned to start down the stairs—and flailed wildly as her foot landed on something that slid out from under her. The laundry basket went flying. She felt herself pitching forward, and at the last minute, just as she knew she was about to tumble down the stairs, her left hand snagged the handrail. Her body pitched forward, but she hung onto that rail with everything she had, as her whole body turned sideways and slammed against the rail.

And suddenly, she wasn't moving anymore.

Her heart was racing, her knee felt like someone had just given it a three-sixty twist, and her shoulder sockets ached from catching the full force of her weight.

But she wasn't moving.

The world came back into focus. Aiden was crying. No, *screaming*, and as she began to straighten up, she heard Beverly's voice raised in alarm as she rushed into the house.

"Shelley? What happened? Are you all right?" Beverly charged up the steps two at a time.

Shelley slowly released her death grip on the banister and lowered herself into a sitting position on the second step. "Aiden," she called. "Aiden, come here."

She craned her neck to look up at her son. He didn't move. "Mama, I'm sorry," he sobbed.

"Aiden," Shelley said sharply. "Come here." She patted her thighs, and her son came forward and crawled into her lap, putting both arms around her neck and clinging as he continued to cry.

Beverly's concerned gaze met Shelley's over the top of his head. She eased onto the step beside Shelley. "What happened?" she mouthed.

"I fell," Shelley said quietly. "I was about to come down the stairs and I tripped over something." She looked at the laundry basket lying at the foot of the stairs, and then at the clothing strewn from top to bottom. "I caught myself, but obviously I didn't manage to hang on to the laundry basket."

Aiden was still crying, and she rubbed his back. "Honey, I'm okay."

"I'm s-sorry, Mama." His little voice hitched as he tried to speak between sobs. "I w-won't leave my t-t-trains there anymore."

"Your trains?" Shelley began to understand as Beverly leaned down and picked up a small wooden train from the step just below them. "Is that what I stepped on, Aiden?"

Her son cried harder. "Yes." It was a wail of anguish.

"Shh." Shelley continued to rub his back. "I'm okay, honey. It's all right."

"I p-promise I won't hurt you anymore, Mama."

Shelley's heart nearly broke right in two. "Oh, Aiden, accidents happen. You didn't hurt me. I wasn't looking, or I wouldn't have stepped on your train."

"But I hurted your knee too."

In point of fact, Shelley's knee was killing her, and she suspected this little escapade may have added a few weeks to her recovery schedule. But she'd never tell her son that. And she was horrified to realize he'd been blaming himself. No wonder he'd been touchy and easily upset recently. "Wait," she said. "Were you trying to hurt me when you ran into me that day?"

Aiden drew back, his mouth open in an indignant scowl. "No!"

"Well, then, it was an accident." She hugged him close. "We learn from accidents. What have we learned from these last few?"

Aiden thought for a moment. "No more toys on the steps."

"It might be good to keep upstairs toys only in your room," she agreed gently.

"Uh-huh. And I won't run in the living room anymore."

"Oh. So you'll run in the kitchen?"

Aiden giggled. "No, silly. I won't run in *any* room."

"Okay. That sounds like a deal." Shelley held up the train Beverly had set on the step beside her. "Would you like to go put this away now?"

"Yeah!" Aiden grabbed the train, jumped up, and ran to his room.

Shelley looked after him, shaking her head with a fond smile. Quietly, she said to Beverly, "So much for not running in the house."

Beverly smiled, but her eyes were sober. "How's the knee feeling?"

Shelley shook her head. "Like ... I don't know what, but it doesn't feel good."

"Let me help you down the steps. Then I'll get you some ice."

Shelley nodded. With Beverly's help, and the other hand bracing her on the banister as she moved, she managed to ease down the steps without jarring her leg too much. Even so, she was biting her lip hard enough to hurt by the time Beverly got her onto the sofa.

"Leg above heart level," her friend said, very carefully lifting Shelley's foot by the heel enough to slide a throw pillow beneath it. Quickly, she hurried to the refrigerator and returned moments later with not one but two ice packs and clean dish towels in which she wrapped them before packing them around Shelley's knee.

"Talk to me." Shelley tried to smile. "Get my mind off how much this is going to add to my recovery time."

"It may be much better tomorrow," Beverly said. "It might be hurting like the dickens, but perhaps you haven't done any serious damage."

"I hope not." Shelley closed her eyes for a moment and prayed. When she opened them, she said again, "Talk to me."

"About?"

"I don't know. Tell me about your job. Or the job you think you'd like to have."

Beverly looked at her strangely. "Don't you want to talk about *your* career?"

Shelley shook her head. "I can't think about that right at the moment. You talk, I'll listen."

"All right." Her friend exhaled deeply. "When I moved here and changed my job so that I could work at home part-time and only commute a little bit each week, I thought it was going to be the perfect setup. Instead, it's made me despise that drive even more. Go figure." She shook her head. "And the accident I had at the beginning of the month didn't help."

She fell silent, and Shelley had to prompt her. "So you were helping me develop my business plan, and it occurred to you that *you* could be doing something different with your life."

"In a nutshell," Beverly agreed. She looked at Shelley. "I'm seriously considering trying to develop a consulting business helping people with small businesses as well as larger corporations—as Margaret suggested."

"That would be perfect for you. You've been such a huge help to me." Suddenly she felt stricken. "It never even occurred to me to pay you. Oh, Beverly—"

"Of course you're not paying me." Beverly looked mildly affronted. "I did it as a friend, Shelley. And actually, I owe you for giving me the chance to see that it's something I might enjoy."

She went on to tell Shelley about the conversations she'd had with other consultants. "I really think I might do this. I probably would concentrate on helping people get their businesses started on the right foot, but with my background, I could also offer budgeting skills."

"You could teach a course on how to start your own business," Shelley told her. "That would be one way to get your name out there to a wide variety of people."

"Great idea!" Beverly looked more excited and enthusiastic than she usually did.

Shelley heard the back door open then, and Dan's deep voice interspersed with Emma's little treble floated into the room. "Hello," she called.

"Hey. Give me a minute to get this munchkin out of her snowsuit," Dan said.

"Beverly's here," Shelley told him.

A moment later, Dan appeared in the doorway between the kitchen and living room. "Hi," he said. "Are you guys discussing business again?"

Shelley nodded. "Some."

"Great." He looked at Beverly. "We finally have come to an agreement on just about everything we need for this new kitchen. I've already ordered some of the materials. Shelley got the deciding vote on colors, but I've talked her into ceramic tile on the floors."

"Won't that be slippery?" Beverly immediately had visions of one of the children slipping and getting a concussion.

Dan shook his head. "They have antiskid tiles now that work well for kitchens."

"And I love the look," Shelley said. "I wasn't even going to consider it because of the cost. Vinyl is so much cheaper."

"But this will last much longer," Dan reminded her.

She smiled at him. "Yes, dear."

Dan's smile faded as he suddenly realized that Shelley was icing her knee. "Are you all right? Did something happen?"

She took a deep breath. "I tripped and nearly fell down the steps. Luckily, I caught myself. But I think I gave this knee a bit more of a twist than it appreciated."

"Do you need to go back to the doctor?"

Shelley wanted to say *no* immediately, but she forced herself to be honest. "I'm not sure yet. Let's see how it looks and feels tomorrow."

CHAPTER TWENTY-FOUR

Margaret was ready to tear out her hair. Strand by strand, perhaps.

She held out the heavy sketch paper on which she was working and studied it. She was working on one of the pen-and-ink sketches for the historical booklet. Since Diane had shared all her research yesterday, an image of a storm-battered ship sheltering in the cove had insistently nudged at her, begging her to put it on paper.

Everything had gone well—until she'd started drawing the people kneeling on the deck praying. Her figures looked out of proportion to the size of the ship, and even to each other. What in the world...? True, she hadn't worked in this medium in a long time, but she always sketched in a basic plan for the painting she planned, and she shouldn't have lost her touch to this extent.

Rising, she threw down her pencil in disgust, just as a figure passed the window and turned into her doorway. A moment later, Diane entered, jangling the bell over the door.

"Good morning," she sang.

"'Morning." Margaret surveyed her friend. "You sound chipper."

Diane grinned. "I feel chipper. I *finally* got Jules Benton to agree to meet with me again and answer more questions about that National Register nomination."

"Oh, good. I'm glad something's going right for someone around here today."

"Uh-oh. What's the problem?" Diane took off her knitted hat and shook her head, freeing her brown hair to fall about her shoulders.

Margaret held up the sketch. "I'm beginning to wish I'd never agreed to draw these sketches for the booklet, that's how poorly this is going."

Diane studied the sketch. "What's wrong with it? This is exactly how I envisioned this event. Nice job."

"The people are all wrong." Margaret pointed with the end of a pencil.

Diane pursed her lips as she studied the sketch. "I see why you're not satisfied, although they don't look *terrible.*"

Margaret began to laugh. "But I notice you didn't say they looked good!"

"Well...no," Diane admitted, beginning to chuckle as well. "Oh, Margaret, I'm sorry. This is taking you away from your painting. We don't have to put sketches in this book."

"Yes, we do. I'm determined now. I will *not* let a silly pen-and-ink series get the better of me."

Diane laughed as Margaret turned back to the counter and snatched up a folder. "Here are three of the sketches. It's just these last two that are taking a little longer."

"Great." Diane took the folder. "I'll scan them in for the mock-up of the booklet. When it's time to be printed, I'll let the printer work directly from these, since he'll get a much higher quality image."

"How are you coming with the rest of it?"

"Pretty well. I've gotten all the material written, and most of it is laid out, even with the photos. I left spaces for your sketches. When it's finished, I'll give the completed copy to Beverly to take to a printer for estimates."

"It may never be finished," Margaret muttered as she picked up her sketch again.

"If one's giving you trouble, why don't you go on to the next?" Diane suggested. "I do that with my writing." She grimaced. "Not that I've been doing much of that lately."

Margaret, bent over the sketch with a soft eraser, glanced up at her. "Why not?"

Diane shrugged. "I'm having a little trouble getting this second book started. And I've been busy with this booklet."

"Maybe the booklet is a nice break," Margaret said, "and as soon as it's done, you can start fresh with your book."

"I hope so." *If I can ever find the perfect angle.* But she nodded. "Yes. I should be able to start it tomorrow." But she knew she probably wouldn't. Every day, she decided that tomorrow she'd get back to work on her book. And every tomorrow, something came up that demanded her attention, and she put off starting her book for yet another day.

* ★ ★

Diane left the gallery and walked briskly along Main Street to the municipal building annex. As she walked, she went over the information she had about the National Register of Historic Places nomination. Which was, sadly, precious little. When she'd called the council president at home, he'd finally agreed to meet her today to discuss the nomination. She was hoping he had had time to resolve whatever concerns he had about sharing information with her. She was convinced the man knew more about it than he had admitted. He'd acted so...so *shady*.

Jules Benton was already in his office when Diane reached the building. Angela, the secretary, was as cute as ever, this time in a baby blue cowl-neck sweater. She flashed Diane a big smile and said, "He's already back there. He said to tell you just to come in."

"Thanks." Diane headed for Benton's office, taking off her coat and carrying it over one arm.

The office door was open, and yes, the office was still as awful as Diane remembered it. Benton was seated behind his desk, but when he saw her arrive, he hurried to take her parka and hang it on his coat tree. "Would you like some coffee?" he asked. "I have a new blend of French roast." He looked anxiously at her. "It's not for the faint of heart, though."

Diane chuckled. "I love coffee. That sounds delicious." And who would have thought that Mr. Benton would be a connoisseur of gourmet coffee?

When their drinks were made to perfection, he carried both mugs back and handed her one. To her surprise, he took the seat beside her rather than going around behind his desk again.

Taking a sip, Diane said, "Ahh. This is delicious."

Benton looked delighted. "I'm glad you like it."

"And it's warm. It is really frigid outside today."

"I know. I walked downtown and about froze my ears off."

Considering the sparse hair the man sported, Diane could believe that, even if he'd been wearing a hat. She took a deep breath. "The last time I was here, you seemed worried when I tried to talk to you about the historical nomination. Given the interest in developing the land—"

"Which the council has decided not to pursue," he inserted.

She nodded. "I think it's more important than ever to have the lighthouse declared a protected property."

Benton nodded. "But it's a little more complicated than that."

"How so?"

The council president sighed. "Settle back, and I'll tell you the whole story."

Astonished, Diane did indeed relax into her chair. She hadn't even gotten out her thumbscrews yet—figuratively speaking—and he was ready to share information with her!

Benton cleared his throat. "I wasn't on the council then, so this story is secondhand, mind you. About ten years ago, one of the summer people talked about this National Register just like you are. He had a pot load of money that he pledged to use for renovations, and the council told him to go ahead with the nominating process. He had some specialist come in—" He scratched his head. "Don't know exactly what that guy did, though."

"Was he an architectural historian?"

Benton nodded. "I think that mighta been it. Anyway, this fella started with the state and jumped through all the government hoops and filled out a million forms. It took something close to six months to get it all done, but the guy kept coming back clear through the fall and talking about it. He finally came in one day all excited and said the Keeper of the Register approved it."

"But that's wonderful! So what happened? Is it on the National Register?" Diane couldn't understand this. If the lighthouse was already registered, why didn't anyone know it?

Jules Benton's face fell. "Well, not really. The way I heard it, the council got through the winter and started wondering about it. And then summer came, but the fella never came back. Couldn't understand it. Finally, one day toward the end of the summer, they got a call from the fella's son. Seems the man passed away."

"Oh, how sad. He worked so hard and then never got to see the fruits of his labor."

Benton nodded. "Ayuh. And then they found out there wasn't going to be any money coming. I guess the heirs got into a wrangle, and it got into the lawyers' hands, and by the time they were done nobody was speaking to anybody else." He lapsed into silence.

After a moment, Diane couldn't stand it. "So what happened to the registration?"

The man shrugged. "Nothing. The council didn't have any money to preserve the lighthouse, so they just kept quiet about it. No sense in getting people all excited about something that didn't work out."

Perhaps not, but it appeared the council had completely overlooked the potential donations that the right kind of publicity could bring in. And besides... "I don't think that simply because it's listed, you have to restore it," she told him. "The property owner—the town, in this case—still can do whatever you want with it. Nothing, if that's what you choose. But having it listed may qualify you for special grants or other funds."

Benton looked surprised. "Wish I'da known that."

All you had to do was read the Web site. But Diane bit her tongue. "So what's the status of the lighthouse now?" she asked.

"It's listed as a historic property. And that's about all I know about it."

"Where's the documentation?"

"In this file." Benton reached onto his desk and handed her a thick accordion file full of papers and one ring-bound document.

Diane gaped. "You're giving it to me?"

"Ayuh. And there's a whole bunch of mail that's come in since it got listed. Nobody ever opened it because we weren't going to do anything with it anyway."

Diane was dumbfounded. They could have been offered money, for all he knew! "Mr. Benton, why did you try so hard to avoid me when I approached you to discuss this?"

Benton's shoulders drooped. "I felt guilty for letting the ball drop on the registry deal. My wife's health isn't good, and I was hoping you'd give up and go away..."

"And you could sell the land to developers," she said grimly.

"Oh no," he hastened to assure her. "That's the last thing I want." He heaved a sigh and rubbed the back of his neck with one hand. "I feel stupid."

Diane had to smile. "Please don't. As you said, you've had a lot on your plate. And the timing of all these events was terrible."

Benton nodded. "But you're going to take care of it now?"

Diane nodded. "Is that all right with you?"

"Absolutely," he said "It would be great to know that our lighthouse is safe."

"Thank you," she said. "I'll look through all of this and report back."

Benton nodded. "That'd be great. You're officially the Lighthouse Preservation Committee, Ms. Spencer."

★   ★   ★

Dan took Shelley to the doctor late Tuesday afternoon while his mother came in and kept the children.

Upon their return, after the boisterous welcome the kids gave them, Dan helped Shelley into the living room recliner, where she could sit and ice the knee as she'd done since she fell.

"What's the verdict?" Frances asked anxiously. "Are you going to need surgery?"

"No, Mom," Dan said. "Stop dramatizing. She doesn't need surgery."

"The doctor doesn't think I did anything too awful," Shelley reported, putting a hand on Dan's arm. "He wants me to ice it today and tomorrow, and then begin using my crutches again." She flicked a finger at the edge of the brace. "Although he made no promises about when I could stop wearing this."

"What a relief." Frances put a hand to her heart. "I've been worrying myself sick ever since you called."

Dan cleared his throat. "I've got to get back to work. I'll be a little late, Shel, because I want to get my hours in."

She nodded. "That's all right." Dan bent and kissed her and then left the room.

Shelley sighed. "I feel like I'm going to be stuck in this thing forever."

Frances eyed the brace. "You're going to have to be extra-careful for a while."

Shelley felt herself bristle at the implied criticism. But then she tried to look at the comment in another light;

Frances was worried about her. "I know," she said, choosing her words carefully. "I guess I'm just going to have to depend on you to help me out for a while longer."

Frances beamed. "I've enjoyed it. I've never gotten to spend much time alone with you without Dan around. Watching you bake is just amazing. I just know your business is going to take off like a rocket once the fellows get this kitchen finished."

Touched beyond belief by the unexpected praise and support, Shelley felt tears sting her eyes. Before she knew it, the words in her head came right out of her mouth. "Thank you, Frances. Sometimes you make me crazy, but then you say something sweet like that, and I forgive you instantly." Horrified, Shelley clapped a hand over her mouth. "I am so sorry," she mumbled from behind the hand.

Frances began to laugh. "Don't be sorry! You're not saying anything I haven't heard before from my own kids. I only irritate the ones I love, y'know." She came over and gave Shelley a warm hug around the shoulders. "Hey, I forgot to tell you—I have the scoop on your friend Beverly."

"Oh?" Shelley wondered where in the world Frances would have seen Beverly. They didn't exactly move in the same worlds.

"Did you know she's been coming to church at Old First?"

"I'd forgotten." Now Shelley was *really* curious.

"She was there last Sunday, and she brought a man with her."

Shelley nodded. "She's been seeing a man named Jeff Mackenzie. They went out to dinner the other night too."

Frances fanned herself. "My, oh my, was he attractive."

Shelley laughed. "I concur."

"I couldn't get over there fast enough to introduce myself," Frances said. "What a lovely couple they make."

"Don't let Beverly hear you say that," Shelley said. "She's not quite ready to claim him as her boyfriend."

"Oh, give her time," Frances said conspiratorially. "She will."

Then the older woman snapped her fingers. "Speaking of handsome men, your husband has a birthday coming up. Do you want to have a family celebration on Sunday?"

Dan's birthday was on Sunday the twenty-ninth, just five days away. Shelley already had a new polo shirt, a DVD he'd wanted, and a power sander that Dan had drooled over but knew he could never afford. She'd managed to find a reconditioned one through one of Dan's father's contacts, and she could hardly wait to give it to him. "That would be great," she said to Frances. Then she had an idea. "Would you want to take the gifts along now so he doesn't see them until Sunday? He'll think I didn't get him anything."

Frances grinned. "That's a great idea. Are those the wrapped gifts in the top of Emma's closet?"

Shelley nodded and laughed. "It was the only place I was pretty sure Dan would never look."

CHAPTER TWENTY-FIVE

Margaret popped into Diane's house after work on Wednesday, file folder beneath her arm. "*Ta-da!* Done," she said, handing the folder to Diane with a flourish.

"You finished the sketches." Diane's face lit up. "Come on in." She closed the door and flipped open the file, perusing the artwork while Margaret took off her coat.

The first one, of a swimmer that looked suspiciously like Margaret herself towing another person through the waves toward the beach, was exceedingly well done.

"You've got the figures of your people just right," Diane told her.

"Finally," Margaret said. "It took me long enough."

Diane whisked aside the sketch to view the second and sucked in an audible gasp.

It depicted the burning church, and it was absolutely riveting. Drawn from the perspective of a person on a ship, all that could be seen in the foreground was a hand clasping the rail of a ship. Just beyond it, white-capped swells made it clear that the ocean was very rough, as did the slight angle at which the rail was tilted, as if the ship had just crested a wave and was skating down the other side. In the distance, the beach gave way to dunes. Behind the dunes were glimpses of vegetation, but what really riveted the viewer was a fire engulfing a building, visible only through a valley that cut between two dunes. Tongues of flame bursting from the windows and through the roof, and black billows of smoke even darker than the night sky rose above the conflagration. Above the church, nearly obscured by the smoke, was a steeple, the cross at its top still standing—clearly for only moments more—and plainly visible. It gave Diane chills.

"What must this have been like?" She swallowed, moved by Margaret's uncanny rendering of the hideous event. "Can you imagine being on that ship, thinking you were probably going to die in that storm—and then seeing that light?"

"It would leave a lasting impression," Margaret agreed. "No wonder Jeremiah Thorpe was so faithful, building the lighthouse and the church, and then rebuilding the church after that fire. It must have seemed like a heavenly directive when that ship anchored in the cove, and that parish realized that their devastating loss had saved over a hundred lives."

Both women were silent. Diane felt on the verge of tears for a moment. Finally, she said, "I almost feel as if Orlean Point is sacred ground. God certainly had a plan for that piece of land, and Jeremiah heard His word loud and clear."

Margaret nodded. "I'm so glad we are beginning to think about restoring the lighthouse. It's a vital piece of Marble Cove's history."

Diane ushered her into the living room. Fishing her phone out of her pocket, she said, "I've got to call Beverly. I can have the final draft of this booklet ready for her to take to a printer this week." After making the phone call, she said, "Beverly's coming over. She wants to see the sketch of the fire." She shook her head. "That really is amazing, Margaret. And I love the way you managed not to have to deal with drawing in people."

Margaret laughed. "It was inspired by desperation, I admit. I worked on those swimmers forever, trying to get them right, and finally, I set it aside to work on the other piece, because the image in my head was simply screaming to be set down on paper. And later when I returned to the swimmer sketch, it came so easily I couldn't believe it." She smiled. "I'm pretty certain that I had some divine inspiration as I worked on these."

A soft rapping on the door preceded Beverly's arrival, and Diane called, "Come in."

Beverly let herself in and smiled when she saw Margaret. "Hey there. You finished the sketches." It was a statement of fact, since she knew the booklet would not be ready otherwise.

Margaret nodded, grinning. "Feels like I lifted the weight of the world off my shoulders. Isn't that silly? I was really beginning to wonder if I'd lost my touch."

"It's not silly at all." Diane glanced over at her friend. She knew that feeling well. Almost every day when she got up and couldn't find a single thing to write, in fact. "I think we all feel that way from time to time."

"I'm also worrying about the talk I asked Louellen Lumadue to give. What if no one shows up?"

"We'll show up," Diane promised. "And we can spread the word."

"Why don't you send a notice to all the local churches?" Beverly suggested. "Surely there's at least one person from every congregation that is interested in angels or art and would enjoy her talk."

"That's a great idea!"

"My specialty." Beverly winked.

"Hey," Diane said. "I heard a rumor about you. You've been spotted with Jeff Mackenzie, and local gossip says you're going to be married soon."

"Heavens, no!" Beverly looked horrified. "Really?"

Diane couldn't keep her composure. "No," she said, laughing, "not really. But I might start that rumor if you don't give us details. You were seen having dinner together at Spinella's."

Beverly shrugged, her smile coy. "We went to dinner, we had a nice time. End of story."

Margaret's eyes narrowed. She turned to Diane. "She's hiding something."

Diane nodded. "Uh-huh." She surveyed Beverly. "So are you going out with him again?"

Beverly hesitated and then smiled. "Yes," she admitted. "He invited me to attend the symphony in Augusta with him."

"That sounds wonderful!" Diane said. "You said yes, didn't you?"

Beverly merely smiled. "I did."

"Shelley's going to be mad that she missed this gabfest," Margaret noted. "Want me to run over and get her?"

Beverly shook her head. "She almost took a header down the stairs Monday; she twisted her knee and is off her feet again for a couple of days."

Diane was dismayed. Her poor young friend seemed to have one challenge after another, and they just never stopped. *God,* she prayed, *if you must add challenges to someone's life, give them to me rather than poor Shelley, okay? She's dealt with more than her share by now!* "Poor Shelley," she said. "I'll visit tomorrow and tell her everything we talked about." She turned to Beverly. "Speaking of men, which we were a moment ago, I ran into someone who asked about you."

Beverly looked puzzled. "Who?"

"Dennis Calder. He specifically wanted to know if you were seeing anyone exclusively right now. His words exactly."

"What did you tell him?" Beverly's voice sounded strangled, and she'd begun to blush.

"I said you dated, but you weren't in a relationship. At the time, it was true."

Beverly shrugged. "It still is."

Diane suddenly sat up straight. "My goodness, I haven't even offered you a drink or a snack. I have a few of Shelley's chocolate chip cookies left. Anyone in the mood?"

"Oh, me, me." Margaret waved her hand madly in the air as Diane hopped up and went to the kitchen.

The other two women followed her. As Diane turned to the counter to grab the cookie tin, she saw a note lying there that she'd scribbled earlier in the day.

"Oh, I almost forgot to tell you: I called the National Register of Historic Places today, and I explained what happened with the lighthouse nomination. The lady I spoke to was extremely helpful. She's going to send me some additional information. She suggested we work with the local historical society to create a group dedicated to preserving and maintaining the lighthouse."

"Preservation and maintenance require funds," Margaret pointed out. "What if we sent letters to everyone we can think of whose life was changed by a miraculous light sighting, or who witnessed it? They might be more favorably disposed to support us."

"Excellent idea!" Diane flipped over the piece of paper and grabbed a pen to jot down Margaret's thought.

"Maybe if I can get the booklet printed fast enough, you can take a copy with you, and see if they'd like to sell them there."

★   ★   ★

Dan picked up Shelley from the Cove two nights later after she'd worked for the first time since she'd twisted her knee on the steps.

She was limping and her knee hurt badly; she could hardly wait to get home, take some painkillers, and get ice on it.

"How was the evening?" Dan asked anxiously. "Looks like you're hurting."

"It was tough." She nodded and sighed. "I can't wait for February to be over, and our new kitchen to be completed. It'll make things so much easier for me."

Dan nodded. "I know. I'm anxious to get started. Dad says he can begin to help next Monday."

"That sounds great." Shelley smiled over at him in the cab of his truck.

When they pulled into the driveway, a strange car was parked out front.

"Who's here?" Shelley asked.

"I don't recognize that car." Dan shrugged. "There wasn't anybody here except Mom when I left."

Shelley couldn't really hurry, but at last they entered the back door. And she saw Allie Fox sitting at the table having a hot drink with Frances. Although she liked the young woman, she was so tired and sore that she almost dreaded the effort being social would take.

"There she is," Frances sang as Shelley and Dan came through the door. "Oh, honey, you looked exhausted. Dan, you take her right into the living room, and I'll get the ice packs."

"Hi, Allie," Shelley said. "I'm sorry I wasn't here when you arrived."

"No problem," Allie said. "I just stopped by to drop off a couple pairs of pants that have gotten too short for Bryce. Aiden's a little shorter, so I thought perhaps he could use them."

"Thank you." Shelley appreciated the thought. Clothing was ridiculously expensive. Dan hung up her coat and shepherded her into the living room, and Allie trailed along.

Frances bustled in a moment later with ice packs and a glass of water. "Here," she said. "I thought you might want some painkillers too." She pulled up a nearby footstool and gently began to place the ice packs around Shelley's knee.

"Thank you." Shelley accepted the items gratefully.

"No thanks needed," Frances said. "You know I'd do this for any member of my family." She rose when the ice packs were arranged to her satisfaction. "I'll get out of your hair now and let you rest." She got almost to the door before she turned back around. "You decide what you want to bake tomorrow, and I'll come do your running for you in the afternoon."

"Oh, that's all right—"

"Don't argue with your elders," Frances said. "I'll see you around one tomorrow."

"All right," Shelley said meekly.

As Frances put on her coat and exited through the kitchen door, Allie stirred. She'd been very still and quiet while Frances was busying herself.

"Your mother-in-law is *awesome*," Allie said in a tone that indicated she was absolutely serious.

Shelley's eyebrows rose. "I'm not sure that's the first word I'd use to describe her." She grinned, and Allie chuckled.

"I visited with her for a little bit before you got home. I know all Dan's brothers' and sisters' names, how many grandchildren there are, your anniversary..."

"I believe it." Shelley shook her head. "She is a font of information—an overflowing font, most of the time."

"Yes, but you're so lucky, Shelley. It's so nice to see how much she loves you. To her, you're truly a part of her family. Another one of her children."

Struck by the words, Shelley could only nod. Frances hadn't grated on her last nerve tonight like she often did, but it was more a shift in Shelley's perspective than any change in her mother-in-law's behavior. *You're truly a part of her family.* She was a part of the Bauer family, Shelley realized. And she acknowledged that until recently, *she* hadn't been completely willing to accept *them*.

Thank You, Lord, for my mother-in-law and Dan's whole family. Please remind me to appreciate them every day.

Allie stayed only a few more minutes and then took her leave. After her new friend left, Shelley realized that she hadn't even noticed Allie's nervous giggle tonight.

CHAPTER TWENTY-SIX

M argaret was in high gear on Saturday afternoon.
"Allan, I need this table over here. Adelaide, go
check and make sure the bathroom is clean. Diane? Do you
think Shelley will be here soon with the food?"

Louellen's informal chat was scheduled for 2:00 PM. Oh
heavens, what if there wasn't a crowd? It had been thrown
together so quickly that she hadn't had time to arrange
nearly as much publicity as she normally would.

Or even worse, what if *no one* came? Surely some folks
would. She'd rearranged the window to include the three
new paintings, and she'd hand-lettered a sign in calligraphy
asking people if they could find the angels in the artwork.
She'd been surprised at the number of people who had found
most, but not all, and then had come inside and demanded
Margaret show them the ones they'd missed.

Surely some of those people would come to hear Louellen.

Beverly walked over to her. "It's almost one thirty. I'm
going to unlock the door and turn over the sign now, all
right?" Margaret had closed the gallery that morning to
clean and prepare for Louellen's talk.

"All right." She bustled over to the counter to be sure everything was sparkling and free of dust. While she was occupied, the bell over the door jingled. She turned around in time to see a couple who had stopped in earlier in the week to ask about the angels.

The bell over the door barely stopping ringing after that. The gallery quickly filled with people.

Louellen arrived at one forty-five and was openly staggered by the crowd. Her eyes sparkled, she chatted with the early birds ... if Margaret didn't know better, she'd swear it couldn't be the same lackluster woman she'd heard speak only two short weeks ago.

Margaret and Allan had borrowed fifty folding chairs from Our Savior, their church, and by five minutes before two, every single one was filled. Allan, Adelaide, Diane, Beverly, and even Dan, who'd come with Shelley, were standing in the very back. Also with them were a new friend of Shelley's and, to Margaret's surprise, her mother-in-law Frances. Shelley and Beverly's father, Mr. Wheeland, were the only two of their little family of friends who were seated, for obvious reasons.

Margaret took a deep breath and stepped up to the front of the room after saying a quick, silent prayer for a warm reception for Louellen and an interesting topic for the crowd that had assembled. "Good afternoon, ladies and gentlemen. Today it is my privilege to introduce ... "

Louellen appeared to genuinely enjoy herself. And the crowd loved her. She told the story of her mother's passing, her painting, and Adelaide's discovery in simple, concise terms. "I believe in divine inspiration," she told those listening. "If any of us doubt for a second the existence of a Higher Power, seeing the detailed work in the Hand that guided mine during the creation of these works should banish all doubt. I had no idea I was including angels in my paintings." She continued to speak for a few minutes more, and then took questions. Voices peppered her with queries, and Margaret finally had to intercede, or she feared Louellen would be there for hours.

Handing Louellen a bottle of water as she stepped away from the table where she'd laid her notes, Margaret said, "That, my friend, was superb. Thank you so much."

"Thank *you*," Louellen responded. "I owe you a great deal, Margaret. I woke up this morning inspired by a new theme, and that hasn't happened in a very long time."

"What's the new theme?"

Louellen smiled. "Angels. It will be a novel experience to paint them on purpose."

Margaret laughed. "I can't wait to see them."

"Mom! Mom!" Adelaide was usually very polite, but for some reason, she was excited enough to interrupt.

Margaret laid a hand on her shoulder. "Excuse me?" she prompted.

"Excuse me," Adelaide said. "Mom, we sold all the paintings." She looked up at Louellen. "All your angels have homes."

Louellen's mouth fell open. "All six paintings? All at once?"

Margaret was as stunned as Louellen. Several people had indicated interest earlier, but no one had pulled the trigger and purchased. To have every single one sell in one afternoon was outstanding.

Louellen enfolded Margaret in a hard hug. "Thank you," she whispered.

"For what? You're the one who did six stellar pieces that sold so fast." Margaret patted Louellen's arm as the other woman released her.

"Yes, but you—you gave me back the joy in my work. That is a gift beyond measure."

★   ★   ★

The four friends gathered at Margaret's house after dinner that evening.

Allan had taken Adelaide to a new movie that she had been excited to see. Margaret begged off, realizing that she could invite her friends to an informal gathering of the "Newport Four." Now the quartet gathered in Margaret's comfortable living room, assembled around one of Allan's low Scandinavian tables.

Shelley had brought a new brownie recipe she called the Sweet Shoppe Rockslide. In the pan, the brownies were covered with caramel, and then topped with tiny brownie cubes and roasted almonds with caramel ganache drizzled over the top. Shelley had cut the completed sweet into brownie-sized squares and arranged it on a pretty clear glass platter with a frosted snowflake design on it.

Margaret had heated apple cider and made coffee. She and Shelley went with cider, while Diane and Beverly stuck to coffee.

"I'm still in shock," Margaret proclaimed. She deftly scooped up a black-and-white cat that occupied Allan's recliner and plopped herself down in its place. The cat stretched, yawned, and decided to stay, curling itself into a loudly purring ball of fur in Margaret's lap.

Beverly perched on the edge of one of Allan's handmade chairs. There were two more cats on the couch, and she didn't have Margaret's confidence with the animals. She couldn't bring herself to march over there, gather one up, and move it. Didn't cats bite? Adelaide's had always seemed pleasant, but maybe they didn't like being handled by strangers.

Margaret laughed, breaking into her thoughts. "Beverly, what's wrong? You're eyeing poor Lizzy like she's about to attack you."

Beverly felt herself growing red. "I've never spent much time around cats before. I don't know what they're going to do."

Diane's eyebrows rose. "Seriously? Beverly, look at those cats. Do they look like they're going to move? That would require an expenditure of energy, and I'm pretty sure none of them are so inclined."

Shelley sighed. "I like cats. I had a cat when I was a kid, until my mother gave it away. But I guess now that we have Prize, we won't be able to have a cat."

"I don't see why not," Margaret said, sounding surprised. "Cats and dogs can get along if they're properly introduced."

"And if the dog doesn't get too excited about something small that runs from him," Diane added.

Margaret cleared her throat ostentatiously. "We did not get together to talk about cats," she said. "I want to bask in the glow from Louellen's incredible success today."

"And in *January*, no less." Shelley shook her head. "Every business owner in town dreads the beginning of the new year. Sales are always horrible. I've already been thinking about what I can do with the Lighthouse Sweet Shoppe to generate sales during those months."

"My pride and joy," Beverly said fondly, smiling at her younger friend. "You have done a great job preparing your business plan."

"You've done a great job helping me understand what I need to be thinking about," Shelley said. "If it wasn't for you, I don't know that I would even have considered long-range planning. Maybe eventually, but right now? I'm so consumed with getting my kitchen set up and the business basics organized that I'd never even considered that."

"You really should consider start-up business consulting if you're serious about a new career, Beverly." Diane nodded for emphasis as she looked up at Beverly.

Shelley picked up the fat orange tabby and plunked it in her lap, then patted the seat next to her. "Come sit down," she invited. "This cat's too busy being lazy to pay any mind to you."

Beverly smiled and took a cautious seat next to Shelley. The cat narrowed its eyes at her, purring loudly, then flopped backward and let Shelley rub its belly. "I am thinking seriously about it," she admitted to her friends. "It might just take me a while before I launch into it full time."

"How wonderful!" Shelley clapped her hands. "All four of us will be self-employed businesswomen. We ought to start a club or something."

"We *have* a club," Margaret pointed out.

"Oh, I guess we do." Shelley beamed.

Diane reached into her large bag and pulled out copies of the mock-up of the historical booklet. "Here's the completed thing," she said. "We have a job to do tonight. Everyone has to read through it and look for typos. You're all going to be editors."

"Does that mean we get listed in the foreword?" Beverly asked.

"She could just dedicate it to us," Shelley hinted.

Diane snorted. "I'm not even putting *my* name on it. This is a Marble Cove production. A lot of people in this town contributed to it, even though some of them have passed away."

"I'm so glad you figured out the nomination story, Diane." Shelley reached for the booklet Beverly passed to her. "It warms my heart to know our lighthouse is going to be protected forever."

★   ★   ★

Shelley left shortly after they reviewed the booklet. Diane and Beverly lingered a few minutes longer and left at the same time.

It was as frigid as January in Maine usually was, but the night was crystal clear. Stars hung in the sky, shining like diamonds, and the snow reflected the light of an almost full moon.

Diane paused at the edge of the sidewalk in front of her little house. "I'm going to stand here until you're inside," she told Beverly.

"That's silly," Beverly objected. "We're in Marble Cove, not Manhattan."

"Still," Diane said, "it never hurts to be cautious."

"All right." Beverly smiled, happy to humor her friend, and Diane gave her a quick hug before she went on her way. Suddenly, she stopped in her tracks. "Diane!" It was a hoarse whisper.

Diane took the few steps to Beverly's side. "What's wrong?"

"I don't know." Beverly pointed in the direction of Orlean Point, where the lighthouse stood, a lonely sentinel abandoned after so many decades of being needed. A shiver ran down her spine. *A light!*

A steady glow illuminated one window of the lighthouse, as if someone were home, perhaps baking bread or carving a decoy. It was a warm and inviting light.

"What do you feel?" Diane whispered.

Beverly shrugged. "Nothing." She tried to reach out into the darkness. Was there someone or something out there in need of aid?

No.

She knew it as surely as she knew her own name. That was a peaceful light, a reassuring light. A light that said *I'll take care of you.*

Author Bio

Best-selling author Anne Marie Rodgers has published more than forty novels since 1992, the last nine for Guideposts Books. She was the launch author for Guideposts' *Stories from Hope Haven* series and has been a finalist for the prestigious RITA Award. Anne Marie has been involved in animal rescue efforts for many years. Currently, she volunteers at Centre Wildlife Care, rehabilitating injured and orphaned wild animals, and serves as the coordinator of the Orphaned Kitten Program in State College, Pennsylvania, where she and her family make their home. She considers irises, beaches and babies of any species some of God's finest creations.

A CONVERSATION WITH
ANNE MARIE RODGERS

Q. Each of the four women in Miracles of Marble Cove began her working life in a career other than the one she is pursuing in the series. What career did you pursue prior to being a writer?

A. My undergraduate degree was in special education, and I was working toward a Master's in school administration when writing hijacked my life. Teaching handicapped children came about in part because of my experiences growing up with my Down syndrome cousin Billy, and I spent nine years teaching special-needs children and teens in Virginia and Maryland before my husband and I began a family. Writing initially was a way to have a career while being at home with young children, but the children are grown and gone now, while the words are still flowing.

Q. If you were to start over in your life or career as our friends in Marble Cove have done, what would you like to do?

A. An animal lover since childhood, I would pursue some sort of career working with animals, whether in a medical setting, as a researcher, or in a rescue facility.

My dubious math skills would probably prevent me from considering veterinary work, although I have considered getting an AA in veterinary technology to improve my skills and understanding of the work I do with animal rescue. I've always thought working in the field of animal language capability would be fascinating. What, exactly, are those whales and dolphins saying? The great apes? What cues am I completely missing in my daily interactions with my own pets? What might I unintentionally be telling them? Yes, I admit it: I would love to talk with the animals!

Q. *The lighthouse in Marble Cove is mysterious and even miraculous. What unexplainable event(s) have you experienced in your life?*

A. In August 2001, the ceiling of my church's sanctuary collapsed. It was a Tuesday afternoon, and by the grace of God, the room was not in use. Moments earlier, an organist had completed a rehearsal. There had been a wedding and Sunday services there the prior weekend. Had this happened during one of those events, there surely would have been many deaths and injuries; an enormous air conditioner crashed down onto the pews where seven members of my family were seated that last Sunday morning. What a miraculous blessing it was that no one was harmed! We worshipped for a year in our fellowship hall until the repairs and renovations were complete. It gave a truly new perspective to that old chestnut about a church being the people rather than the building. And yet I will never forget our first Sunday as a congregation worshipping again in the space we all had once taken for granted. Everyone present felt the Holy Spirit sharing in our joy.

In December 2004, my younger daughter was involved in a very serious car accident. Earlier that day, she had accompanied the high school choir's performance of the "Hallelujah Chorus" from Handel's *Messiah*. She remembers being pinned in the car...and the next thing she recalls is standing by the side of the road. She had placed her phone in her handbag behind her seat...and yet she had it in her hand during her first moments outside the car. The doors wouldn't open; the windows were smashed...but she had not a scratch on her. We have no idea how she got out of the car (or maybe we do!). The car was totaled, the dashboard shoved back within inches of the seat...and amazingly, her only injury was an apparent concussion. Later, it became apparent that she had suffered more traumatic brain injury than was first observed. How thankful we were she had completed her concert before the accident! We had several very difficult years afterward...and yet two more miracles came our way. Her intellectual capabilities were undamaged (very helpful, since she took the SATs only a month later!), and after several years of therapy and healing, she is once again the bubbly, enthusiastic personality she was before the accident. We were blessed beyond measure throughout this entire experience and are thankful for the miracles we have witnessed.

Q. Have you ever been involved in preserving a landmark or other historical place for posterity?

A. I have not, although my mother is a member of the historical society in our hometown. She also is a member of a museum board that oversees a collection of local artifacts, including the pottery of John Bell, a Pennsylvania potter from the nineteenth century. Although I have not followed in her footsteps in this regard (yet!), I had a fascinating experience when my home church began a pastoral search some years ago. As a member of the committee, I had the responsibility of putting together an extensive report. The information included demographic statistics, financial reports, a historical overview of more than two hundred years of our history, a summary of the physical structure, the results of congregational surveys regarding members' feelings and hopes for the future, details about the church's governing structure and various outreach efforts, photographs, and many other details I've forgotten. I learned about aspects of my church's ministry of which I was unaware, got a solid understanding of who we were and where we wanted to go, and developed a strong sense of pride in the tradition and history of my faith.

Baking with Shelley

Chocolate-Covered Cherry Cookies

½ cup real butter, softened
1 cup sugar
1 egg
1½ teaspoon vanilla extract
1½ cup flour
½ cup baking cocoa powder
½ teaspoon salt, divided into two ¼ teaspoon amounts
¼ teaspoon baking powder
¼ teaspoon baking soda
1 jar maraschino cherries (10 ounces)
1 cup semisweet chocolate chips
½ cup sweetened condensed milk

Preheat oven to 350 degrees.

Cream butter and sugar together in a mixing bowl. Add egg and vanilla; mix well. In a separate bowl, combine flour, cocoa, ¼ teaspoon of the salt, baking powder and baking soda. Gradually add to the creamed mixture.

Drain cherries, reserving 1½ teaspoon of the cherry juice. Pat cherries dry.

Roll the dough into balls. Place two inches apart on ungreased baking sheets. Next, use the back of a round ¼ teaspoon measure to press the center of each ball to make a perfect hole.

In a saucepan, heat chocolate chips and condensed milk until chips are melted; stir until smooth. Remove from heat. Add reserved cherry juice and remaining salt; stir well.

Place a cherry in the hole in each cookie. Cover each ball with the chocolate-cherry glaze.

Bake for eight to ten minutes or until set. Cool on wire racks.

FROM THE
GUIDEPOSTS ARCHIVES

This story by Giorgina Reid of Jackson Heights, New York
(as told to Kathryn Slattery), originally appeared in
the August 1989 issue of *Guideposts*.

As a teenager in New York City, I worked part-time for then-Congressman Fiorello LaGuardia, later mayor. He was called "the Little Flower" because of his first name— and because he was just over five feet tall. I rode with him in the elevator one day, and I'll never forget what he said. "Trust in God," LaGuardia told me. "Believe in yourself and you can do anything."

After study in New York and in Rome, I started a long career as a textile designer. I met my husband Donald, also a textile designer. We dreamed of having a place to go every weekend from our apartment in Queens, and in 1960, as we neared retirement, we made our dream come true. We bought a darling two-bedroom cottage in Rocky Point on Long Island's north shore, with its own little beach and a breathtaking vista of Long Island Sound.

We began hearing horror stories from neighbors about erosion eating away the bluffs that the houses were built on.

A storm could chew away ten or twenty feet of property at a time. In March 1962, it happened: A violent nor'easter, coinciding with the highest tides of the month, slammed into Long Island. From our apartment in the city, we listened to reports of catastrophic damage: piers and houses swept away, the shoreline carved into new contours.

As the storm lingered for three days, we knew nothing about the fate of our little cottage. When it was over, we drove with great trepidation to Rocky Point. Our cottage, thank the Lord, was intact. But not so the bluff our house was built on. The rains and winds had washed away about ten feet of our land. Deep gullies had been etched into the bluffs, and our small beach lay obliterated by piles of debris.

As we surveyed the devastation, the words came to me again: *Trust in God. Believe in yourself and you can do anything.* Suddenly I noticed millions of reed stems, three to eight feet long, pencil-thin, and topped by a feathery plume, blown in from a nearby marsh. I didn't know it then, but I'd been given a gift from the sea.

That day, Donald and I began trying to save our property. With the washed-up lumber we built retaining walls and stuffed reeds and sand between them. We worked our way up the one-hundred-foot bluff, refining our method until, in the end, we had created a series of terraces, filled with reeds and topped with sand. But would our homespun system work?

The answer came on June 15, 1963, when another nor'easter dumped more than four inches of rain in less than eight hours. Several houses went crashing down onto the beach. But the bluff under our house stood intact, thanks to the reeds.

I was astonished by all the useful properties of the remarkable plants. When placed at the bottom of the retaining walls, they acted as seals, preventing the sand from sifting out. Their hollow stems served as tiny pipes perfectly suited for retaining rainwater—a miniature underground irrigation system. When they decayed, they blended with the roots of plantings above, holding the soil together like millions of tiny fingers.

It was all so elegant in its simplicity. Soon I had all the neighbors using my technique. I patented my method and wrote a book titled *How to Hold Up a Bank*.

Then I learned about the plight of the lighthouse at Montauk Point. The lighthouse, on Long Island, has stood for almost two centuries, flashing its beacon south over the Atlantic and north across Long Island Sound. It had been commissioned by George Washington. When completed in 1797, it stood safe and secure atop a sixty-eight-foot-high bluff known as Turtle Hill, set 297 feet back from the ocean. But after nearly two centuries of erosion, the lighthouse stood a precarious fifty feet from disaster.

A stone revetment built by the Army Corps of Engineers helped diminish the pounding surf, but big hunks of the bluff still came sliding down. Unless something was done quickly, the tower would go too. And if that wasn't bad enough, the Coast Guard had announced plans to replace it with an ugly steel stanchion.

I made up my mind, then and there, that I wouldn't let this wonderful piece of our history disappear. The Little Flower's words came back to me: *Trust in God. Believe in yourself*... I contacted the Coast Guard, asking permission to try my "reed-trench terracing" method on what was left of Turtle Hill. I knew what they were thinking: *Why, she's just a little old lady.* I *was* little, just four feet and eleven inches, and beyond the age of retirement. But since previous attempts at stemming the bluff erosion had failed, the Coast Guard had nothing to lose, so they wrote back with an enthusiastic yes.

Donald and I began spending weekends combing the Long Island shore for washed-up reeds, raking them up, stuffing them into potato sacks, and taking them out to Montauk Point, where we buried them in the terraces. Local residents came to help too. We made the trip each week for nearly twenty years to help preserve this beautiful landmark, which still stands on Long Island.

Who would have dreamed that I, a city girl, would unlock nature's secret for erosion control? But in the Bible, God often used the least likely person to accomplish His purposes. I believe He used me. After all, with trust in God and a belief in yourself, you can do anything. Just like the Little Flower told me.

Read on for a sneak peek of the next exciting book in
Miracles of Marble Cove!

Unexpected Treasures
by Melody Carlson

The two women had just reached Orlean Point Light
when snowflakes began to tumble from the steel-
colored sky. Diane pulled her polar fleece cap down more
snugly over her ears. "Seems like the weatherman was right
after all," she said to Beverly. "That winter storm looks like
it's about to make an entrance."

Beverly nodded as she zipped her jacket up to her chin.
"Feels like the wind is picking up too. We should probably
head back."

Diane peered up at the lighthouse. "Don't you worry, old
friend," she told the tall structure. "Come summer, we're
going to do all we can to get you fixed up."

"Speaking of preservation." Beverly's brow creased as
they picked up the pace, walking directly into the wind now.
"I really want to help with Old First Church's."

"After that last storm, parts of Old First are literally
falling to pieces and the water damage is serious."

"I just heard about that in church this morning." Diane
shoved her free hand into her jacket pocket. "It seems

someone from Old First approached our pastor, and our church has agreed to help. I'm not sure what we can really do, though. Maybe some kind of fund-raising event?"

"I'm sure we wouldn't turn down any offers of financial help, no matter how small. But I'm afraid it's going to be a pretty expensive project. I've been researching online for some ideas for doing a big fund-raiser."

"And it's such a lovely old building," Diane agreed. "It would be a shame for Marble Cove to lose it."

"It certainly would." Beverly pointed to a lone figure walking toward them on the boardwalk. "Is that Margaret?"

Before long, the three converged on the boardwalk. "I was getting worried about you two," Margaret told them as they all hurried back toward town together. "The sky was getting so heavy and dark looking that I thought you might get lost in the blizzard."

Diane laughed. "So you came out here by yourself to rescue us?"

Margaret shot them a sheepish smile. "Truth is I just needed some fresh air."

"Anyone care to get a coffee at the Cove?" Diane asked.

"Count me in," Margaret said.

"A nice hot mocha sounds lovely to me," Beverly agreed.

They hurriedly turned on to Main and, shaking off their accumulated snow and peeling off portions of their outerwear, the three of them burst into the welcoming warmth of their favorite coffee shop. The smell of fresh-roasted coffee beans and the sight of Shelley's baked goods in the glass case made Diane's stomach rumble happily.

The friends placed their orders and made their way back to their favorite corner table. Diane wished that Shelley could join them, but knew that she and Dan and the kids were spending the afternoon at his parents' today.

"Beverly and I were talking about fund-raiser ideas," Diane told Margaret as they settled in.

"Who needs a fund-raiser now?" Margaret frowned as she sipped her coffee.

Beverly explained about the state of Old First. "If we don't do something soon, we could lose a whole section of the building. And that would be a real shame."

"Our church has decided to help," Diane told Margaret. "I thought a spaghetti supper might be a fun way to contribute."

Margaret shook her head in a dismal way. "I'll bet it'll take millions to fix up that old place. And it's not even on the National Register, is it?"

"I'm not sure," Beverly admitted. "But it should be."

"Maybe I could look into that," Diane offered.

"I don't know," Margaret said with unexpected skepticism. "You can't save everything. I don't want to rain on your parade, but just because something is old doesn't mean it needs to be rescued. Especially when you consider the economic instability of our times. I'm sorry to say it, but some projects are just going to have to fall by the wayside."

Beverly looked dismayed. "I understand what you're saying, Margaret. But *Old First*? That seems so wrong to me. It's such a lovely old building. The architecture is so